THE ENGINEER OF BEASTS

A RICHARD JACKSON BOOK

ALSO BY SCOTT RUSSELL SANDERS

FICTION ■

Wilderness Plots

Fetching the Dead

Wonders Hidden

Terrarium

Hear the Wind Blow

Bad Man Ballad

NONFICTION ■

D. H. Lawrence:
The World of the Major Novels

Stone Country
(with photographs by Jeffrey A. Wolin)

Audubon Reader
(editor)

The Paradise of Bombs

·The ENGINEER of BEASTS

SCOTT RUSSELL SANDERS

ORCHARD BOOKS **NEW YORK**
A DIVISION OF FRANKLIN WATTS, INC.

Orchard Books
387 Park Avenue South
New York, New York 10016

Orchard Books Canada
20 Torbay Road
Markham, Ontario 23P 1G6

Orchard books is a division of Franklin Watts, Inc.

Manufactured in the United States of America
Book design by Mina Greenstein
The text of this book is set in 11 pt. Sabon
10 9 8 7 6 5 4 3 2 1

Library of Congress Cataloging-in-Publication Data
Sanders, Scott R. (Scott Russell), 1945–
The engineer of beasts / Scott Russell Sanders.
Summary: Thirteen-year-old Mooch runs afoul of the
repressive authorities controlling her floating domed city,
by helping an old engineer build realistic robot animals
and by seeking her spiritual roots with the wild animals
left on the outside.
ISBN 0-531-05783-6. ISBN 0-531-08383-7 (lib. bdg.)
[1. Science fiction.] I. Title. PZ7.S19786En 1988
[Fic]—dc19   88-2647 CIP AC

For seven of the next generation:

CHRISTOPHER AND LAURA

MAHADA AND ADRIAN AND NOAH

DAVID AND BETH

■

Fooling around, the clown is really performing a spiritual ceremony.

—Lame Deer

■

It is the business of the future to be dangerous.

—Alfred North Whitehead

PART ONE.

PART ONE

1·

"Call me Mooch," were the girl's first words upon emerging from the lion's jaws.

Before he could make out these words, Orlando Spinks had to pry her loose from the lion's rubber teeth. Before he could do any prying, Orlando had to wake up. At the age of seventy-one, plagued by a tricky back, he no longer slept well at night, but he made up for his insomnia by napping at work. Thus Orlando was dozing in the control room of the New Boston Disney, from which he reigned over his menagerie of robot animals, when a hooting siren jerked him awake. He clapped the pith helmet on his bald head, surveyed the monitors, then rushed to the cat house, where he found a bunch of school kids swarming around the lion's cage and yelling bloody murder.

About as many of the schoolies were cheering for the king of beasts as for the victim, whose lower half protruded from the grinning lips. Some were yelling, "Save her!" or words to that effect, while others hollered, "She's dead meat!" Instead of hanging slack or jerking about in terror, the girl's legs—clad in baggy, purple trousers—stood firmly planted on the floor of the cage. She had jammed the mechanism by thrusting her head and shoulders into the gaping mouth when it was in the midst of a speech about the vanished jungles of Africa. In place of the lion's voice, there now issued from the cavernous throat a child's bemused humming.

"Meddlesome kids! Always poking their noses into things. How's a man supposed to run a disney?" Orlando muttered as he climbed into the cage, switched off the lion, and levered the jaws apart. "Now come on out of there, you."

The girl, still contentedly humming, went on tinkering with the lion's innards. She only had a few more switches to set. In any case, she was not one to jump whenever a grown-up said boo.

"Come *out* of there!" Orlando insisted.

More humming. With a grunt, he seized her by the waist and dragged her out. What emerged for inspection was a girl of thirteen, her grease-covered hands clenched in boxing position, a screwdriver gripped in one fist and a circuit probe in the other. Between her teeth she held a flashlight. The front of her purple shimmy-shirt warned in neon letters OUT OF MY WAY, and the back proclaimed EAT MY DIRT. A pile of incandescent red hair rose above her foxy face. Her eyes, glaring from deep sockets, were the inky green of new dollar bills. She removed the flashlight and bared her teeth in a worrisome grin, as though she had not yet decided whether to smile or bite. Afterward, during his brief stay in jail, Orlando was to recall this first impression of the girl as a fair warning of the troubles to come.

"Who the devil do you think you are?" he said.

"Call me Mooch," she answered without lowering her fists.

Outside the cage the schoolies murmured and swayed, gawking at her for any sign of injuries. The boys admired the swell of her new breasts through the shimmy-shirt. The girls wondered why she didn't cover her freckles with makeup and her snarled hair with a wig. "Mooch the pooch!" one of the children hooted.

"Go recycle your brain!" the girl shot back. Turning on Orlando, she demanded, "And who're you?"

He stiffened, drawing his short frame to its maximum height. He touched the brim of his pith helmet and smoothed the creases of his khaki safari suit. "I'm the chief engineer," he said.

"The one who makes all these boffo beasties?"

"I build and repair the animals, yes. Now, see here—"

"Then you're just the guy I wanted to meet." Transferring the screwdriver and flashlight to her left hand, she thrust her right one toward him.

Polite even when irked, Orlando gingerly squeezed the girl's hand, feeling the pickpocket nimbleness of her fingers. What she felt was an old claw bumpy with scars and toughened at the tips with calluses. What she saw was a tiny, bow-legged, fidgety leprechaun of a man with a face like a worn-out boot. The jungle helmet bulging over his white fringe of hair made her think of a fried egg.

"How do you do," said Orlando in some confusion, pumping the mouse-quick hand.

When the schoolies detected no sign of blood around the girl's middle where the lion had clamped its teeth, they lost interest in the scene and shuffled away down the aisle of the cat house, some heading toward the panther and leopard, some toward the griffin and sphinx. Everyone departed, that is, except for a gangly boy who skulked near the cage and pretended to be cleaning his fingernails with a toothpick, all the while casting sidelong glances in the direction of Mooch.

Dropping the girl's hand as though scorched, Orlando snapped, "Can't you read?" To dramatize his point, he read the warnings aloud, in capital letters: "DANGER! KEEP OUT! WILD BEASTS!"

"You call this *wild*? This juiced-up pussycat?" Mooch patted the lion's mane, which had the stringy texture of frayed nylon rope. "There's more wildness in my left little toe than in your whole kitchy-koo zoo."

This was a sore point with Orlando. "Why, you cheeky brat!" he sputtered. "Where's your teacher?"

"I didn't come with a teacher."

"Your juvenile officer, then?"

"I didn't come with any juvee, either."

"Your parents?"

Mooch put on a sadsack frown. "I don't have any parents. I'm just a poor little orphink. Boo hoo."

This provoked a snigger from the tall, knobby boy who had stayed behind to spy on her. Noticing him for the first time, Mooch hollered, "Ratbone, you utter creep! If you don't quit sneaking around after me, I'll tie your ears across your nose and blindfold you!"

Nature had indeed afflicted the boy with huge ears, twin scoops of pink, translucent flesh, which now turned rosy from embarrassment. "Quit calling me Ratbone," he mumbled, then slunk away behind a talkie-feelie booth that was shaped like a giant panda. His face loomed above the panda's shoulder, giving the impression—thanks to those remarkable ears—of a swiveling radar screen.

"Maybe you came here on your own," Orlando told the girl, "but so help me God you're going to leave with an Overseer, just as soon as I can put in a call." He lifted the wristphone to his lips.

"Hey, come on, mister. Why make a stink? I didn't break anything. In fact, your pussycat here is running better than before. I fixed him so he won't be making any more whacko speeches. Nothing but natural sounds." Once again Mooch patted the lion's ropy mane, whereupon the beast yawned, shuddered, and let out a prodigious belch.

Since Orlando never programmed such rude noises into his robots, this brought him up short. He dropped his arm, leaving the call to the juvenile officer unmade. "How did you do that?" he asked wonderingly.

"Easy as pie," she answered, then proceeded to sketch a diagram with her finger on the dusty floor of the cage to show how she had altered the sound-loop on the lion. This dazzling explanation was only the first of many surprises she would spring on Orlando. She had taken courses in cybertronics at Get-a-Job Tech, but had learned even more about machines through tinkering with the security devices at the orphanage. Videos, computers, light-gates, locks— you name it, she had taken every gismo apart and put it back together again.

Orlando narrowed his eyes to wary slits. "How come you're monkeying with all that security stuff?"

"So I can skip out of that orphanage whenever I feel like it."

"Then you really are an orphan?"

"Would I lie?" Her gaze took on the velvety innocence of moss. "Come on, let's take a load off our feet, and I'll tell you all the gory details."

■

ALWAYS a sucker for a story, Orlando followed her outside the cat house to the lake, then across the water on lily pad stepping-stones to Monkey Island, where they settled themselves on a fiberglass log in the shade of a plastic banana tree. The boy named Ratbone sneaked after them and kept watch from shore. Mechanized monkeys, chimpanzees, and baboons capered over the slopes of the island, going through their spiels like door-to-door salesmen. Every thirty seconds, a hippo rose above the lake's surface and yawned pinkly, then submerged, giving way to a hydra that lifted its nine snaky heads like periscopes and peered in nine directions.

A never-never look stole into Mooch's money-green eyes as she began her tale. Her parents, she told him, were tribals, renegades who stayed outside in the wilds, hiding, when almost everybody else moved into the Enclosure. They lived with a bunch of other back-to-the-earthers beside a lake not far from Old Boston, in a great round hut woven like a bird's nest of branches and reeds. "That's where I popped into the world, in that leafy hut, and I landed on a bearskin rug."

"Real bearskin?" said Orlando, who was the son and grandson of taxidermists. The mere thought of fur made his palms itch.

"One hundred percent genuine." The dreamy look in Mooch's eyes did not keep her from checking to see how much of the story Orlando was buying. She went on with her tale.

From the moment she landed on that bearskin, naked and bawling, her own skin carried the smell of wild beasts. Until she was three, she rode everywhere on her father's back, tied to a board and wrapped in a blanket like a papoose, and drank nothing but her mother's milk. The clan imitated the ancient ways of the Indians, with a dose of precautionary science thrown in. They painted their faces, wore feathers in their hair, danced to the moon, prayed to the four winds. They also filtered their water, purified the soil where they raised their crops, and took medicines to ward off disease. Still, when Mooch was five, a plague swept through the tribe, killing everyone but Mooch herself.

It was November, the fields brittle and bare, an early snow falling. There was food enough in the leafy hut to keep her through the winter, but not enough wood. When the fire burned out, she wrapped herself in the bearskin and lay shivering as the snow fell. She slept. It could easily have been her last sleep. Instead, in the pitch dark, she woke to feel herself being snatched into the air and carried through the night. As though slung in a hammock, she rode in the bearskin, which was pinched in a fierce grip behind her shoulders. A hot, clammy breath panted against her neck. By and by, the claws of whatever was carrying her began to click against stone, and the chuffing breath echoed back from nearby walls. Mooch was lowered to a gritty floor and squeezed between two enormous shaggy bodies. After getting the best of her terror, and persuading herself that the beasts were not going to eat her right away, she began to enjoy the cozy warmth. She snuggled down between the two mounds of flesh, which gave way slumberously, like two yielding, rumbling, furry volcanoes.

Morning light revealed not two but three shaggy mountains, a mother black bear and her yearling cubs. Their den was a cave, its stone floor littered with leaves and twigs and crackly bones. That was where Mooch lived, keeping warm between the dozing animals, feeding on bear's milk, until her adopted family began to stir from hibernation in the spring. The mother accepted her as one of the cubs, and the cubs nuzzled her, romped with her, sniffed and licked her. Mooch learned their speech, but at night she whispered English words to herself, so that she would not forget the language of humans. She learned the smells of danger and the sounds of weather, learned to use her hands like paws to snare fish, learned to avoid the oil-slick ponds and the gray, poisoned zones in the woods. During the warm months she ate roots and berries and green sprouts. When the cold returned, she moved back into the cave, dozed through weeks of snow and frost, waking only to feed on the mother bear's wild and musky milk.

So the winters and summers passed. Mooch was nine when the health patrollers found her, scrubbed her down until she thought her skin would come loose, sprayed her with antiseptic, and shipped her inside to the nearest orphanage, The New Boston Home for Little Wanderers.

"And ever since they locked me up in that smothery place," she concluded, "I've been stealing out every chance I get."

"Like today?" Orlando asked.

Mooch nodded. "There's no way I'm going to stay bottled up in that place until I'm eighteen. I'd sooner die." Her face squinched up, as though from a bad smell. "It's the putrid pits." Raising her voice, she called out, "Isn't that so, Ratbone, you eavesdropping snoop?"

The gangly boy, who had been pacing back and forth along the shore, now froze in place as though stabbed by a searchlight, his ample ears once again flaming with embarrassment.

"He's an orphan, too?" said Orlando.

"Yep. Another little wanderer," Mooch replied. "And a big pain in the rear end. Every time I escape, he's right behind me, his tongue hanging out like a soggy belt. Hey, Ratbone," she yelled, "come on out here and meet the guy who makes all these wimpy beasts."

The boy ducked out of sight behind a clump of inflatable cactus.

"Wimpy?" Orlando puffed up with indignity. "Young lady, these beasts are accurate replicas—"

"Don't shovel me that sludge! Hippos yawning by the clock? Monkeys juggling? Snake-headed monsters blowing bubbles? And how about that speechifying lion? Lions couldn't talk, and even if they could, they'd have talked about sunlight or the crunch of antelope bones, not about village life on the African veldt."

"Well," he conceded, "I have to jazz things up a bit for the customers. Show business is show business."

"That's what I came here to palaver about. Box office. The way to bring in folks is to give them a taste of wildness. Let the animals be themselves, like they would be outside."

"If there *were* any animals outside," Orlando observed with a melancholy air.

"What you need around here is a helper who knows the beasts," Mooch went on. "Somebody raised by bears. Somebody who's read all the eco books, watched the nature feelie-films, tromped through holograph jungles. Somebody like me. Make me your apprentice, mister, and we'll turn this disney into a place that will stand people's hair on end."

The notion of wildness appealed to Orlando, and so did this fiery girl. But the prospect of visitors with hair standing on end made his own scalp—where only a fringe of hair still grew—tingle with fear. The instinct of self-preservation led him to say, "I'm managing just fine without an apprentice, thank you."

■

WHEN ORLANDO returned her to The New Boston Home for Little Wanderers—Ratbone trailing behind them at a spy's distance—Mooch did not kick or scream. She merely twitched her lips, squinted her unsettling eyes, and promised, "I'll be back."

13 ■

2.

Bertha Dill, the orphanage director—a plump woman of fifty or so, but painted and patched up to look years younger, like a reupholstered couch—told Orlando a quite different version of Mooch's history.

To begin with, the girl's name wasn't Mooch. Her legal name, derived from the tangled circumstances of her birth, was Emitty Harvard Tufts. She was the first and last fruit of an experiment performed at the Tufts University bioengineering lab, in which a frozen egg from a Nobel laureate at the Massachusetts Institute of Technology was joined in a glass dish with frozen sperm from a Nobel laureate at Harvard University. (In fact, Bertha Dill, a woman of great delicacy in sexual matters, spoke not of egg and sperm but of "the maternal offering" and "the paternal contribution.") The resulting child, who was supposed to be a genius, turned out to be a sneaking, lying, thieving, conniving, low-down, trouble-making scamp.

"You don't like her?" Orlando asked.

"In my official capacity, I'm not allowed to hold an opinion," said the director, her voice dropping two notches, "but privately, Mr. Spinks, I can tell you that I would gladly swap Ms. Emitty Harvard Tufts for a migraine headache."

"Queer sort of name," he said. "I can see why she prefers being called Mooch."

" 'Harvard' and 'Tufts' are perfectly straightforward," the director replied. "As for 'Emitty,' that's the closest we could come to 'M.I.T.' We couldn't very well call her 'Massachusetts Institute of Technology,' could we now?"

"So she wasn't born in the woods and raised by bears?" Orlando mused regretfully.

Bertha Dill rumbled with laughter. Her towering hairdo, dyed a nightmare black, threatened to collapse from the tremors. "Don't tell me you fell for that one? Oh, my!" She patted her quaking bosom. After regaining a degree of composure, she went on to explain that baby Emitty, the insufferable vixen, was rejected by the pair of psychologists who were to have adopted her. They disliked the infant's red hair, her freckles, her grassy stare, her ugly triangular face, and her vulgar manners.

"I thought all babies were vulgar," Orlando said.

"Believe me, this girl broke the records for vulgarity." The director closed her eyes for several moments, as though to draw a veil over the infant Emitty's gross deeds.

"And nobody else would adopt her?"

"There were legal constraints. After all, she was an experiment. And three university bureaucracies were involved, plus all the scientists. She was born in a snarl of red tape. They're still fighting over who owns the patent for her."

"She's *patented*?"

"Indeed she is, although who'd ever want to make a duplicate of her is more than I can say."

"Funny, she doesn't seem such a bad kid."

Thrusting out her lower lip, Bertha Dill let go an indulgent breath that sounded like a swift leak in a balloon.

"Pardon me for saying so, Mr. Spinks, but you strike me as someone who has never had any children of his own. Am I correct?"

Orlando shuffled his feet, and then gazed down at them as though trying to remember whose feet they were. "I was never okayed for parenting," he admitted.

"Few of us are, few of us are. No reason to be ashamed. But had you raised children, Mr. Spinks, you would not have been so easily fooled by little Ms. Tufts."

"You're probably right," said Orlando, aware of how blind he could be in the business of the heart. Still, unable to erase that image of the girl's legs protruding from the lion's mouth, he could not prevent himself from adding, "How about apprenticing her out?"

"We've tried her in four places, my dear Mr. Spinks, and each one shipped her back in less than a month, along with a catalog of damages."

Orlando remembered how swiftly Mooch had reprogrammed the lion to belch. When it came to machines, at least, he was not likely to be fooled. "She's awfully clever," he said with confidence.

Trembling, the director proclaimed, "The child is a walking catastrophe."

■

NEVER CERTIFIED for breeding, never married, an only child himself and therefore without even nephews or nieces to sharpen his eyes, Orlando had always looked upon children as one looks upon the waves of the sea. Some big and some little, some quiet and others loud, kids poured in their hundreds through the disney each day. Why, out of all these indistinguishable faces, did this one girl stick in his mind?

Orlando's mind was not a place where things human

were prone to stick. As a baby, he started counting his toes soon after he discovered them wriggling at the ends of his spindly legs. Ever since, he had been climbing about in the airy scaffolding of mathematics, like a man at a building site clambering over the frame of a skyscraper. Machines appealed to him because they were the incarnations of formulas, precise and clean. Of all machines, robots were his favorites, because they actually thought in numbers.

Precise and clean himself, Orlando might have been one of his own mechanical creations. Everything about him was tidy—the crisp safari suit he wore as a uniform, the angular motions of his arms when he talked, his whittled speech, his trim, white beard and fringe of hair, the creases that rayed out from his bright, squinty eyes. Even at seventy-one, Orlando still had the compact, symmetrical body of a tightrope walker. Like the machines over which he fussed and fretted all day, he gave off the medicinal tang of lubricating oil.

The disney was laid out meticulously in the shape of a spoked wheel, with Orlando's private quarters and the workshop and control room gathered in a single round building at the hub, and with aisles of exhibits forming the spokes. The plastic thatch covering the central building—an imitation jungle hut—was combed as neatly as Orlando's hair. In his workshop, every tool could be found in its appointed place. Stuffed heads of moose and buffalo and other surly beasts—legacies from Grandfather Spinks—gazed down in impeccable ranks from the walls. Their fur was periodically vacuumed. In his private quarters, Orlando kept house like a finicky sea captain.

All in all, he was not the sort of man to ally himself with a walking catastrophe. No one had less of a taste for trouble. You could have searched that dilapidated organ, his heart, without discovering any murderous hankerings. You could have shone searchlights into the basement of his brain without finding the least cobweb of malice. His intentions were as innocent as butterflies.

And yet Orlando Spinks, that fastidious man, in love with the clarity of numbers and the obedience of machines, wished to program into his robot animals a streak of wildness. Which is why, in the days following his interview with the director of the orphanage, he kept thinking of that rude, rebellious, messy girl who called herself Mooch.

■

WILDNESS, or at least the simulation of wildness, had been the Spinks family business for several generations. Orlando had learned the trade of beast-engineering from his father, who had learned zoo-keeping from *his* father, who had stuffed animals for a living back in the days when there were still animals to stuff. Orlando could just barely remember when freshly-killed deer, lashed to the hoods of cars, were delivered by weekend hunters to his grandfather's taxidermy shop in Old Boston. Swordfish arrived in trucks, stiff as boards. Bedraggled pheasants were pulled from coat pockets, rabbits from hats. Once a neurosurgeon drove all the way down from Maine with the carcass of what he claimed to be the last black wolf in the White Mountains. Obeying the doctor's instructions, Grandfather Spinks fitted the wolf with glass eyes of a demonic red, bared its fangs, sharpened the claws, and sprayed the fur with varnish to make the hairs on its back stand up menacingly. After the supply of large trophies dwindled away, Grandfather stuffed raccoons and possums, frogs and mice, even preserved beetles and moths and the occasional praying mantis. When the supply of insects and rodents also dried up, Grandfather abandoned taxidermy as a doomed craft, like blacksmithing or balladeering, and took a job shoveling manure and scrubbing elephants at the Franklin Park Zoo. For a man who had labored so long with dead animals, he was surprisingly good with live ones, and eventually rose to become the zoo keeper. In his spare time he purchased at auction and lovingly restored the moth-eaten moose heads and leathery crocodiles that would decorate Orlando's workshop many years later.

Then one day, in a lapse of judgment, Grandfather Spinks died from teasing a gorilla, and Orlando's father succeeded him as keeper of the zoo. His first official act was to shoot the gorilla. Since there were no more great apes in the zoo, and none in the jungle, and none in the whole world for sale, that cage remained empty. One by one, during the years of Orlando's childhood, the animals withered from old age, or choked to death on candy wrappers, or caught lethal viruses from the syrupy air, or died in some other manner. As the cages fell empty, Father Spinks began filling them again with mechanical models, which he sewed up in the preserved skins of the dead beasts. The earliest of these mechanimals, as he called them—or mechs, for short—were crude, able to do little more than wave their paws and grunt. But with each new model, Father Spinks refined his art, until the later mechs began to dance and sing and tell jokes and sign autographs. The zoo was transformed piecemeal into a disney, an amusement park populated entirely by robot clowns dressed up in fur.

This was the enterprise that Father Spinks moved into New Boston soon after Orlando's fifteenth birthday, at the Enclosure, a jumbled and crazy time when the several million citizens of Old Boston were also moving inside, together with gameparks and hospitals and racetracks and the universities that would later give life and three names to Emitty Harvard Tufts. It was not a long move. New Boston floated on the ocean just a few kilometers east of the stumpy remains of Cape Cod. The rest of the Cape—along with Old Boston, San Francisco, Tokyo, Buenos Aires, and most of the world's coastal cities—had been flooded earlier in the century by the rising oceans. Floods were the least of the dangers that forced humankind to build the network of floating metropolises and take refuge indoors. Poisoned air and water, exhausted soil, radioactive dumps, and a thousand other menaces had changed the earth into a hostile planet.

Once the domes clamped down over the cities, and flexiglass travel-tubes bound the cities together in a global web, and extractors began mining the oceans, and recyclers began filtering the air, and the Enclosure was sealed tight in all its manufactured perfection, Father Spinks, who was inside, had to give up all notions of capturing wild animals, which were forever and always outside. He contented himself with his menagerie of mechs. Orlando worked beside him all day, training his fingers in the intricacies of gears and circuits, then at night he studied at the robotics school. While still a teenager, the boy was fashioning animals so lifelike that they made visitors speak, in hushed tones, of sorcery.

After Father Spinks drowned while entangled in the arms of a malfunctioning squid, Orlando became chief engineer of the disney. The title was misleading insofar as he was the *only* engineer. Robot drones picked up trash and hosed the walkways and sold tickets, but otherwise Orlando did everything, from stitching up tears in tattered hides to replacing chips on memory boards. For several years he kept the disney just as his father had left it, as a shrine to the old man. But eventually, wearying of the gigantic mice and congenial tigers which Father Spinks had favored, Orlando introduced frankly imaginary beasts, such as unicorns and griffins and mermaids. By shuffling together parts of various animals, he could make new ones. The body of a goat joined to a serpent's tail and a lion's head made a chimera, for instance. An eagle's head stuck on a lion's torso yielded a griffin. Orlando worked out dozens of permutations which had never been dreamed of in the bestiaries. Before long, the visitors who shuffled past the exhibits no longer knew or cared which of the animals had once lived on Earth and which were imaginary.

By the time Mooch came along to jam herself down the lion's throat, the gawkers who streamed through the disney were unlikely to have met any sort of beast, real or mythical, anywhere except in Orlando's park. Those younger than fifty had lived all their days inside the Enclosure. Trees and birds and sharks and bears, no less than dragons, had become for them the stuff of legend.

3.

Nicknames bred like cockroaches in the hallways of The Home for Little Wanderers. No amount of scouring or poisoning could defeat the roaches, and no threats from Bertha Dill could stamp out the nicknames. Given her plumpness and her sour expression, it was inevitable that the orphanage director should be referred to as Dill Pickle. The orphans usually shortened this to The Pickle. To be hauled into the director's office was to Get in a Pickle. The Home itself was The Pickle Jar. The brawny guards who kept watch over the gates and broke up fights were variously known as Bickle, Dickle, Fickle, and so on right through the alphabet. The orphans called themselves LWs, by which they meant, not Little Wanderers or Lazy Waifs, but Lethal Weapons. Using their own private labels for the staff and for one another, they filled the corridors of the Home with the buzz of secret conversations.

Mooch was engaged with two other girls in one of these whispery conversations when the mustachioed guard known as Fickle collared her and marched her away to Bertha Dill's office. The Pickle loomed behind the bare, gleaming plateau of her desk, which no clutter was allowed to mar. The frown of disapproval on her face seemed to Mooch as permanent as a geological feature.

"Emitty," said Bertha Dill, "you would try the patience of a saint."

"And you're not a saint, are you, ma'am?" replied Mooch, on whom The Pickle had used the same line before.

"No, not a saint." The director made an effort to smile and failed. "However, I do pride myself on being able to stomach a great deal from rebellious children before I give up on them."

Mooch thought of a wisecrack having to do with The Pickle's stomach, but said only, "Are you giving up on me, ma'am?"

"Not yet, Emitty, not quite yet." Elbows flattened on the desk, Bertha Dill wove her fingers together and used them like a sling to brace her sagging jowls. "However, I must warn you that I have reached my limit. I've just had an interview with Mr. Orlando Spinks concerning your shenanigans at the disney—"

"He's kind of a sweet old geezer, isn't he?" Mooch interjected.

"—and I've persuaded him not to press charges," Bertha Dill went on. "But that is positively the last time I'm going to bail you out. I do not care to hear complaints about you from any more policemen or shopkeepers or funny little engineers from amusement parks. One more escapade like this lion business, and I'll have to expel you from the Home."

"Where to?" Mooch asked hopefully.

"If you're lucky, to the Female Training Institute, where the psycho-chemists will find just the potion needed to make you into a docile young lady."

Lord save me from chemmies, thought Mooch. "And if I'm not lucky?"

"To the Cape Cod Refarmatory."

Rumors about the place circulated in the orphanage, but they were as vague as they were grisly. Mooch was not even certain of the name. "You mean re*form*atory, ma'am?"

"I mean exactly what I said. Re*farm*atory. A prison farm for juvenile delinquents."

"What do they grow?" Mooch asked.

"Adult delinquents, as nearly as I can tell."

"How about animals?"

"There are cows, I believe, and hogs, perhaps chickens and sheep. Altogether a stew of unruly beasts. No doubt you would fit right in."

"It's really on Cape Cod?" said Mooch. The name conjured up in her visions of wind, sand, grass, unsimulated sky. *"Outside?"*

"There's a dome, of course. The idea is to improve your character, not kill you. But there's no city around it, no video arcades, no playzones. Just barracks and fish-tanks and fields. A grim place indeed." The erosion lines of Bertha Dill's frown deepened as she put on her sternest glare. "I do sincerely mean what I say, Emitty. The very next time I catch you running away and getting into mischief, I will kick your fanny out. Is that clear?"

Mooch knew there was a time for sassing and a time for putting on the veil of meekness. She answered primly, "I'll remember, ma'am, and try to behave."

"Try hard," replied Bertha Dill, who prided herself on seeing through all the dodges and disguises of children. "And if you fail," she added, "perhaps when I send you away I'll ship Garrison along to drive you crazy."

■

GARRISON RATHBONE, the boy who trailed Mooch to the disney in a fever of devotion, could not help being called Ratbone. Already tall and skinny, at the age of thirteen he was stretching out so rapidly that his knobby wrists and ankles immediately began sprouting from the cuffs of brand new uniforms. Unable to keep pace with his lengthening bones, his pale skin looked as though it had been laundered with a killer detergent and dried in a furnace. There were stretch marks on his forehead. He was perpetually tired. Nothing could stir him to effort aside from chasing Mooch and dreaming of space travel. His ears and nose, like his feet and hands, seemed to have been designed on a scale even larger than the rest of his gangly body. His exuberant yellow hair, no two strands of which pointed in the same direction, gave him the look of someone who had recently clawed his way ashore from a shipwreck.

Mooch considered him the ugliest thing she had ever seen going about on two legs. She thought he gave off an odor of berserk hormones. Anybody who could live in this hive of an orphanage, inside this plastic bubble of a city, and dream of moving to even more sterile colonies in space was, in her opinion, a dumb cluck.

For his part, Garrison believed that Mooch must have been standing first in line on the morning when brains and beauty were handed out.

Naturally, she would not give him the time of day.

Garrison hated his nickname, but Mooch loved hers. She would plot revenge against any grown-up who called her Emitty, and any child who made that mistake she would promptly clobber. She was called Mooch less because the nickname echoed her legal one than because she was the champion sneak in the orphanage. Anywhere she set her mind to go, she could go. She was able to slip like a wraith past the most vigilant guard. She could fool the most ticklish alarm, undo the stubbornest lock. With her nimble fingers she could snitch your belt while shaking your hand, and with her bare toes she could tie your shoelaces to a chair leg. She never stole from the other kids, but she filched like a bandit from the Home, especially keys from the guardroom and sweets from the kitchen. Her fellow orphans claimed that she could make herself invisible, but in fact she merely possessed such utter stealth that people could look straight at her without seeing her. Even Garrison, who was so alert to her presence that he divided the universe into the zone of Mooch and the zone of not-Mooch, would sometimes have to locate her by picking up the cadence of her breathing with his tremulous ears.

■

THE EVENING after her session with The Pickle, Mooch was lounging on the bunk in her cell, eating pilfered choco-bars, playing solitaire with a deck of cards that once belonged to the janitors, listening through earphones to a tape of whale songs stolen from the library, and brooding. Never short of subjects to brood about, at the moment she was lamenting the cruel joke of her birth. Why had the genes of two Nobel scientists, scrambled together in a glass dish, inflamed her with a yearning for escape from this clockwork Enclosure that science had built? Why had she been sentenced to live in this floating city, where not even dogs or cats roamed, let alone buffalo, and not so much as a blade of grass ever grew? To put it briefly: Why had she been born three centuries too late to be an Indian?

The lonely bleating songs of the whales filled her with oceanic longings. She kept her eyes lowered to avoid seeing the walls of her cell. They were painted shocking pink, a color she loathed but one which Bertha Dill believed to have a soothing effect on hyperactive troublemakers. Most of the orphans were allowed to put up holos and light-tapestries and other hanging stuff, but Mooch—a hardened mischiefmaker who needed the full benefit of color therapy—was ordered to leave her yucky walls bare. She dodged around this ruling as she dodged around most others. The pictures she drew of the animals who visited her in dreams were stuck up here and there with gum. A map of the night sky as viewed from the peak of Mount Katahdin at the winter solstice hung by threads over her bunk. On the inside of the door she kept a grizzly bear poster which had been liberated from the Home's antique collection of *Wild and Woolly Wonders* magazines. During room checks, she could snatch down the poster, drawings, and map and slide them under her mattress while the guard's key was rattling in the lock.

In keeping with the same color theory, Garrison Rathbone's cell over in the boys' dormitory was painted mustard yellow, a hue designed to rouse some energy in his languid frame. He might have been living inside a stainless steel box for all the notice he gave to the shade of his walls. Holographs of pockmarked moons and shimmering stars were plastered over the walls in any case, and the view was further obscured by models of spacecraft dangling from the ceiling. Much of the time, when not skulking after Mooch, he slumped in his beanbag chair with a drawing pad or book, or slouched before his computer console, long arms and legs folded like the wings of a collapsible drying rack.

On this particular evening, while Mooch was brooding to the accompaniment of whale song, Garrison lay sprawled on the floor of his room, sketching a design for a space station. Guided by rulers and compasses and French curves, the light-pen skated over the creamy film. The doughnut-shaped station, viewed at a tilt, became an ellipse, and then imperceptibly, ink stroke by ink stroke, it turned into a mouth. And not just any mouth, but the captivating thin-lipped mouth of Mooch. Recognizing what his fingers had drawn, Garrison felt a jolt of desire.

Although it was the quiet hour after supper, when the orphans were forbidden to stir from their cells, and although Garrison had scarcely enough energy to straighten his legs, he tiptoed downstairs, across the exercise yard, past the dozing matron, and upstairs into the girls' dorm, where he knocked at Mooch's door.

Even above the bleat of whales, she recognized the hesitant bony sound of his knuckles. She groaned. Removing the earphones, she rolled from her bunk and slipped over to the door. She laid her cheek against the grizzly bear poster and hissed, "That you, Ratbone?"

"Roger," he whispered back, lapsing as he often did into astronaut lingo.

"Roger who?"

"I mean yeah, it's me. Garrison."

"Get lost."

"I just wanted to see if you're okay."

"Why shouldn't I be okay?"

"I was afraid maybe that lion hurt you somehow."

"He didn't lay a tooth on me."

"You really gave me a scare, getting chomped like that."

"I didn't get chomped, for Pete's sake."

"You sure?"

"Sure I'm sure! You want to come in here and check my belly for bruises?"

There was a spell of silence, during which Garrison chased away the butterflies of dizziness. "I didn't *say* that," he protested, although in truth he found the idea warmly appealing. "I was worrying about you, is all."

His tone was so forlorn that she relented enough to whisper, "Okay, okay. Thanks a bundle. Now you can quit worrying because I'm a big girl."

"You're not mad?" He put his fingers against the metal skin of the door in hopes of catching the vibrations of her voice.

"No, I'm not mad. Now clear out before the guards nail you."

"I'm gone," he murmured.

He was certainly gone from Mooch's thoughts even before his clumpy footsteps quit sounding in the hall. But Garrison's visit had the effect of making her think even harder about the lion, the disney, and that quirky old keeper whose heart she must win. The way to the engineer's heart, she imagined, lay through his beloved machines. Show him what she could do to liven up his robot animals. Drive them wild. Knock his socks off. Without a thought for Garrison, Mooch lay on her bunk and schemed.

Meanwhile, back safely in his mustard yellow cell, collapsed in his beanbag chair, Garrison fell asleep over a textbook on rocketry. He dreamed, not of alien planets, but of the pale meadow of Mooch's belly.

4.

The nearest thing to a curse Orlando Spinks allowed himself was *Dad burn it!* and even this he used rarely, lest he wear it out. But as he struggled to make the lion stop belching and resume its lectures, he uttered the oath five times before noon. It took him altogether several hours and half a dozen more *Dad burn it*s to undo the girl's mischief, she had been so ingenious in her tinkering.

Whenever any part of his menagerie broke down, Orlando could not rest until it was fixed. Since there were some two hundred mechanical beasts in the disney, plus innumerable zip-carts and vending machines and robot drones and other breakable gadgets, all of them assaulted daily by mobs of children, he got very little rest. His workshop was always littered with the bodies of mechs awaiting repair. Even without insomnia, he would have been forced to spend most nights, electro-probe in hand, gazing like a surgeon into the bowels of some ailing machine or other. Thus he had formed the habit of napping in the control room, one ear cocked for sirens, a tool belt draped over the arm of his relaxer chair.

More than his usual tidy-mindedness prompted him to sweat over fixing the lion. Tomorrow was the monthly Senior Day at the disney, when nobody under seventy would be admitted. On a typical Senior Day, those who pottered through the exhibits would average between ninety and a hundred years old. The sight of them made Orlando feel like a spring chicken. For a spell he could ignore his own aches. Their gossip about synthetic livers and nylon hip joints made him thankful that he still had all of his original equipment. Alert to signs of decay in themselves, the old folks diligently noted any least wobble in the machinery of the disney. With their prying canes and their eyes renewed by cataract operations, they found out the slightest flaw in Orlando's exhibits. "That hyena is leaking oil," they would inform him. Or "That phoenix doesn't set its tail feathers all the way down on the fire." Or "That giraffe's got a kink in its get-along." What a chorus of complaints they would sing about a belching lion!

Orlando had instituted Senior Day when he himself turned seventy. He still didn't feel old, but he noticed that many of the bewigged and wrinkled elders who had been visiting the disney for years were looking downright decrepit. Give the old gents and ladies a chance to hobble around or cruise the sidewalks in their zip-carts without being jostled by kids, he figured. Give them a little quiet so they can hear themselves think.

This monthly influx of old-timers had become the occasion for meetings of a secret lodge called Seniors Against Gravity, or SAG. Those who belonged to this organization could be identified by the split-fingered handshakes they gave one another and by their drooping, orange hats, rather like oversized hot water bottles, which flapped against the sides of their heads as they strolled. At a climactic moment in the SAG rituals, these limp, rubbery hats were pumped full of air, and the inflated shape was revealed to be that of a gigantic fist. This transformation symbolized the prime belief of SAG, namely, that life is a prolonged struggle against gravity. Arthritic knees, flaccid breasts, discouraged hearts, tired blood—what is old age but the accumulated effect of gravity? What is youth, giddy and supple, but a condition of weightlessness?

Orlando was familiar with their creed from having attended a series of introductory lectures. But he couldn't bring himself to undergo the initiation and actually join, partly because he did not fancy wearing the orange balloon hat, partly because he was too much of a nuts-and-bolts man to swallow their various schemes for defying gravity. Some members placed their hopes in levitation, others in astral traveling, some tried out the latest pills, others encircled themselves with helium-filled doughnuts and bounced along, and still others slept upside-down in harnesses while breathing a mixture of restorative gases. Animal magnetism, interstellar ether, orgone rays, flying carpets, and most other forces known to quackery or science had been called into play.

Never initiated into SAG, Orlando was not allowed to observe the mystic rites they performed at their monthly gatherings in the disney auditorium. He knew about the ceremonial inflation of the hats from eavesdropping on his old cronies, who complained of leaks in their headgear. By watching from outside, he knew the members left their shoes at the door, even those who rolled to the meeting in zip-carts, and they all proceeded into the room in their stocking feet. By pressing his ear to the wall of the auditorium, he could pick up tremors from their droning voices. But he did not recognize a word they were saying. "Picka cowski pep" was a typical expression. "Pucka reemy poo" was another. Perhaps they used an ancient language. Midway through the ceremony, the entire building began to hum—whether from chanting or from the gravity-defying gadgets wielded by various members or from one of the occult forces they summoned up, he could not say.

■

FOR THIS meeting of SAG, Orlando had been asked by the leader of the group to stage another one of his bang-up shows.

"Like the one you did with the dog ventriloquist, remember?" said Humphrey Tree, the pleasant old butterball who currently held the post of Exalted Sagamore.

"That was a pretty good one," Orlando admitted.

"Or the boxing kangaroos," said Humphrey.

"Did you like them better than the dolphins?"

"The ones that did ballroom dancing?" Humphrey stroked his chin, from which a few pale whiskers sprouted like the rootlets of potatoes. "Hard to say, hard to say. I'll tell you what I didn't like, though. I didn't like the yodeling peacock."

"That was pretty much of a flop," Orlando agreed.

"Whatever you do, just be sure and make it uplifting." The Exalted Sagamore arched his white caterpillar eyebrows in a plea for laughter. "You get it?"

"Get what?"

Over ninety, something of an uncle to Orlando, Humphrey had been firing puns and jokes at him for half a century, but Orlando still often required an explanation or a dig in the ribs before he could see the humor.

"Uplifting," Humphrey explained, "as in morally elevating, but also as in rising from the ground." Hooking his thumbs together, he wagged his fingers to mimic the flight of a bird. "Now you see?"

"Oh, sure, I get it now," said Orlando, giving him an obedient chuckle.

■

AFTER RECEIVING this invitation, Orlando put his mind to work on the subject of uplift. Eventually he devised a plan that made a bubble of pleasure form in his chest. What could more vividly illustrate the triumph over gravity, he reasoned, than the spectacle of an elephant standing on its head? What, indeed, except to behold that same elephant launch itself skyward by expelling a jet of air from its trunk? A week's labor went into the preparation of this trick. It was indeed a trick, for the jet from the elephant's trunk only seemed to boost it from the ground. The actual hoisting was accomplished by means of winches and transparent cables.

On the morning of Senior Day, Orlando put the elephant through its paces one last time, and it performed flawlessly. Late in the afternoon, the initiates filed into the auditorium for their secret rituals, wearing limp orange hats and floor-length black capes imprinted with the symbols of uranium and plutonium. (They considered radioactivity to be nature's own way of thumbing its nose at the tyranny of matter.) Orlando stood outside awaiting his summons. Nervously he ran a finger along the creases in his freshly-laundered safari suit. Not long after the point in the ceremony when the building vibrated like a tuning fork, the Exalted Sagamore himself opened the door and said, "Show time, kiddo."

Orlando adjusted the angle on his pith helmet and strode inside. The members were clustered near the stage in zip-carts, helium-filled doughnuts, wheeled breathing-boxes, and other contraptions. Following Humphrey Tree down the aisle to the podium, smiling self-consciously, Orlando noticed with regret that all the balloon hats were as flat as pancakes. He had been hoping to spy one in its full glory.

"Fellow SAGites," declared Humphrey, with a sweep of

his cape, "I give you our generous host—a man known to you all as a friend of our cause, the master of this disney, the supreme wizard of machines—Mr. Orlando Spinks!"

The roomful of wheezy old lungs broke into cheers. By far the loudest noise proceeded from the mouth of Grace Palomino, a ninety-year-old dynamo in a blue wig. She was Humphrey's wife, and a devoted one, with enough gusto left over to dote thoroughly on Orlando, for whom she was something of an aunt, as Humphrey was something of an uncle. Perched on a seat in front, she exposed her acrylic teeth in an ear-to-ear grin.

Her smile put Orlando at ease. Although he was by nature shy, the sight of an audience never failed to ignite in him a flicker of the Spinks family showmanship. He climbed onto the stage and stood before the curtain. He raised his arms. "Thank you, thank you, ladies and gentlemen! Hold your applause—and throw money!" He thrust out his pith helmet in the attitude of a beggar with a bowl, then laughed and slapped it back onto his head. "No, no. Seriously, now, it gives me great pleasure to offer you today an act never before witnessed on land or sea. I have spared no effort or expense to bring here for your delight and instruction—from the wilds of Oklahoma—the incredible—the stupendous—the one and only—SUMO THE ELEPHANT!"

He punched a button on the controller that was buckled to his wrist. The houselights went down and the curtain parted, revealing a scrim on which was projected the holographic image of a jungle. Monkeys could be spotted dangling like hairy question marks from the boughs. Snakes festooned the looping vines. Off to one side, a tiger was quietly gnawing the remains of a unicorn. Lightning flashed and thunder crackled.

The spectators oohed and aahed, then burst into applause as the elephant lumbered on stage. It slouched up to Orlando and pretended to lean against him. He smacked it in the ribs. "Stand up straight, you big oaf!"

The elephant promptly rose onto its hind legs and aimed its trunk at the roof.

"Not that straight!" Orlando cried.

Sumo flopped back down onto all fours.

"That's better! Now say hello to the folks!"

With a flap of its huge ears, the elephant gravely bowed.

"Good boy, good boy. How about a little dance?"

The bucket-sized feet did a barefoot version of the old soft shoe. Each number drew louder and louder applause.

"Now show us a little ballet!" said Orlando.

The elephant posed on one chubby hind leg and slowly pirouetted.

"All right, now, Sumo, let's wake up those folks in the back row."

The elephant curled its trunk and loosed a deafening honk. This was greeted with laughter and whistles, even from those elders who had in fact been catching a little shut-eye in the rear seats.

"Tune up your hearing-aids, ladies and gentlemen! Squint up your eyeballs! You are about to see and hear wonders!"

Keeping up a jaunty patter—not his strongest point—Orlando ran the elephant through the rest of the performance. A game of catch with a beachball was followed by the working of simple arithmetic problems, the reciting of an ode to peanuts, and a brisk flurry of hopscotch. As the finale approached, the opening bars of "The Flight of the Bumble Bee" sizzled from overhead speakers, quite loud, so as to drown out the noise of meshing gears and grinding winches.

"And now, ladies and gentlemen," Orlando shouted above the dizzy music, "watch closely, for Sumo is about to attempt the most difficult, dangerous, and *uplifting* routine ever performed by a pachyderm on this or any other stage!"

As programmed, the invisible cables hoisted the elephant's rear end until the beast appeared to be standing on its forelegs. Thinking this the whole stunt, the audience clapped lustily. Next came the headstand, which inspired more clapping. Then, tip of trunk pressed to the floor, grunting as though from herculean effort, the elephant ponderously rose until it seemed to balance on its slender snout. Whistles, thumping of canes. Then came a blast of air from the trunk and the enormous gray bulk lifted from the stage. Frenzied cheers!

Flushed with pride, Orlando stood admiring his handiwork. Proud as any parents, Humphrey and Grace beamed at him.

At this point, Sumo was programmed to settle gently down and then bow in parting. But instead, the elephant hovered there like a blimp above the stage. In mid-air it began to shimmy.

Orlando madly poked buttons on the controller. Nothing doing. "Dad burn it!" he muttered. "What's wrong now?"

Suddenly "The Flight of the Bumble Bee" was cut off, the sound of cannons boomed from the speakers, the huge body seemed to erupt, and from the raised hindquarters shot a stream of brown and green and yellow lumps. At first glance, and against all logic, Orlando figured these must be samples of what Grandfather Spinks used to shovel from the elephant's pen at the Franklin Park Zoo. But on closer inspection, as one lump after another thudded to the stage, he recognized them for what they were.

"Our shoes!" cried the SAGites. They clumped their stockinged feet in glee. They howled with delight. They tossed balled-up credit vouchers at Orlando. The engineer of beasts had surpassed himself with this final display! Imagine, a volcano of shoes!

Bewildered, Orlando glanced from the erupting elephant to the cheering crowd and back again. He shrugged, put on a goofy smile of humility, and soaked in this downpour of praise. Then slowly it dawned on him that his orderly life had been knocked out of kilter for a second time by that quick-fingered orphan.

■

WHILE THE SAGites were sorting through the heap of footwear on stage and laying claim to their own shoes, Orlando unhooked the elephant from its cables and drove it back to the workshop. He checked it over for signs of tampering. Behind Sumo's left ear he found a chalked message: GREETINGS FROM YOUR FUTURE APPRENTICE. Dag nab it, he swore to himself. That girl. He was about to phone the orphanage and lodge another complaint when he thought to look behind the right ear, where he found the message: PLEASE DON'T RAT ON ME.

Just then a tooting of horns drew him to the door. Humphrey Tree and Grace Palomino had driven by the shop in their zip-carts to thank him again for the marvelous show. Shriveled by their great age and hunched over the steering wheels, they might have been wizened kids in dodgem cars. They had taken off their ceremonial capes and rubber hats and were dressed in the grungy-gray jumpsuits they wore for scavenging. The cargo bins at the rear of the zip-carts were piled high with junk.

"I don't see what we can do next month to top that, kiddo," said Humphrey.

"I haven't laughed so hard since I had a look at my last face-lift," said Grace.

Orlando gazed at his toes. "It was nothing."

"My favorite was that bit with the shoes," Humphrey said.

"Yes, oh my!" Grace declared. "The whole show was one big hoot—the floating in the air and stuff—but the gag with the shoes proved you really are a wizard. However did you do it?"

Orlando hemmed and hawed before replying, "I had help from an elf."

"Come off it," said Grace.

"Or maybe it was a gremlin," Orlando added.

"Elves and gremlins!" said Grace. "Why all this humble pie, dearie? Take credit where credit is due. Nobody else is going to blow your horn for you."

Humphrey beeped out shave-and-a-haircut on the horn of the zip-cart. "Just a little joke," he said. "I couldn't resist. Well, so long, kiddo, and thanks again. Gracie and I have to go unload our day's haul." He jerked a thumb back over his shoulder at the tarp-covered mounds of junk in the cargo bins.

"Ta ta!" said Grace.

Pouring the juice to their zip-carts, the two old scavengers went cruising away toward the mountains that loomed beyond the disney. Orlando watched them go, reflecting on the hydraulics involved in the launching of shoes, and admitting to himself that it really was a pretty slick trick.

5 ∙

The mountains of New Boston closed each night between twenty-two and twenty-four o'clock to allow for cleaning. Even in this spick-and-span metropolis, where dirt cost more per kilo than sugar, a mountain could become remarkably filthy in a day's time. Children climbing in the flexiglass trees shook down a litter of twigs. Cups and wrappers and peel-off lids spread about the vending machines like glacial moraines. Deltas of metal shavings accumulated at the ends of pedbelts. Hikers who refused to ride the belts, toiling instead uphill with the aid of pikestaffs, often punctured the inflatable rocks, which then cluttered the mountainsides like cast-off skins. Idlers on benches pared their fingernails and some even blithely spat on the walkways.

There were four of these mountains in Natureland Park, out at the edge of the city. All that separated them from the curving, translucent shell was the disney, whose lighted hub and aisles looked, from the mountain peaks, like a stationary Ferris wheel. The summits rose just high enough to give a view into the upper-story windows of the New Boston skyscrapers. Molded with quickfoam around aluminum skeletons and named after the corporations that financed their construction, they were supposed to make up for the mountains of stone and earth from which the citizens had been cut off at the time of the Enclosure. These days only old-timers, gazing at the pointy hills, could remember the mountains of Maine and Tennessee and Oregon.

Each night, as the last of the strollers withdrew at twenty-two o'clock, detergents gushed from nozzles on the peaks and scoured the slopes. Drains siphoned the run-off into recycling vats down below, where the muck was reduced to its original elements, which would be refashioned eventually into some new doohickey or other.

Mt. Hexxon, tallest of the four mountains, was honeycombed with caves. Stalactites dangled from the ceilings, mushrooms sprouted from the floors, albino crayfish speckled the ceilings, bats glided through the dank air, every feature having been made out of some rubbery gunk. Hidden tubes dripped water into murky pools. The hollow chambers echoed with the grunt of circulating pumps. No matter what your opinion of caves, these were pretty gloomy holes. The psycho-architects who had designed Natureland Park, as they had designed every last nook and cranny of the Enclosure, believed that even space-age citizens would need some place for making stone-age retreats. The citizens thought otherwise. Each year fewer and fewer people ventured down into these clammy pits. Those who did often returned gasping from the blackness. So the lower caves were slowly filled by the groundskeepers with out-of-fashion vegetation, deflated rocks, broken trees, shattered creekbeds, sacks of frogs, tangles of snakes. These shaggy and bulging items only rendered the darkness more frightening. After a few spelunkers lost their wits in the labyrinths, the Overseers closed all the entrances to the caves, leaving open only the ventilator shafts.

■

IF, LIKE Humphrey Tree and Grace Palomino, you were looking for some hidey-hole where you could stash away tons and tons of junk, then Mt. Hexxon was just the place. They had been collecting junk for years from the streets of New Boston, not from any habit of tidiness, but, on the contrary, from a desire to spring a messy surprise on this oppressively tidy city. The two old scavengers usually reached the foot of the mountain at twenty-four o'clock, an hour they persisted in calling midnight, even though midnight looked no different from noon under the eternal blaze of lights in the domed city.

Because of the SAG meeting at the disney, however, tonight Grace and Humphrey arrived early. The cleaning fluid was still pouring down the slopes. So they sat in their zip-carts talking over old times, which in their case stretched back almost nine decades. They had known one another since kindergarten days in the suburbs of Old Boston. They married right after college, then served in the Pollution Corps together, moving around the country as, bit by bit, the whole of North America was declared uninhabitable. They knew the history of one another's wrinkles. Over the years they had come to smell alike, a mixture of wintergreen and fish oil. The sum of their weights hardly varied, so that if Humphrey put on a kilo or two, Grace lost the same amount, and vice versa. By now they had loved one another so long that the edges of their personalities were fuzzing together. When either one began a sentence, the other one could finish it.

Humphrey broke a spell of silence by chortling.

"That Orlando!" said Grace, divining the source of the laughter.

"Those shoes!" Humphrey exclaimed.

"To think little mister sober-sides—"

"—grew up into such a card!"

"What a shame—"

"—he never married."

"No kids," Grace lamented.

"He'd have been great with kids," Humphrey agreed.

They both sighed, for Orlando was the closest thing to a child they themselves had ever had. When Grandfather Spinks ran afoul of the gorilla and again when Mother Spinks ran off with the dictaphone salesman and yet again when Father Spinks died in the arms of the squid, Grace and Humphrey, as friends of the family, had stepped in to comfort Orlando. From boyhood on, every time he caught a cold, they sneezed. Every time he picked up a new scar, a matching scar formed on their own hearts.

"It's hard to believe—" Humphrey began.

"—he's getting old like us," Grace concluded.

"Bald as a billiard ball."

"Still cute as a bug."

Never cute by any standard, Humphrey at ninety-three had a face that brought to mind a crumpled brown sack. Fortunately, Grace never gave a hang about looks. After his stint in the Pollution Corps he became a chip inspector, a tedious job from which he was now blessedly retired. His eyes and heart were electronic, and one hand was synthetic, but otherwise he still got by with most of his original joints and organs. Due to his monumental appetite, he had accumulated a big man's body on a small man's frame, so the flesh now sagged over his skeleton like a garment he would never grow into. Grace was a bit younger, a retired tap-dancer, not so quick on her feet since acquiring new hips and ankles and knees. Shriveled now, she possessed the antiquated beauty of a palace awaiting restoration. When she was feeling her oats, she ran circles around Humphrey.

Their youth was so far in the past it had taken on the blurry contours of myth. Grace was half convinced her mother the oceanographer used to ride whales. Humphrey was persuaded that his father, a coal miner, had brought him ingots of goblin iron hot from the center of the earth. Orlando's youth they could summon up more clearly.

"Remember when he was about three or four and we gave him that toolbelt with the loop on it for his pliers?" Humphrey recalled.

"He wore it slung down low over his hip like a six-gun," said Grace.

"And remember when he was a teenager—"

"—how the girls chased after him—"

"—and how fast he ran—"

"—straight to his workshop."

"Always nuts about machines."

"Instead of tickling girls he tinkered with gears."

"And look at him now! Still tinkering."

"Still a bachelor."

"You know, Gracie, there's something to be said for falling in love while you're young."

"Before you know any better," she replied.

"Before you get stuck in your ways."

"Before you start worrying about pain and separation and death and all that bluesy stuff."

"Bingo," said Humphrey.

Uneasy about the drift of their talk, they clammed up for a while and listened to the purr of golden-oldies playing from the tapebox on Humphrey's hat.

■

AT LENGTH the cleansing of the mountain was finished and the gates opened. Driving their zip-carts, which as usual were heaped with junk, Humphrey and Grace climbed the mountain's glistening flank. Everything shone as if newly made, the quickfoam gullies and hillocks, the flexiglass bushes and trees, the concrete paths. Below, the avenues were marked out in a grid of lights, immaculate, unblemished, as if New Boston had just that moment crystallized out of the air like a snowflake. This sterile perfection, false to everything they knew about the funk and mess of living, made them grit their teeth.

While they had the peak to themselves, Grace and Humphrey climbed out of their zip-carts and peeled back the tarps and showed one another the treasures they had collected on their separate rounds that day.

"Twenty-seven cans," Humphrey announced, pointing out a few of the highlights in his cargo bin, "five rags, two zippers, a pair of boxer shorts, a melted joy stick, and volume three of *The Anarchist's Handbook*."

"Don't we already have the fourth volume?"

"It's down there somewhere." He tapped his foot on the roof of Mt. Hexxon.

"Lord only knows where," said Grace. "But just look here at this hubcap and this perfectly good catcher's mitt." She put on the mitt, which swallowed her birdwing of an arm halfway to the elbow. "Chuck it in here, babe!" she sang, smacking a fist into the pocket.

Humphrey tossed her a doorknob, which she caught handily. "Any spoons?" he asked. Because of his gargantuan appetite, he coveted spoons above all other loot.

"No," said Grace, "but here's a fork."

"Ah, there's my sharp-eyed lass!" So saying, Humphrey kissed her full on the puckered lips. That was one of the fringe benefits of growing old: you could smooch whenever you liked and tell any busybody who objected to go take a flying leap.

"And would you believe seven wigs?" said Grace.

"Isn't that a record for wigs?"

"I do believe it is. And they're good thick ones, too."

The blue wig that Grace was wearing had been acquired in this manner, as had the music-box hat worn by Humphrey, as indeed had the better part of their entire wardrobe. Her knee-length boots, for example, had been salvaged from a trash can beside the wading pool in Marconi Plaza.

They did not scavenge as a way of making ends meet, but as a hobby, almost an art. Unlike Old Boston, whose streets in the latter days before the Enclosure had swarmed with bums and beggars and dumpster-pickers, New Boston fed and housed every last soul. Collecting junk was not easy in that sanitary city. Along with the mountains, the streets and towers and plazas were flushed daily, each quarter of the city at a different hour; and the recyclers down below gobbled everything. No space station gliding in orbit, no ship cruising to the stars could have been tidier than New Boston afloat on the sea. By timing their rounds carefully, however, Grace and Humphrey scoured the avenues just ahead of the detergents, and thus managed to find, on most days, a cartload of trash: discarded clothing, broken heels, foam cups, advertising flimsies, toys, leaking batteries, wire, belt buckles, electronic gadgets, spare body parts.

People sometimes left stale food or wounded furniture

in their path, thinking these old geezers had somehow fallen through the welfare net into poverty. Most people, however, encountering the two scavengers, pretended not to see them. The Overseers regarded them as harmless eccentrics. What did it matter if they hoarded rubbish? They planned to make it matter, one day when their mountain was filled with junk. They would give this glittering city something to chew on.

After the day's discoveries had been admired, Humphrey and Grace shoved aside one of the pumped-up boulders, disclosing the mouth of a ventilator shaft, and through this opening they dumped their junk into the hollow crown of Mt. Hexxon. As they listened to these new prizes clattering or whumping onto the hoard of rubbish below, they exchanged the sly prankish look they had been exchanging on conspiratorial occasions since kindergarten.

Once the boulder was back in place, they sat for a while atop the mountain, basking in the artificial sunlight, gazing down on the city. The icy glitter of the streets reminded them of winters when they were living in Watertown and the Charles River froze hard and they could skate all the way past Cambridge to the dam. That ice had gleamed with the same sinister perfection.

Grace felt a cuddly mood coming on. "You know what I could do with right now?"

"What's that, chickiepea?"

"A cat."

"Now, Gracie. Don't start in again."

She craved all manner of pets, as Humphrey craved all manner of food, but most of all she longed for a lapful of cats. Nothing about the move into the Enclosure caused her more grief than the prohibition against pets.

"I'd settle for a cross-eyed tom with its tail chewed off," she muttered.

"I keep telling you Orlando could *make* you a cat."

"I mean a *real* one. What I want is a four-legged, willful, cantankerous fur ball that glares at you through slitty eyes and goes its own merry way."

"Orlando ought to be able to whip you up something along those lines."

"Aaargh," said Grace.

Hoping to distract her, Humphrey pointed at the sky and exclaimed, "Will you look at that!"

Lavender clouds had begun spurting from vents on the neighboring peak of Mt. Pepsicoke, storm clouds that would never drop rain or snow but would merely hover beneath the dome like bruised angels.

"So big deal. Clouds."

"But look at the sickly purples they're using," said Humphrey.

Grace perked up. "You're right. The old storm clouds used to remind me of those dark purple lilacs we had out by the compost bins on Lincoln Street. Purple so deep it looked like grape jelly."

"Grape jelly," mused Humphrey.

"Lilacs," said Grace, realizing her mistake.

"Orange marmalade."

"Remember how they drooped," Grace insisted, "and the bees would swarm around them and get so loaded up with pollen they could hardly fly?"

"Honey! Oh, lordy, baking powder biscuits! Strawberry preserves. Blackberry cobbler. Cherry pie. Stewed rhubarb." Humphrey's tongue flicked across his lips, probing the wrinkles as if prospecting for those vanished flavors.

Once he began reminiscing about old-time foods, you

just had to let him run down. So while he drooled through his epic of jams and jellies, Grace figured she might as well recall her own vanished pleasures: the slither of wool against her skin, the smell of dung from police horses, the raspy summer sound of locusts, the ooze of hot tar between her toes on a country road, the squirm of a kitten. So the two old people ambled on separate pathways of reminiscence back to the dead-and-gone days from before the building of New Boston. They ended up gaping at one another, startled by the length of their memories, measuring how old they were by the remoteness of these things.

"All the same," Grace declared, "I wouldn't go back to those days for love or money. If we were still living outside, we'd be dead."

Humphrey agreed. "Killed thirteen different ways by poisons and radiation, starved to death, and shot full of holes in the bargain. Not to mention getting fried by ultraviolet light and sizzled by microwaves and eaten up by acid rain."

"One of those alphabet chemicals—DDT or PDQ or PCB—would have rotted our bones."

"Druggies would have bonked us over the head."

"Those teenage rowdies!"

"The greenhouse effect!"

"Smog!"

They clicked their tongues in perfect rhythm. At this point the first visitors of the new day were gliding up the slopes on pedbelts or dawdling up the walkways on foot, children tugging at leashes, kids wearing the masks of their favorite video stars, occasional old people as barefaced as Humphrey and Grace, all of them so fresh-looking they might have just been taken off a shelf and unwrapped.

"Here comes the enemy," said Grace. She stood up, beating the dust from her jumpsuit, stamping her boots on the mountain's flimsy skin. The nearby trees wobbled and boulders bounced.

"More powerful than an earthquake," Humphrey observed.

"You'd better believe it," said Grace.

6·

After the stunt with the elephant and the shoes, Mooch lay low for a spell, waiting to see if Orlando would squeal on her to The Pickle. That little prank was a calculated risk. One more complaint and Bertha Dill might very well ship her fanny to the chemmie dump or the prison farm. But Mooch figured the only way of winning over the engineer was by showing how good she was at his own mechanical art. True, he didn't come running to the Home and begging her to become his apprentice. But he didn't squeal on her, either. So there was hope.

When several days passed without a call to the office, Mooch reckoned it would be safe to pay Orlando another stealthy visit. On Sunday, freed on a five-hour pass, she ducked past the robot gatekeeper at the disney, hid away in the hall of dinosaurs, and then, while Orlando was making his rounds of the exhibits, she jimmied a lock and slipped into the workshop.

It gave her a scare to see the stuffed animal heads glooming down from their mounts near the ceiling. Buffalo, antelope, musk ox, wolf, moose—her glance darted from one to another, and came to rest on the grizzly bear. As on her poster, the lips were curled back, teeth bared in a snarl. Imagine a day when such creatures walked the earth! On all the heads, the glass eyes shone, the fur bristled as though freshly groomed.

The entire shop was amazingly neat. Tools hung against their own painted silhouettes on pegboard racks. Gray steel cabinets lined three walls. Inside the cabinets were drawers, inside the drawers were cubbyholes, inside the cubbyholes were parts, each one identified with typed labels—enough parts, it seemed, to repair all the beasts on Noah's Ark. A lucky thing, too, because the rest of the shop was filled with broken animals. Laid out on benches, wires sprouting from eye sockets, cogs and shafts gleaming through torn fur, they might have been so many anesthetized bodies awaiting operations. The place looked clean enough for open-heart surgery.

Here was a chance to make herself indispensable, thought Mooch, as she looked over the wounded mechanimals. She pitched right in to work on the nearest hulk, which was a python with a kinked spine, and before long she was hooking vertebrae together and sliding the long ribcage back into the tube of skin. The card she left propped against the snake's nose read COMPLIMENTS OF YOUR HELPER, and on it she drew in red ink the pawprint of a bear.

On the next few Sundays, always sneaking into the shop while Orlando was out, she repaired a centaur's knee joint, renewed the feathers on the head of an ostrich, patched a leak in a camel's hump, replaced a servomotor in the tail of a mermaid, and touched up the spots on a leopard. Each time she left her card. On the last of these visits she discovered a new casualty in need of a fix, this one a coyote with a blotto memory board. Patiently she tested the chips and replaced the defective ones. And then, because the monitor showed Orlando still busy outside answering questions from a bunch of gawkers, she decided to venture a step beyond innocent repairs. Before stuffing the electronics back inside the fur, she programmed the coyote to say a few chummy words when next it spied its master.

■

MOOCH was snug in her bunk at the Home, playing two-handed solitaire with a girl from across the hall, when Orlando slumped back into the workshop. It had been a tough day—an overflow crowd, trash ankle-deep in the aisles, two clean-up drones on the blink, a vending machine smashed by customers angry over being charged for burnt soydogs, an alligator's jaw dislocated by a kid who propped it open with a baseball bat, visitors asking endless dumb questions. I really could use some help, Orlando was thinking as he trudged into the shop.

It did not surprise him to find the coyote, out of commission that morning, now sitting up alertly on the bench. Like a fairy mending the cobbler's shoes at night, the girl had been fixing mechs on Sundays for the past several weeks. The cards she left behind were stuck in the frame of his bathroom mirror, as a reminder for him to thank her if he ever laid eyes on her. She was an elusive kid. What did surprise Orlando was to behold the sleek, dusty-golden coyote leap down from the bench, lift a forepaw in the air, and say in a syrupy voice, "Howdy-do, boss."

Orlando raised his own hand in greeting, then dropped it quickly when he realized what he was doing.

"I know you've had a bummer of a day, boss," the coyote went on, "and that's the very thing I want to jaw with you about. So before you switch me off or go soak your feet or pop a headache pill, let me bend your ear a minute. You listening?"

"Yes," Orlando replied uncomfortably. He could not bring himself to be rude even to a machine.

The coyote clacked its fangs in seeming approval. "Truth is, I worry about you, boss. You take on too much. Look at this humongous big disney—ten zillion widgets to break down—and only one of you. Now, I ask you, is that wise? To work yourself down to a frazzle? And what about me and the rest of the hairy crew? Where'd we be if you keeled over? Up a creek, is where. I'm talking responsibility here, boss. I'm talking forethought."

"That girl put you up to this, didn't she?" said Orlando.

Unfazed by the interruption, the coyote merely paused, mouth open, until Orlando had finished, then it resumed: "Who's going to run this place when you kick the bucket? Who's going to carry on the Spinks family tradition? Are you just gonna let this fabuloso empire of machines fall apart after you're gone? Think of it, me and the other mechs being sold for scrap! The disney torn down and in its place a crummy zappo range or feelie palace! All your life's work gone down the tube! Hey, boss, you still with me?"

"I'm with you." In spite of himself, Orlando was feeling the rasp of anxiety, like a coarse file grating back and forth on his skull.

"But don't despair, boss. There's a simple solution."

"Let me guess. I should get myself an apprentice?"

As before, the coyote only paused, waiting for silence, then continued as though Orlando had not spoken: "All you've got to do is find yourself an apprentice."

"From The Home for Little Wanderers, by any chance?"

"What you need is a kid with no family strings attached. An orphan, say. Like from The Home for Little Wanderers."

"A girl, perhaps?"

"I'd go for a girl, if I were you. She's got the deft fingers. She's teachable. She's neat. The best age is around thirteen—old enough to work on her own, not so old that her head's filled up with boys."

"And I suppose you have the ideal thirteen-year-old orphan girl in mind?"

Instead of coming out with the name of Mooch, as Orlando had expected, the coyote sat up on its haunches, aimed its muzzle at the ceiling, and broke into a wheedly rendition of "Daisy, Daisy, give me your answer, do." In place of "Daisy," however, the coyote inserted the name "Orlando," which gave the song a ragged rhythm.

Amazed, the engineer burst out laughing. He sobered up quickly, however, when the coyote crooned, "I'm half crazy, all for the love of you." It always made him nervous to hear love dragged in.

■

FAIR ENOUGH, thought Orlando, as he lay that night on his astro-lounger in the control room, unable to sleep. The coyote had a point. Rather, the *girl* had a point. He was not getting any younger, and neither were the beasts. It would be worth putting up with a kid underfoot in exchange for a little help. No two ways about it: she knew how to use her hands. She would make things messier for a while, but she could be trained to pick up after herself. She would learn soon enough to rise and sleep on his regular schedule, to eat what he ate, to adopt his monkly habits. Her talk of bears and wilderness was no more than that, he felt certain—merely talk. The orphanage director, that cushiony woman with the sour name and sour face, must have been flattering herself, bragging on her own patience, when she spoke of the girl as a walking catastrophe. Behold me, Bertha Dill, suffering the slings and arrows of this outrageous child! Dog piddle, thought Orlando. Pure dee bushwa. Would a truly rotten girl spend her Sundays clearing up the backlog in some old coot's repair shop?

Besides, if the girl caused him any grief, he could ship her back to the Home with a list of damages.

Before he signed on as a surrogate parent, though, he wanted to consult with his own surrogate parents, Humphrey Tree and Grace Palomino. Surely they must have felt some jitters when Mother Spinks ran off with the dictaphone salesman and Father Spinks drowned in the squid's embrace and they were left in charge of a wet-eared youth.

"We didn't feel the least bit uneasy," Grace told him next morning at breakfast. "Isn't that right, Humphrey?"

Humphrey nodded from across the table. His mouth—as usual when he found himself in the neighborhood of food—was fully occupied with eating.

"Ours was a different case entirely," said Grace. "We'd known you since you were in diapers. We'd seen you toddle around in your first tool belt. We'd spanked your bottom. Isn't that right, Humphrey?"

"Mmmph," the ancient gentleman replied around a wad of toast.

"When your parents abandoned the nest, so to speak," Grace went on, "we knew just what sort of bird we were taking under our wings. But what do you know about this girl? It's the prankster we're talking about, right? The sweetie who made the elephant spew out shoes?"

"She's the one," said Orlando.

"What's the scoop on her, then?" Grace asked.

He told them everything he knew about Emitty Harvard Tufts, beginning with his rescue of the girl from the lion's mouth, roaming back to her conception in a test tube and forward to her meddling with the coyote, not omitting the numerous tales of rebelliousness he had gleaned from Bertha Dill.

"Snap her up," Grace urged him at the conclusion of his report. "I like her spunk. I like her grit. She's just what you need around here. A kid like that could take a load off your shoulders. Loosen you up. Besides, the poor thing deserves a break. Imagine, patenting a baby! What do you say, dumpling?"

Humphrey waved a half-eaten bagel in token of agreement. Like his wife, he surmised that such a rambunctious girl, with her craving for the wilds, might be just the sort of person to understand why two old geezers would stuff an aluminum mountain full of trash. She also had the perfect build for slithering down through the caverns of Mt. Hexxon on a certain mischievous mission.

■

"If you can tame her," Bertha Dill told Orlando in her office later that day, "I will eat my hat."

In windless, rainless, sunless New Boston, hardly anybody wore hats, least of all Bertha Dill, who spent too much on her high-rise hairdos to risk mashing them down. But the expression lingered from the old days of weather.

One of the rare souls who did wear a hat—not so much to cover his bald scalp as to complete his safari costume— Orlando now pressed the pith helmet to his chest, turning it nervously with tiny inching movements of his fingers along the brim. Unencumbered, his white fringe of hair stood out like a parasol.

"And if I can't tame her," he said, "I can always return her, is that right?"

"Unfortunately, yes." The director frowned. Her face, powdery with makeup, gave the impression of a rumpled bed. The image was reinforced by the ruffled white dress she wore, a garment voluminous enough, Orlando estimated, to serve as a king-sized sheet.

"No time limit?" he said.

"Not before she turns eighteen."

"What happens then?"

"If you kick her out, she's got to fend for herself."

"And if she gets into trouble then?"

"That's the Overseers' problem."

Mention of the Overseers gave Orlando pause. Even in his childhood, when their less mighty counterparts had been called the police, these weapon-toting enforcers had terrified him. "What's to worry?" Father Spinks used to scold. "Did you knock over a bank while I wasn't looking? You rub somebody out? No? Then relax, the cops are here to protect us law-abiding folks." But Orlando could not help feeling a shiver of guilt whenever he encountered one of those blue uniforms. He imagined the police carried in their heads photos of suspects, one of which looked like his spitting image. Now the uniforms were a metallic gold, bulging with a dozen pockets in which the Overseers carried stunners, light-probes, radios, sniffers, truth-drugs for interrogations, and who knew what other lethal devices. The sight of a gold figure in its mirrored helmet riding the pedbelts or gliding overhead in a shuttle made him break into a sweat.

Bertha Dill, with her claxon voice, pried him loose from the grip of these reflections by demanding, "So what's it going to be? You want an apprentice or not?"

Her chair creaked as she leaned forward expectantly on the desk. The flesh of her elbows spread in doughy rolls.

Her powdered face took on the eager look of a saleswoman about to unload the last outfit in a discontinued line.

Shoving aside his frets, reminding himself of the ingenious coyote, the elephant, the lion, the mechs repaired as though by fairies, he said firmly, "Where do I sign?"

■

MEANWHILE, the object of their conversation, advised of the news by a matron, was racing through the halls of the girls' dormitory, pounding on doors and screaming in jubilation, her red locks floating behind like the tail of a meteor.

From the boys' dorm across the yard, Garrison Rathbone recognized the voice. It was the quiet hour before supper, when all good Little Wanderers were supposed to be studying, so Mooch's hollering broke over the Home like a trayful of china clattering to the floor in a hushed cafeteria.

Garrison knew the likely meaning of this frenzied racket, because every time Mooch was chosen to be an apprentice she carried on this way. Shutting the fractal geometry text around his forefinger to keep his place, he went down and stood in the yard and listened with a heart swollen by sadness to her exuberant shrieks. It did not make him feel any less miserable to recall that her previous four apprenticeships had ended in disaster, and that on each occasion she had returned to the Home within a few weeks. He feared she might behave herself this time, hit it off with the old engineer from the disney, and never come back. No longer able to see her every day, no longer able to listen to her giggling with friends in the grub line, deprived of her like an astronaut deprived of air, he would suffocate from grief. What a waste! A dude like him, smart as a cyber, not bad looking in dim light, brimming with love, and nobody to spend his riches on.

After a while the racket died down. The light went on in Mooch's room and her silhouette, familiar to Garrison from long evenings of observation, flitted across it as she packed. She would be taking down the grizzly bear poster from the door, the star charts from the ceiling, the pictures of dream-animals from the walls, with nary a thought in her noggin about him.

Heavy with sadness, he could not move. He was still sulking there in the yard, geometry book dangling forgotten in his fist, when Mooch and the old bow-legged engineer came out of the girls' dorm. They walked side by side, a cautious distance apart, the old guy putzing along in his khaki shorts and white helmet like an antique Boy Scout, Mooch slinking along in her OUT OF MY WAY shimmy-shirt and her black jeans that were painted with tiger stripes. Mooch was talking a blue streak in her usual breathless way, gesturing flamboyantly. She carried only a small zippered bag, which gave off the clink of tools. The engineer was lugging her two suitcases.

Garrison had prepared himself to stand there beside the walk, inconspicuous as a lamppost, and not say a word as she strolled by, just to show he was capable of heroic suffering. But when it became clear that she really was going to flounce on by, arms gesturing, voice lilting, he broke down. In agony he cried, "So long, Mooch!"

She turned her green eyes on him, looking right through him to his bones, and said cheerily, "Oh, toodle-oo, Rat-bone. Have a good life!"

Orlando Spinks gave him a crooked smile, tugged lopsided by the weight of the suitcases. He recognized the moonstruck orphan boy with the unfortunate ears.

"You coming back here to visit?" Garrison asked.

"Not on your life," said Mooch, picking up her pace.

"How about if I come see you at the disney?"

Orlando chirped up: "Come right along any time you like, young man. Tell the ticket drones to page me and I'll give you a pass."

"Is that all right with you, Mooch?" Garrison called after her as she hastened away. "Mooch?" he cried again, his voice breaking. *"Mooch!"*

7.

During her first weeks at the disney, Mooch was on her best behavior. If only she could last a month, she would break her old record for length of apprenticeship, and she hoped by then to have made herself so useful to Orlando that he might never send her packing. She played no tricks, did what she was told, bit her lip whenever a wisecrack rose from her belly. Obediently she wore the hideous safari outfit while on the job, helmet and shorts and all, even though she hated exposing her knees.

Orlando marveled at her docility. Without a complaint, she rose before he did every morning, powered up the drones, greeted the first visitors as they shuffled through the gates; then she made her circuit of the exhibits, answering endless queries. In her spare moments she worked in the shop repairing whatever was broken. At day's end she put the tools away, and made sure everything was locked up after the last idler departed. Where, then, was the hellion spoken of by Bertha Dill?

"Just you wait," warned Bertha Dill, when she called to check on Mooch's progress. "That girl is hatching something."

"I'm delighted so far," Orlando replied.

"Mind my words. Sooner or later she'll make you eat bitter soup."

The only time Mooch said no to Orlando during those early weeks of the apprenticeship was when he asked her to work up another gag for the next meeting of the Society Against Gravity.

"The elephant and the shoes knocked them out," he said.

"Sorry, I can't do it," Mooch replied. "No more animal jokes for me."

This baffled Orlando. What were the beasts *for* except to amuse visitors? Could her refusal be the opening shot of an insurrection? There was an iron firmness in her voice, so he let the matter drop. Besides, Mooch had taken over so many of his chores that he was left with ample time to prepare a quartet of singing orangutans for the SAG meeting. Their barbershop harmonies brought down the house.

After the meeting, astride zip-carts that were loaded with junk for a run up Mt. Hexxon, Grace and Humphrey congratulated him on his splendid luck. What a find, this girl! What a helper! Privately they grumped because she was not turning out to be the minx they had been hoping for. She was bidding to become little Miss Manners, instead of a two-legged hurricane that would shake Orlando from his tidy snooze. And however could they speak with such a dutiful girl about their naughty designs for Mt. Hexxon?

"None of my cats was ever that obedient," said Grace.

"No cat in history was ever obedient," Humphrey pointed out.

"What slander!" Grace cried.

"The girl's better than a robot," said Orlando, "because you can teach her to do any job under the sun, and you never have to show her how to do a thing more than once."

"Is that her only advantage over robots?" Grace asked with a challenging flip of her blue wig.

Orlando pulled at his beard. "Well," he replied at last,

"she's better company, that's one thing. She hums when she's working, and at breakfast she tells me her dreams. Weird ones, about animals. Can you figure that, her dreaming about animals when she's never met one in the flesh?" He pinched a lock of the beard and drew it out like white taffy, adding thoughtfully, "I guess I'd have to say I *like* her, which I wouldn't say about any of the drones."

"I'm relieved to hear that," said Grace.

As for Garrison, who took up Orlando's offer of a free pass, the boy came snooping round the disney whenever he could slip away from the Home. The sight of Mooch's knees, bare and pink beneath her khaki shorts, made his pulse gallop. But he knew better than to say a word in praise of them. Most of the time he kept his distance, to avoid getting sliced by her sharp tongue. But some days the force of his desire would tug him close to her, and then he would mumble, "How's it going?" or "The gang's really missing you at the Pickle Jar."

Mooch had to admit she also missed a few kids from the Home—especially two or three girls with whom she could let down her guard and really talk—but she did not miss Ratbone, with his tall klutzy frame and his ears like solar collectors and his aura of hyperactive hormones. Yet in her new obedient guise, she was polite even with Ratbone, treating him as just another one of the gawkers who pestered her with questions all day. Say, Miss, did aunteaters eat uncles as well? How much luggage could an elephant carry in its trunk? Is it true that dragons had asbestos lips? How could unicorns eat grass without plowing up the ground with their horns?

By nightfall, when the fake sun glowing on the dome of New Boston was turned off, Mooch's head buzzed from the nitwit questions. What would those dingbats make of a real elephant? Would they shut their traps in the face of an actual grizzly?

She slept in a storage room adjoining the workshop, on a pallet she had made with a bunch of deerhides left over from the days of Grandfather Spinks. The skins had been expertly tanned: after all this time they were still supple. The pungent odor they gave off, like the inside of an old shoe, was how she imagined a tipi would smell, or a bear's den. At the Home she had occasionally dreamed of animals. Now, perhaps because of the deerhides, beasts came to her almost every night. They did not speak, but merely presented themselves, filling their skins to perfection, staring at her with eyes that were fathomless and forlorn.

■

THE SCUFFED black metal trunk in which she had found the deerhides also held other heirlooms from Orlando's father and grandfather. There were framed taxidermy licenses, prize ribbons from the Massachusetts state fair, a powder-blue tuxedo, a set of rainbow-striped suspenders, a tennis racket, a Mickey Mouse watch, and, at the bottom, underneath a layer of brittle newsfax, were seashells, feathers, fossils, and bones. Mooch handled these treasures delicately, fingers trembling. One of the bones, about the size of her pinkie, was hollow. Most likely a bird's. And if a bird's, why not an eagle's? When she blew into it, out came a soft whinnying squeal. There was an answering call deep in her blood.

Orlando gave her permission to do whatever she wanted with these moldering items. "I couldn't bring myself to throw the stuff out," he said. "But if you take a fancy to anything, it's yours."

"Even the skins?"

"Anything at all."

That night, after examining all the riches in the trunk, and having asked Orlando to identify the many articles that were strange to her, she chose a squirrel's paw, an owl's skull, a compass with a fidgety needle, a sealed pouch of Red Man tobacco and a corncob pipe, a starfish as pink as a baby's ear, a crystal of milky-white quartz, and a turtle shell with a clatter of small bones inside. These were to make up her medicine bundle. She wrapped them in a red fox fur, tied the bundle with a shoelace, and tucked it beneath her pillow. The bone whistle she hung on a string about her neck and did not take it off even in the shower.

Before wishing Orlando good night, she asked him again if he minded her using the deerhides.

"I don't mind at all," he answered. "Lord knows *I'll* never have any use for them. They've been sitting in that trunk since Father and I moved from Old Boston. Fifty-odd years. I remember a psychiatrist brought them back from a hunting trip in Canada and paid to have them tanned. He was going to have them done up into lampshades for his waiting room, but he never came back for them."

"I've got plans for them," said Mooch.

"Be my guest."

Stitching awkwardly by the light of a gooseneck lamp during the next few evenings, she made herself a doeskin dress, with fringed sleeves and a skirt that reached her ankles. Out of the leftover scraps she fashioned a clumsy pair of moccasins. She wore the dress and moccasins at night after the disney closed. Her fiery hair she did up in braids, tying the ends with strips of rabbit fur. Hidden beneath the helmet all day, at night the braids came down, and she stuck two gray feathers behind her left ear.

Orlando was startled the first time he saw her in this

get-up, but he merely scratched the wrinkles in his neck and said nothing. He was a long way from understanding her infatuation with Indians. In his eyes, they had been crude, superstitious, overgrown children, one of history's dead ends. But so long as she did her work conscientiously, how she dressed in the off hours was her own business.

"You don't know where I could lay my hands on some porcupine quills, do you?" Mooch asked him when she turned up for supper in the squaw outfit.

"I'm afraid I don't."

"Guess I'll have to make do with beads." She ate a bite of her fish patty. Then she turned her ruddy, pointy-chinned fox face toward him and said, "Do you figure these are eagle feathers?"

"I would have guessed turkey," said Orlando, squinting at the long gray plumes that sprouted from her braided hair. "But your guess is as good as mine."

"Then I declare them eagle feathers," she announced.

At supper again not long after, an hour when she figured his blood sugar—and therefore his resistance—would be low, Mooch asked him, "Is it okay if I decorate my room a bit? Do a little painting, hang a few things on the walls?"

"So long as it's neat," said Orlando.

She made a hammock from the deerskin pallet, knotting ropes into a web and suspending them from the corners of the room. Standing back to admire the effect, she thought spider-webs must have looked like this. Below the hammock, on the vinyl floor, she marked out a circle with black electrical tape to signify the creation, and inside it a cross to show the cardinal directions. She always slept with her feet pointing east.

Over the next few evenings, with touch-up paints from the shop, Mooch drew on her ceiling and walls the animals that came to her in sleep. Long-legged antelopes, shaggy bison, mountain goats, a coyote with lifted snout, a pack of tawny wolves on the run, rattlesnakes, a broad-winged hawk, a snowy owl, a raccoon: the beasts loomed around her in miniature glory. Above the hammock she painted a surly black bear.

Ducking into the room one night to check on her progress, Orlando felt as though he had stumbled upon a sacred cave.

"What do you think?" she asked.

"It's—" He groped for an adequate word, then murmured respectfully, "Mysterious."

Mooch climbed into the hammock, her face tilted in the direction of the rising sun by the medicine bundle beneath her pillow. She contemplated the bear, dark as a thundercloud above her, and said, "That's what I'm after. The old mystery."

■

A MONTH passed, then two, three, and still no catastrophe. On the contrary, the disney ran more smoothly than ever. There were days when every single mechanimal, every drone, every talkie booth and vending machine functioned without a hitch. Orlando's back stopped hurting. His insomnia relented. He took to bedding down again in his thatched hut and slept like a babe, knowing Mooch would respond to midnight alarms.

Her work in the shop made him shake his head in wonder. She understood machines the way someone blessed with perfect pitch understands music. She could peer into a snarl of wires that was more tangled than a plate of spaghetti and quickly see the one misplaced strand. She could sniff out the tiniest flaw in a circuit. Gears were transparent to her, and motors yielded up their secrets.

Not since his father's death had Orlando so enjoyed himself in the workshop. Her presence there beside him—chatting about her life in the orphanage, humming snatches of song, making a continual soft patter—was like having a fountain play in the room. As they tinkered, Mooch begged him for stories about the old days before the Enclosure. She wanted to know what it felt like to walk through woods, to swim in a river, to feel dirt with your bare feet. Orlando answered as best he could, dredging up memories from his childhood. He had never been one to take much notice of the world, and so his impressions even from the day before were fuzzy. Those from sixty years ago were enshrouded in fog.

"Forests were messy," he said. "A lot of dead trees, and bushes straggling every which way, and litter underfoot."

"You could feel the wind?" Mooch asked eagerly. "And you could hear it swishing through the branches?"

"I suppose so," he replied.

"And you'd come to a creek and kneel down to look at the tracks in the mud, and take off your shoes and go wading across?"

"The streams were polluted. I kept away from them."

"How about animals? You must have seen scads of them."

"I saw quite a few in Grandfather's taxidermy shop."

"Live ones, I mean."

"Well, there were still a few mangy dogs and cats. And once I saw a rabbit. It was brown, I think, and had long ears."

Mountains, he recollected, were large and lumpy, waterfalls were noisy, the ocean was a vast and muttering expanse of gray. By way of apology for his vagueness about the country, he reminded her that he was, after all, a city boy. What about stars, then, Mooch wanted to know. You couldn't see them through the streetlights. How about the moon? Hidden by smog. Pigeons? Sparrows? Lead poisoning. Mosquitos? Butterflies? Ants? Done in by pesticides.

"Then tell me about weather," Mooch persisted. "Even in the city you must have had weather."

"Oh, sure. It rained every little while. In winter it snowed. Sometimes it got boiling hot. When the weather was lousy, I stayed indoors. You could go all over Boston through tunnels and skywalks without sticking your nose outside."

"But when you did get caught in a storm, how did it feel?"

After a moment's reflection, he said, "The rain was, you know, *wet*, and the snow was cold."

Mooch eventually gave up asking him questions about the wilds. His answers were too depressing. She preferred the vibrant green world she knew from books and films and dreams.

To prime herself for those dreams, each night before going to bed, when the disney was quiet and the life of the city was a distant roar, she put on her moccasins and fringed doeskin dress, retrieved the turtle shell from her medicine bundle, and went into the workshop. There, under the impenetrable gaze of the stuffed animals, weaving her way among the benches, she beat on the shell to make it rattle and whistled through the eagle bone and pounded her feet on the floor and danced, reverently danced.

8.

On Mondays, when the disney was closed, Orlando and Mooch could putter for hours in the shop, with Grandfather's collection of trophy heads encircling them like a glum board of supervisors. On one of those leisurely Mondays, while reconditioning a panda, Mooch asked him, "Have you ever thought of giving the mechs a touch of wildness?"

"Now and again," Orlando confessed. He recalled how angry the girl had made him that first day, after her rescue from the lion's mouth, when she had accused him of running a playpark full of wind-up toys. She had been right, of course, which irked him all the more.

"I was thinking," she explained, "we could give folks a better show if we made our beasts more like the genuine article."

"That's easy to say," he replied testily, having also given the matter some thought over the years, far more years than this girl had lived. "But what does it mean to be wild, anyway? Is it simply a matter of being vicious? Living by tooth and claw? Infested with cooties? Prey to disease? Driven by instinct? Unpredictable? Filthy? Incapable of reasoning or speech? Prone to howling in the middle of the night?"

"Those will do for starters." She turned on him the full

wattage of her green eyes, which quite disarmed him. "What do you say?"

"Hmmm." Orlando thought of his father and grand-father—the taxidermy shop and the zoo—the Spinks tradition of simulating wildness. At the same time he realized how much he wanted this girl to approve of him, to be at ease with him as a daughter might be with her father. "Hmmm," he said again, more leniently.

"Can't you see it, making our own nature sanctuary smack dab in the middle of Plasticville? Giving the animals back their souls? Wouldn't that blow people away?"

Little suspecting where his remark would lead, he told her, "I don't suppose it would hurt to liven things up a bit. How should we begin?"

■

THEY BEGAN with dirt. Instead of cleaning the mechanimals every week, they permitted them to gather dust and loose hair and grease. Orlando was persuaded to overcome his distaste for dirt by Mooch's argument that wild creatures would be encrusted with mud and cockleburs and twigs, not to mention pee and poop. "Not to mention them," he agreed.

She put a word in with Humphrey and Grace, who kept a lookout for suitable items of filth on their scavenging runs.

"Things are looking up," Grace told her husband.

"She does seem to be coming into her own," said Humphrey.

They saw in her once more a girl after their own hearts, one who would cheer at news of volcanoes and squint in awe at the tiny faceted eyes of a bee.

From the disney cafeteria Mooch collected food scraps, which she massaged into the animals' fur to give them a ripe aroma. Orlando made up signs explaining to visitors that such squalor was typical of beasts in a state of nature. He kept reminding himself, when dust balls dangled from the beard of the goat and a stench of rotting food arose from Monkey Island, that he was not merely indulging Mooch's whim, but was pursuing an educational purpose.

Their next move was to rearrange the exhibits. Aside from the clustering of monkeys on their island and cats in a house of cages and dinosaurs in a panorama, all the beasts were displayed alphabetically, just as Father Spinks had left them. Thus aardvarks stood next to ant-eaters, griffins beside giraffes, zebras cheek-by-jowl with zombies. However the beasts might have arrayed themselves in the wilderness, Mooch pointed out, surely they would not have done so alphabetically.

"No doubt you're right," said Orlando.

"Why don't we put the forest creatures with other forest creatures," she proposed, "and fish with alligators, the snow leopard with the abominable snowman, and like that?"

"You tell me what goes with what, and I'll shuffle them," said Orlando. Whatever his prowess at engineering, he knew himself to be in the dark in matters of biology.

The temporary detachment of beasts from their labels led to confusion among the visitors. Without labels for guidance, the onlookers would mistake panthers for penguins and polar bears for skunks. Indeed, as the food scraps began to rot in earnest and the filth supplied by Humphrey and Grace turned rancid, many of the beasts came to be mistaken for skunks. More than one gang of school children yelled rude variations on the cry of "Pee-ew! Those oinkers *stink*!"

"That was their general custom in the wild," Orlando would answer genially.

Fortunately, the Overseers, who cruised through the disney several times a day on their electric cycles, knew even less of biology than he did, so they permitted him to rearrange the exhibits and besmirch the beasts to his heart's content—provided, of course, that calm was preserved.

How to relocate the imaginary beasts was a puzzle, because in most cases their habitat was ill-defined. Dragons and trolls could be placed in caves with bats and bears. But where should you put a griffin? Among the eagles, in keeping with its front half, or among the lions, in keeping with its rear? Should centaurs be sent out to graze with horses, or should they be assigned to the apehouse out of respect for their human torsos? Sasquatches had been reported everywhere from the rain forest of Colombia to the airless heights of the Himalayas, yet none had ever been captured; so where did you exhibit this hairy, shambling monster? Orlando was beginning to understand why his father had opted for the alphabetical order.

In the end, he and Mooch herded all the unplaceable beasts—the feathered serpents and snake-haired gorgons, the whiskered growlers and long-fanged snuffers—into a huge pit, where the creatures milled around like a nightmare stew. Mooch had a deep regard for the creatures that dwell in the imagination, but she was glad to have them sequestered from the creatures that dwell in forest and sea.

This monster pit soon became a favorite haunt for visitors, who poured through the gates in undiminished numbers, wigs and moodgowns gleaming in the fluorescent light. Many of them now wore breather masks, to shield them from the stench.

No sooner had the soiling and shuffling been completed

than Mooch declared, "What do you say we do over the voice tapes? Erase the goofy speeches and make them sound like animals?"

Orlando consented. After an initial queasiness over having his orderly empire turned upside down, he was enjoying himself. If the truth be told, before Mooch's arrival his life had become rather dull, grinding on with machinelike precision. Now there was a new spice to his days. Mornings, he awoke with a quiver of anticipation. Who knew what might happen? He was catching some of Mooch's daredevil enthusiasm for wildness, even though he still could not have said what he meant by that slippery word.

■

MODIFYING the voice boxes took over a month. The brown bear no longer told stories about forest fires, but instead merely growled and grunted. The monkeys gibbered instead of reciting jingles. The elephants ceased ruminating on philosophy and began simply ruminating, quietly munching plastic hay. The giraffe stopped bantering jokes about the inconvenience of a long neck, and kept silent.

Only the coyote was left with a human voice. "He's a trickster," said Mooch.

More Indian nonsense, thought Orlando indulgently.

"Hey, boss," Coyote would say to him, stealing up behind on silent pads, "how's every little thing?" The beast was hungry-looking, ribs showing through its dusty amber hide. On long, spindly shanks it pranced around the disney in Mooch's shadow, tasting the air with a pink tongue, poking its narrow muzzle into everything. When patrons reached out for a pat, Coyote would bare its fangs at them and say, "You feel me, I taste you."

Following what she knew from textbooks, Mooch programmed the other beasts to remain silent now most of the time. The woods must have been eerie places, Orlando decided. Quiet as tombs except for wind and water and birds. And even birds kept mum half the day.

Visitors who complained about this silence or about the sporadic bestial sounds were provided with cassettes that played all the old malarkey through earphones.

Mooch turned fourteen while they were overhauling the voice boxes. She had kept the date a secret from Orlando, not wanting him to feel he had to make a bother over her. At the orphanage her friends would have given her stationery they had embossed with her name, or bracelets they had woven from colored thread, or a shimmy-shirt with a jokey slogan, and at lunch everyone would have been served a cupcake in her honor. Living here in the disney with this quirky old man whom she was only beginning to know, she awoke on the morning of her birthday with a sense of abandonment.

She felt so desolate, in fact, that several times before evening she was on the verge of saying to Orlando, "You know, I just remembered today's my birthday." But she kept quiet.

It was all that much greater a surprise when Humphrey and Grace appeared for supper with a pineapple cake and fourteen candles. Orlando gave her a sackful of beads for sewing onto her doeskin dress. They had been tipped off by Garrison, who showed up late, puffing and grinning, when Mooch was taking her first bite of the cake. He had saved his measly orphan's allowance for months to buy her a survival knife that had thirty-two blades.

Mooch's eyes burned as she looked around the table from face to face.

■

THE WEEK following that celebration, Mooch and Orlando asked themselves what else could be done to make the beasts act more like beasts and less like humans dressed up in fur suits. Well, rhinoceroses should not balance balls on their horns, rabbits should not consult pocket watches, gorillas should not play bongos, flamingos should not play croquet. Deciding what all these creatures should *do* was a far more difficult matter.

"Mostly they just slept and ate and hunted," said Mooch.

"That should bring in the crowds," said Orlando. "For the price of admission, folks, you can watch filthy furballs snooze!"

Mooch conceded him a laugh, before saying, "I tell you what. Suppose we make half the ones in each exhibit prowl around and hunt while the other half sleep?"

"What would they hunt?"

"Each other."

Orlando rubbed his hands. The engineering problems would be delicious. "I'm game if you are," he said.

This alteration required another two months of labor. Frogs now gobbled flies, mice pounced on frogs, rabbits gobbled mice, owls murdered rabbits, and high-leaping wolves snatched the owls. At the end of each cycle of destruction, the victims were restored to life, put to sleep, and the former sleepers were awakened for hunting.

Despite some muttering, the visitors applauded this new regime. There was plenty of action. Wherever they turned in the disney, some beast was always slaughtering some other one. Even the cows and sheep, stupidly chewing their cuds, would sometimes be attacked by a mountain lion or a pack of beavers.

Undeterred by grungy hides and this new show of aggression, people still crowded up to pat the beasts. "Nice kitty," they would purr to the Bengal tigers. "Sweet little pooch," they would lullaby to the jackals. They climbed on the zebras and camels and kicked them in the ribs, shouting, "Giddap!"

All this kitchy-coo familiarity outraged Mooch. "They still treat the animals like playthings," she complained to Orlando.

"I seem to recall a young lady who stuck her head in the lion's mouth," he observed.

"I'd never have done that if your old lion hadn't been such a ridiculous, empty-headed goofball."

"I suppose he was."

"If he'd been wild, I'd have steered clear of him. If those jaws of his had really known their business . . ." Mooch eyed Orlando to see if he would catch the hint she had flung at him. He blinked, and it bounced on past. So she exclaimed, as though just then hitting upon the idea, "I've got it! Hey! Why don't we just paint lines around each exhibit, and program the mechs to bite anybody who crosses it?"

"Bite the visitors?" he repeated incredulously.

"Only a gentle munch on the arm, you know, and maybe a lash or two with a tail." When he hesitated, she added, "You want them to respect the beasts, don't you?"

■

THEY CONVERTED the jungle exhibit first. Monkeys would now hurl plastic fruits at intruders, cheetahs would leap on them, pythons would coil about their legs, spiders would skitter through openings in moodgowns and bite with needle teeth. The warning signs declared:

DO NOT CROSS SAFETY LINES.
LIKE THEIR WILD ORIGINALS,
THESE BEASTS ARE DANGEROUS.

Anyone invading the barnyard exhibit would now be kicked by mules, butted by pigs, pecked by chickens, and battered by the stiff wings of geese.

Inevitably, some patrons ignored the warning signs. When this happened, Orlando and Mooch would have to shut off the power beam and go pry the trespasser from the grip of a giant panda, as the case might be, or from beneath the squatting bulk of a stegosaurus. In a number of instances they were forced to fiddle with the programming, when an overzealous beast actually ripped a gown with its claws or bloodied a visitor's nose.

The Overseers, when they caught wind of these innovations, sat Orlando down in the control room for a stern lecture. There were two officers, one a brawny great lug and the other one even brawnier, both in gold jumpsuits covered with bulging pockets. Mooch, who sidled into the room and kept very still to avoid being sent away, glared at these enormous men. She hated bullies, especially ones who swaggered around in uniforms with guns strapped to their belts. When they tilted back the visors of their bubble helmets, they revealed themselves to be surprisingly young. One still had pimples on his cheeks, and the other, trying to grow a moustache, had a silly ribbon of fuzz above chapped lips.

They spoke to Orlando for half an hour, their voices like the rumble of a bowling alley. All their talk added up to the warning that, if anyone got seriously hurt in his diddly little amusement park, Orlando would be in the deepest, darkest trouble.

After they had left, he prophesied bleakly, "Somebody's going to get hurt."

"I wouldn't be surprised," Mooch agreed.

The way she twisted her mouth, Orlando could not tell whether she was reluctant or eager to see the first mangled body. Mooch herself could not have said how she felt.

9·

The first mangled body turned out to be Orlando's. He forgot to extinguish the power beam one day before entering the alligator pool with his oil can. By the time Mooch heard his yelps and cut the power, the gators, with their slashing tails, had broken one of his legs and three of his ribs.

"You see what I mean," said Bertha Dill when she telephoned the hospital. "The girl is bad news."

"It was my own fault," Orlando replied. "I programmed the brutes myself."

Shifting her tone, the orphanage director asked, "So you're not sending the vixen back to me?"

"I wouldn't part with her for the world."

Mooch felt miserable. Not about the alligators, whose fierceness pleased her, but about Orlando's having been the victim. She had grown to love the old coot. He was the first grown-up ever to make her feel that her life was more than a costly experiment gone wrong.

That night, with Coyote on the floor nearby for comfort, she tossed and turned in the hammock, arguing with herself. Only a lunatic would dream of turning a bunch of fur-covered machines into wild animals, she thought wretchedly. And then, with a quivering passion, she thought: I can't bear to live in a world where all the creatures except us have lost their souls.

When Orlando came back from the hospital in the morning, perched in an electric wheelie, she met him at the gate in her doeskin dress, red pigtails, and turkey-feather headdress, her face blotchy from crying. Coyote squatted beside her.

"I'll make them all tame," she blubbed, breaking into tears again at sight of his leg thrust out stiff in its foam cast.

"Don't be silly," he gruffed, more upset by her tears than by his own injuries. "I should have been more careful. More respectful. Isn't that what you were trying to drum through my thick skull? Respect?"

"You mean . . . you don't want them tame?" Mooch caught her lower lip between her teeth.

"No, no! Absolutely not! What sort of lion-trainer would pull the fangs from his cats? Besides, I've been having the time of my life with our tinkering. And just as soon as I'm on my feet again, I plan to get right back to it. Maybe we should add a few more safeguards, though, to protect boneheads like me."

Mooch wiped her eyes with a fringed sleeve. "Then you wouldn't mind if I tried out a few ideas on my own?"

"So long as you're careful—and you leave plenty of tinkering for me."

"Oh, you're a sweetheart!" Mooch bent over the wheelie, landed a glancing kiss on his forehead, then stood away, embarrassed.

"My, my," he said. "I shouldn't have waited so long to break my silly leg!"

It pained her to see his face turn pale when he laughed,

from the broken ribs. And she hated to think of him hobbling around for months in the cast.

Before he could do any hobbling, he would have to keep off that fractured leg for a spell. Old bones are slow to heal, the doctor had reminded him. It was a needless reminder, since Orlando was feeling quite brittle. He chose the control room for his convalescence. In there, at least, he would not be entirely useless; he could watch the monitors and push buttons. Mooch fixed up the astro-lounger as a bed and tuned her wrist-talkie to the room's intercom, so he could summon her day or night.

Grace and Humphrey stopped by to cheer him up, fondly comparing this latest accident to those he had suffered as a boy. They were able to recall those earlier wounds by fingering the scars on their memories.

"It's not that you've ever been clumsy, Orlando," Grace confided, "but you do have a way of losing your temper with machines, and when you do, the machine usually has the final word."

"Like when you broke your big toe from kicking that motorcycle," Humphrey said amiably.

They brought puzzles, books, board games, playing cards, all the old-time distractions they could find in their closets, to help Orlando while away his hours of immobility. Humphrey insisted on bringing sacks of munchies, most of which he finally ate by himself, since the broken ribs had taken the edge from Orlando's appetite.

While the elderly threesome played games and reminisced in the control room, Mooch was busy altering the mechs. The sting of Orlando's accident had worn off, and now she was even more determined to refashion these dumb machines into living, breathing, aching beasts. Instead of making them safer, she would make them more dangerous. Out of fear, people would have to stand back, give them room, maybe even recover a sense of awe. One by one she worked over the mechs, replacing beam receivers with five-year batteries, inserting fight-and-flight routines, stuffing their memories with everything she had learned about their wild brothers and sisters.

On the monitors, Orlando could see her moving from exhibit to exhibit with her tool caddy, the coyote slouching along at her heels, and through the open door between the control room and workshop he could see her performing surgery on mother boards.

"What's up?" he asked her.

"Improvements," was all she answered.

■

As SOON as he was sufficiently mended to roll about the disney in his wheelie, Orlando painted a second warning stripe at a safer distance from the exhibits. Crossing this new line would trigger sirens. He was afraid to think of what crossing the old line would trigger, now that Mooch had been fiddling with the controls.

In addition to the new warnings, the sight of the beast-engineer cruising around in an invalid's chair, his leg in a cast, had a chastening effect upon the visitors.

Several weeks passed without further mishap. Then a gang of teenagers dared one another into invading Monkey Island. They soon regretted the venture. Boulders and tree limbs rained down on them, followed by the monkeys, which leaped from overhanging cliffs with arms and legs flailing. The strength of these little manikins astonished even Orlando, who after all had built them. Their rage could only have come from Mooch. For some reason he could not shut down the power beam, so he had to rescue the battered teenagers with ropes. All were bruised, and three were hospitalized with mild concussions.

The Overseers wheeled Orlando to the local station, and read him the fine print of the laws regarding public hazards. They could revoke his license right now, without further ado. But instead they gave him ten days to clean up his act. At the end of that period, a squad would come round to make sure everything was perfectly safe. In the meantime, the disney would be closed.

"I'm afraid we'll have to tame them after all," Orlando told Mooch later.

"Good luck," she muttered darkly.

Against doctor's orders, he abandoned the wheelie and heaved himself onto crutches, so that he could lurch across the bridge onto Monkey Island. He would begin by disarming those gibbering fur-balls. "Cut the power beam," he said to Mooch.

"It isn't on," she answered.

He gazed across the moat at a pugnacious-looking baboon, which was picking plastic lice from its neighbor. Nearby, a gorilla was torturing a tire.

"Then how are they *running?*" he asked.

"I've been meaning to tell you about that."

"About what?" he demanded warily.

"Well, you see, it didn't seem right to me that we could turn them off and on anytime we felt like it. I figure a creature's not free so long as you can flip a switch and shut it down. So I rigged them up with batteries."

"*Batteries!*" he shouted. From a palm tree on the island a chimpanzee regarded him soberly, like a scholar perusing a footnote. Orlando tried to recall the dangerous moment in which the yearning for wildness had blossomed in his heart. Was it just before or just after he liberated Mooch from the lion's jaw? Sighing, he told her, "Well, I'm going to have to unplug them."

"I wouldn't try that."

"Why? What'll they do?"

"I don't know."

"You don't *know*?"

"That's the point. Nobody knows. Nobody *can* know. They're wild."

Staggering on the crutches, he turned his back on Monkey Island and glanced across the way at a sullen water buffalo, which was idly demolishing its manger. "You mean they might tear me limb from limb?"

"I wouldn't be surprised."

As though to emphasize her point, the coyote at her side licked its pink lips. "There's some mean hombres out there," said Coyote.

Orlando thought hard. The squad of Overseers would be making their inspection in little more than a week from now. If they found even one hazard in the place they would put him out of business. Scowling at Mooch, he said, "How long before those batteries run down?"

"They're five-year go-packs."

"Five *years*!" He closed his eyes, then quickly opened them again as he lurched dizzily on the crutches.

"You want your wheelie?" she asked.

"I want my *disney*. My calm, peaceful, poky old disney."

"But I thought we were turning it into a kind of wildlife sanctuary," said Mooch hotly.

"I didn't want to go this far. The place is too dangerous to keep open. But I can't afford to close it. It's my livelihood. Don't you see that? It's my *life*." He gazed around in despair at the menagerie of growling, pawing, sinister brutes.

The pain in his voice made something snap inside Mooch, and she went dashing away, her face screwed up with loathing—of herself, of Orlando, of the Home and the stupid visitors and the stifling city and the whole deathly Enclosure.

■

WHILE the gates remained locked—a sign out front explaining that the disney was closed for renovations—Orlando tried every trick he could think of to disable the mechs. Fortunately, Mooch had left their territorial imprints alone, so they did not stir from their assigned cages and pools and halls. Thus he could ride his wheelie up and down the aisles without being attacked, so long as he did not cross the warning stripes.

Jabbing the beasts with poles only upset them, and resulted in the loss of the poles. Surrounding the exhibits with energy shields had no effect, nor did he have any luck with neutralizing rays. Soon he was at his wits' end.

Mooch, all this while, holed up in her room and would not come out. She spoke now only to Coyote. Orlando had to work alone, muttering to himself in a fury that gradually changed, over the course of the week, to despair.

His back gave him fits again, and his insomnia returned with a vengeance. At night, from his rumpled bed on the astro-lounger, he could hear the beat of the turtle rattle and the stamp of Mooch's feet as she danced around the hammock in her room. He scarcely slept at all the last few days before the morning on which the Overseers turned up at the gate and blared through a bullhorn to be let in. There were six of them, big hulking bruisers, with melt-guns and batons dangling from their hips.

In their gold uniforms and mirrored helmets, they towered above Orlando, who met them in his wheelie, the game leg jutting before him in its cast like the masthead on a ship. "Gentlemen," he pleaded, "I still haven't quite whipped things into shape. If I could have just a few more days . . ."

"You've had your few days already, Mr. Spinks," the lead officer growled.

"I don't think it's wise, just now, to go—" Orlando began.

The officer cut him off: "We'll decide what's wise and what isn't, Mr. Spinks."

"But, sir—"

"Shut up and keep out of the way."

When Orlando still protested, the officer waved his gauntleted hand. One of the Overseers grabbed the handles of the wheelie and shoved Orlando roughly against a ticket booth.

Panting fearfully, Orlando watched them divide into three pairs and scatter among the exhibits, their helmets gleaming, batons in their fists, melt-guns swinging.

Soon the first scream tore through the disney. In the space of a few minutes, four of the six men came staggering or running or crawling back toward the gate, their jumpsuits tattered and bloody. They dumped Orlando on the ground, hurled the wheelie aside, and pounded him with their batons while they screamed questions at him.

"I don't know *how* they got that way!" Orlando cried, wanting even then to protect the child. "It just seemed to *happen*! I lost all control over them!"

Meanwhile the lead officer was shouting instructions into his wristphone, summoning riot control. Soon the armored trucks would come squealing up, and shuttles would glide overhead, and melters would spew their vaporizing beams, and everything Orlando had made would turn to mist and disappear.

He writhed on the ground and wailed. A boot landed in his ribs, on top of the old fracture, and other boots were drawing back to kick when suddenly one of the Overseers yelled, and they all flinched away and took off running for the street.

Wincing with pain, Orlando sat up to watch them go, then snapped his head round and stared back down the main aisle of the disney. A tide of beasts came surging toward him, snakes and leopards and ostriches, lumbering gorillas, monkeys shuffling arm in arm, prides of lions and families of dragons, one-eyed monsters and monsters with two heads, pandas and camels and goats, and right at the front was a phalanx of elephants, and there atop the largest of these, in her squaw outfit and full war paint, sat Mooch.

The ground shook from the thud of feet. Orlando rolled out of the way to keep from being trampled, and the flame in his ribs made him whimper. He braced himself against the wall of the ticket booth.

"Mooch!" he bellowed. "Don't! Stop!"

She did not speak or wave or even look his way as she went riding past and out through the gate. Coyote was trotting along beside the elephant's feet.

Mooch felt only a great wind blowing through her, burning her with the single pure desire for escape. She would batter down the walls, straight through to wilderness.

Just then shuttles appeared overhead, melters zinging. Orlando shielded his eyes and blinked up at the hovering white machines. The pilots cut down the laggards at the rear of the troop, and then started blasting their way forward through the ranks.

"Not the elephants!" Orlando hollered.

The shuttles glided relentlessly onward, erasing the beasts with devastating sweeps of the melters. Mooch ignored them, her knees tight around the huge swaying neck. She was on fire, and nothing human could put her out.

Orlando dragged himself into the street on his belly, clawing his way. The citizens who had been riding the pedbelts or strolling in the plazas when the stampede broke out had all retreated into buildings. Awestruck faces gazed at him from every window. The beasts had overturned cars, toppled street signs, flattened bubble booths in their march toward the outer wall of the city.

The air tingled from the melters. Here and there a paw or tail had escaped the annihilating beams, and lay among the rubble like discards from a costume shop.

"Don't hurt the child!" Orlando screamed, his voice drowned out by the grind of engines.

The pilots vaporized Coyote. They slaughtered every last creature except for the lumbering elephants, then briefly held their fire. The shuttles hesitated a few meters above Mooch's head like blind, white fish that had blundered into the air. Then one by one they picked off the outriding elephants, until only hers remained. Still she kept on, leaving Orlando farther and farther behind.

"Mooch!" he screamed. "Give it up, child!"

Far down the avenue he could see the elephant lean its vast, wrinkled forehead against the wall of the city. The beast reared on its hind legs and slammed its weight against the translucent barrier, reared and slammed, over and over, while Mooch held on by its ears. She glared crazily ahead, trying by the force of her desire to pierce the dome and see, beyond a stretch of ocean, the lost green hills of America.

At last the melt-beams sliced into the elephant's heaving buttocks and hacked through the spine and knocked out the legs, and down tumbled Mooch, still clinging to the vast gray ears.

Still on his belly, dragging the stiff leg, Orlando squirmed through the crowd of medics and Overseers and buzzing onlookers to where she lay. She was sitting up, dry-eyed. When he reached for her, she pulled away and did not make a sound, her jaw quivering but firmly shut, as if she had caught some rare bird of grief in her mouth and meant to keep it safe.

PART TWO·

10·

The law pounced with tigerish speed. Before the last of the injured Overseers had been released from the hospital, almost before the trampled avenue had been straightened up, Mooch was sentenced to three years in the Cape Cod Refarmatory.

Bertha Dill enjoyed testifying against her. "Since the day they delivered her to the Home, that girl has been a burr under my saddle," she informed the judge, who was too young ever to have seen a burr outside a book or a saddle outside a museum. The orphanage director concluded her testimony by announcing, in the loudspeaker voice so revoltingly familiar to Mooch, "Emitty Harvard Tufts is the queen of disorder."

Orlando was forbidden to speak at her trial. In fact, he was cut off entirely from Mooch. "You forfeited your rights as her master," he was told sternly by the judge at his own hearing. "We can't permit you to mislead the child any more than you've done already." Because this was Orlando's first brush with the law, instead of being sent to prison he was ordered to do two years of public service as a roving repairman. "Let us see if your ingenious hands can mend things as well as break them," said the judge. Orlando would be permitted to spend the nights in his jungle hut, and to keep whatever tools and furs and stuffed animals he could pack inside the workshop. The rest of the disney would be confiscated by the authorities, who planned to rip down the old exhibits and turn the area into a playzone.

The former apprentice and master were kept in separate wings of the jail, and nobody who visited one of them was allowed to visit the other. All their messages were intercepted. Orlando heard nothing of Mooch, and she heard nothing of him. For each, it was as if the other had dropped off the earth.

■

GARRISON RATHBONE had gone to see Mooch the day after the stampede. They met in a visitor's cubicle, sitting in chairs that were bolted to the floor on opposite sides of a wireglass partition. A camera glinted down at them from the ceiling. Their voices darted back and forth through the intercom, diminished, uncertain.

"How're you doing?" Garrison asked.

"How do I look?" Mooch countered.

She wore muffling gray overalls that hid the bruises left by the Overseers' billyclubs. Swelling had narrowed her eyes to slits. Her braids had been chopped off, and several patches of hair had been shaved to allow doctors to stitch her scalp.

"You look awful," he said.

"That about sums it up."

They fell silent. What little she could see of him through her puffy eyes was good medicine for grief. She hardly noticed his radarscoop ears or bulging nose or gawky manner. "I'm glad you came," she said. "You're the only familiar face I've seen."

Garrison's mouth worked on several words before he

managed to reply: "You had me scared. I haven't been that scared since my folks OD'd on narco."

"You and me both. Those guys meant business." Gingerly she touched one of the raw, shaved patches on her scalp.

"What did the lawyer say about them roughing you up?"

"She said I'm lucky they didn't zap me."

He snorted. "About what you'd expect from a court lawyer."

"Careful." Mooch thrust her chin at the ceiling camera.

He eyed her dingy prison overalls. "What happened to your doeskin outfit?"

"They took away my dress, the moccasins, the feathers. They took that wonderful knife you gave me for my birthday. And they tossed everything down the recycle. Poof. Gone."

"Even your medicine bundle?"

"No. I told them that was sacred. A holy relic. They sealed it in plastic and stowed it in the safe."

"That's a little something, anyway," he soothed.

Again they fell silent, both surprised at having already exchanged so many words.

Finally Mooch burst out: "God, I feel stupid. I feel like a two-year-old twit. I thought I could bang a hole in the city. And then what was I going to do? Swim to shore?"

"You freaked out. Who wouldn't freak out, with all those bruisers charging around and waving their guns?"

"I pretended I was saving the animals. I got to where I really thought they were alive, those battery-powered toys. All I did was get them fried."

"Right now you've got to think about saving yourself."

"Save myself for what?"

"Mooch!" he said, and he looked at her so intently that she momentarily forgot her aches. "Don't talk like that. Don't let them break you. Listen, you've got to keep yourself whole."

When their time was up, they both pressed their hands against the divider, but the cool glass kept them from touching.

"Ask Orlando to forgive me," she whispered in parting. "I didn't mean to hurt him."

But Garrison could not repeat her words to Orlando, for the guards refused to let him see the old engineer. Nor could Grace and Humphrey, after visiting Orlando, get in to see Mooch. Grace fumed, but the guards would not uncross their burly arms.

So Mooch was left knowing only that she had ruined Orlando. Thanks to her, the disney had been condemned. His mechs had been reduced to vapor and scrap. He was too old, she figured, to start over. How furious he must be. How he must loathe her.

She never heard the message Orlando had tried sending by way of Humphrey and Grace: "Tell Mooch I'm sorry. I didn't see what she was after until too late. My brain is slower than hers, and tamer. Ask her to give me another try. I'll have a room and a workbench waiting for her when she gets out."

■

EFFORTLESSLY, the law did what the charging elephant and the herd of beasts had failed to do—it punctured the tough envelope of the city and released her. If not to the wilds, then at least to a part of the Enclosure where animals bred and plants grew.

Instead of flying to Cape Cod in a shuttle, as she had hoped, Mooch rode in a transport tube, along with the morning shift of workers. The windowless curving walls of the car were lit up with ads and feeliefilms but showed nothing of the ocean. She might as well have been gliding through the guts of New Boston for all she could see. To avoid the needling stares of the other passengers, she gazed down at the tracer on her left wrist, which lay atop the medicine bundle in her lap. An amber light flashed once every minute from the woven steel band, signalling her location to the Overseers. She had already tried picking the lock, but that only called in a swarm of guards.

No need of a tracer just now, for her other wrist was handcuffed to a cop, who sat next to her in his gold uniform and helmet, the bubble visor pushed up. He was a well-padded hombre, thirty or so, huge like all the Overseers, pouty in the lips, short on words and long on grunts. He dozed.

A dull assignment, Mooch figured, escorting a juvie to a prison farm. She tugged at the handcuff and the cop jerked violently, nearly yanking her arm from the socket. "Whuh? Whuh?" he roared, glaring about him at imagined attackers. His fists were the size of grapefruits.

"How much longer?" she asked him.

He peered at her, as though surprised to find a red-headed girl attached to the end of his arm. He yawned. "Not long."

"When do we go outside?"

"We don't."

"You mean this tube dumps us straight into the farm?"

"Yep."

"Dad burn it!" she muttered, and immediately thought of Orlando. Her oath made a few nearby passengers curl their lips.

The cop shut his eyes and began to wheeze. He lurched

again when the car whooshed to a stop and a robovoice called, "Ree-farm Station!"

Walking beside him onto the platform, her arm chained to his, Mooch felt like a very small dog on a short leash. Three other kids handcuffed to gold-suited Overseers trudged from the neighboring cars, along with twenty or thirty workers.

They shuffled through a security gate, rode pedbelts down echoing aluminum tunnels, then stood in line waiting to check in. Not a window anywhere, not a clue to show they had truly escaped from New Boston. Then Mooch noticed an odd sensation in her legs—a stillness, like the easing of muscles after a long run. The floor was not shaking. All her life she had felt the tremor of the floating city, its buried engines and pumps and the constant thrum of water. Now for the first time she stood on land. Beneath layers of concrete there was dirt. Or maybe sand. The crust of the earth.

She was thinking about dirt and sand, forests and waterfalls and bears, while the cop signed her over to a matron and unlocked the handcuffs. Rubbing her wrist, Mooch said to him, "Enjoyed your company." He grunted, and lumbered away.

The matron was a bony woman, all sharp angles and prickly fingers. She wore surgeon's gloves and a breather mask and sidled up cautiously, as though examining a plague victim. Then suddenly she lashed out a hand and grabbed the medicine bundle.

"That's holy," Mooch protested.

"So's my left little toe." The matron held the bundle at arm's length, even though the fox fur was encased in plastic.

"Put it somewhere safe."

"Don't you worry." The matron flung it in a drawer. Then briskly and wordlessly, as though tearing the wrapping from an unwanted present, she undressed Mooch, tossed her clothes in the recycle, and shoved her into a sani-shower. Mooch lifted her arms and spun inside the white chamber, the jets of air and germicidal beams playing over her body. The last of the bruises had faded to green islands on her pale skin.

She emerged from the shower feeling newborn. But to what new life?

The matron greeted her with a bundle of clothes, everything a serene blue—the color she imagined for clear sky—blue underwear and jumpsuit and workgloves and boots.

"Nice threads," Mooch observed, plucking a sleeve.

"You'll get sick of them soon enough," said the matron. "You'll get sick of everything."

"What's it like here?"

"It ain't no picnic."

"Do we ever get a chance to go outside? Into the wilds?"

The matron grumped, "Save your chat for the warden, punkie."

The warden might have posed for the ostrich at the disney. His fat rump and belly rested on broomstick legs, and above his long neck swiveled a beaky, insignificant head. He wore a black wig, a white lab coat with a smiling sun embroidered over the breast pocket, mint green trousers, and pink socks without shoes. He told Mooch to call him Dr. Bob.

"I'm your friend," said Dr. Bob in an oily voice, pacing behind his desk. The walls were plastered with diplomas in neon frames. His grin appeared to be part of his wardrobe, like the wig. "I'm here to help you become a good girl, a sweet girl, a law-abiding girl. They tell me you have a crazy itch for the wilds! They tell me you fancy yourself a born-again Indian! They tell me you harbor an affection for animals! Is that so? A grown-up, sensible girl like you?" Without giving her a chance to reply and without relaxing his grin, Dr. Bob went on: "Well, my dear, I trust you'll find that life here on the Farm will free you from those silly notions. A few days with our livestock, for example, should cure you of any sentimental attachment to animals." While speaking, he twisted his ropy neck in such a way as to punctuate his sentences with the popping of vertebrae. The joints of his pink-stockinged toes crackled as he paced. "And now," he added, "before I send you off to meet your new chums, do you have any questions?"

"Yes," Mooch said. "How can I get outside?"

The smile hung rather more limply from the corners of Dr. Bob's mouth. "The outside is poisoned, my dear. The outside is ruined. The outside is disgusting. You don't want to go there."

"I *do*," she insisted.

"Well, that's just one of the things we'll have to work on, isn't it?" He beamed down at her from his ostrichy height. "In the meantime, do your best to fit in. Obey your helpers. The other children will explain how things work. And if ever there's anything you need, don't hesitate to call me."

That night in the dormitory, after the matrons had locked the doors, the seven girls who shared the room with Mooch dragged her from bed and beat her up.

"You listen, ketchup-hair," said the oldest and meatiest of the girls, as she banged Mooch's head on the floor. "You belong to us now. We're a family, get it, and you're the runt. You do what we say. No questions. No squeals."

Mooch bit her lip and swallowed her tears. She knew

better than to cry out, knew that would only bring more blows, knew that nobody would answer her cry, least of all the grinning Dr. Bob.

■

ON SATELLITE photos, the domes of the farm looked like frosty bubbles clumped on the northernmost island of Cape Cod. The Cape still went by its old name, although cod no longer swam off its shores and the land itself was no longer a peninsula, but instead had become an archipelago. What used to be hills on the old Cape had been separated into a chain of islands by the rising ocean.

Laced together underground by tunnels, all but one of the domes were filled with livestock, or with algae and krill and soybeans for the livestock to eat. The single remaining dome housed what Dr. Bob liked to call his twisted teenies—the four hundred or so unruly boys and girls. Straightening out bent juveniles was merely a sideline of the farm. It was first of all a meat factory, churning out beef and pork, fish and mutton and poultry for New Boston.

Mooch got a long nauseating look at the place the next morning, when she was shown around by the husky roommate who had banged her head on the floor. The girl's name was Konga. "As in Queen Konga," she told Mooch.

At thirteen this girl had robbed a quickfood shop, a neat job, got away clean as a new tooth; but her old lady finked on her and the Overseers nabbed her and Konga turned mean. Now she was nineteen, halfway through an eight-year stint for stiffing a geek who'd double-crossed her after a holdup. On her next birthday she would be shipped to the women's pen. "And I mean to squeeze all the pleasure I can out of my last few months as top bitch on the farm," Konga proclaimed. She glared at everybody from beneath tangled black eyebrows, saving her fiercest glare for the matrons, who gave her a wide berth. Dr. Bob she called Dr. Blob. "One of these days I'm going to squash him under my foot." Heavy-boned and loud, Konga stomped wherever she walked and spoke only in a shout.

She had to yell in the livestock domes to make herself heard. They went first to the beef dome, where so many cattle were jammed together in steel pens that Mooch had the impression, not of seeing her first live animals, but of looking across a storm-churned, moaning brown sea. Hornless, white-faced, broad as sofas, the cows looked all the same, as though poured from a single mold. Tubes fed chemmies from overhead pipes straight into their necks. Hydraulic platforms under their bellies helped brace them up. They were penned so tightly they could not move. Conveyors ran beneath their muzzles to carry in food, and beneath their tails to carry away the oozy brown manure. The roar of throats and machinery was deafening.

"How long do they stay in here?" Mooch asked in horror.

"Their whole scummy lives," Konga answered.

In other domes, the hogs were a grunting sea of brown, the sheep a bleating sea of gray, the chickens a noodling sea of white. Mooch could not look at a single beast or bird, there were such mobs of them, one snout or beak identical to the next, the fleece more uniform than a carpet, the feathers like soft pavement. And the squeals, the guzzling, the slurping and banging made her head ache. Only the fish were silent, swarming in their tanks, but they left her cold.

In all the livestock domes there was a pungent smell of disinfectants, which barely masked the underlying stink of crowded bodies. It was more foul than the locker room at the Home, riper than the stench of cabbage forgotten in the fridge.

"You guys all vegetarians?" Mooch asked Konga as they walked among the hogs.

The other girl laughed. "Only the ones with weak stomachs. But not me. I can't get enough of that red meat!" She leaned down and bit a hog on the shoulder, and the animal slammed into the side of its pen.

There was an eery silence, by contrast, in the domes filled with algae and krill and beans. The plants grew in rectangular vats, through which a nutrient broth steadily flowed, and the only sound was a gargle of pumps. Here the smell was like the opening of a bottle of vitamins. Mooch found it hard to think of these red and green rugs as alive. They seemed more like soggy crystals, an effervescence of chemicals.

In each dome a few technicians wearing silver jumpsuits fiddled with valves or punched keyboards. Like the commuters Mooch had seen on the tube, they were clearly not inmates, but staffers, their eyes glazed by routine.

"Where're the other kids?" she asked beside a vat of algae.

"The kinks all go to school till noon," said Konga.

"Then what?"

"Therapy after lunch, chores all afternoon, and group gropes after supper. Six days a week. Sundays it's pure therapy."

"What sort of chores?"

Konga raked her blunt fingers through a raft of algae and answered with evident relish, "You'll start the way we all started, hosing down the rear ends of cows."

Again Mooch thought of Orlando, remembering the stories he told about his father scrubbing elephants, and a surge of pain shot through her. She had only moved into a bigger, uglier, more brutal zoo.

Throughout the tour, nothing was said of the previous night's beating—except, at one point, Konga gave a belly laugh and thumped Mooch on the back and hollered, "I do like getting in fresh blood! I'm sick of pushing around the same old wimps!"

11▪

While a wrecking crew tore into the disney, Orlando holed up in the workshop, so as not to see the melters and cranes gnawing at his creation. He lowered the blinds, but could not restrain himself from peeking around the edges. One moment the bulge of Monkey Island still rose against the skyline, and an hour later it was utterly gone. The dinosaur panorama vanished, and likewise the cat house, the monster pit, the rain forest, the meadows and caves and swamps, exhibit after exhibit, the work of decades reduced within minutes to a heap of dust.

Secluded in the workshop, Orlando could still feel the grit of dust between his teeth, could taste it on his tongue. Never one given to spitting, even in private, he now spat frequently and angrily, often missing the bucket. He busied himself with converting one of the disney's popcorn vans into a repair truck. He lined the back with cupboards for tools and parts, mounted a bell on the roof and painted the whole thing a glossy white to make it resemble one of the ice cream trucks he remembered from his childhood. The side panels announced in red:

> ORLANDO SPINKS
> THE MACHINE MEDIC
> EVERYTHING FIXED FREE

He could make this promise because the authorities would furnish the parts and give him a trickle of credit to live on. For two years, he would be a servant of the people.

To keep him honest, the Overseers clipped a tracer band on his wrist. He soon grew accustomed to the flashing amber light, but the band itself was a nuisance, catching on the workbench and snagging his pockets. The tracer did not enable them to read minds, as the God of the Bible was supposed to have been able to do, but it did allow them to follow his every move. They could have spared themselves the trouble, since Orlando had no desire to jump his sentence. He meant to serve his time so faithfully that the Overseers would never have reason to glance his way.

Even before he finished rigging the van, the wreckers had leveled the disney, and a construction crew had begun laying wire and pipe for the arcades of the future playzone. He winced, hearing the wail of their saws and the pop of their welders. The prospect of living in the midst of feelie booths, dodgem tracks, chemmie vendors, eros parlors, and other jazzy funspots filled him with gloom.

"Who knows," Grace Palomino told him with her usual gusto, when she and Humphrey Tree cruised by the shop in their zip-carts, "maybe you'll take up bowling, or spooking, or feelie-fooling."

"Not on your life," said Orlando.

"It's never too late to kick up your heels," said Humphrey.

"I'm keeping my heels on the floor, thanks very much."

The two old scavengers made a point of looking in on him every other day or so, on their way to haul trash up the slopes of Mt. Hexxon. In the rubble of the disney they always found choice pieces of junk to add to their collection, but they did not have much luck in cutting through the black cloud which had engulfed Orlando since the orphan girl's departure.

Having eased him through the loss of his parents and grandparents, Humphrey and Grace knew the symptoms only too well. He glumped around. He broke off sentences in the middle, his mouth sagging, his eyes unfocused. The bow of his legs became more pronounced. In place of his crisply laundered safari suit, he now wore grubby mechanic's overalls, which looked as though he had been using them to swab the floor. His white beard and scraggly nimbus of hair, uncombed, began to resemble a dust-ball. His face, crumpled and sallow, reminded Grace of a fallen cake.

Humphrey began these visits by raiding the pantry, while Grace strove to whip Orlando into shape with some inspirational talk. She thought of it as taming a great sullen bull of sorrow.

Often the scant good she might have done was promptly undone by Humphrey—as on the evening when he returned from the galley with his mouth full of soydog, gazed across the floodlit ruins of the disney and said, "Looks like an ash heap out there."

"Finish chewing before you speak, dearie," said Grace.

"I can't believe how fast they took it down."

"I can't believe you're eating again," said Grace pointedly. "I keep telling him to cut back on his calories, Orlando. It's because of his metabolism. You pass ninety and your metabolism slows down. Like a tortoise. Either cut back on your calories, I tell him, or it's fat city."

Still peering across the ruins, Humphrey said, "I can't even find the auditorium."

"They flattened it yesterday," Orlando announced dolefully.

"Ah, I see where it used to be. Flat as a pancake. Amazing what they can do with this modern equipment."

"Humphrey!" Grace rumbled.

Chastened, the old gentleman took a meditative bite of soydog. "I really am going to have to find some other place where the SAG lodge can meet."

Under her breath, Grace muttered, "It could meet in the space between your ears."

"What's that, Gracie?"

"I keep telling you to get on the stick and find a place," she said, waving at him an arm resplendent with a dozen talkies and watches scrounged from the streets, "but whatever I say goes right in one ear and out the other." Lately she had been thinning out, as though to compensate for Humphrey's expansion, and the baubles clacked noisily over her bony arm.

Humphrey chuckled. "Every time I think about our meetings in the auditorium, I remember that trick with the elephant and the shoes. You outdid yourself that day, my boy!"

Orlando inspected his fingernails, which were rimmed in black with graphite lubricant. Not me, he thought. Mooch. Always Mooch. The least remark was an arrow pointing at her.

To break the mood, Grace slapped her thighs and said: "I know what you need! You need to move house! Get away from all this jumble and racket!"

"Oh, it doesn't bother me."

The scavengers exchanged a knowing glance. Since boyhood, Orlando had been hopeless at lying.

"You should sell this dump and buy a condo in our tower," said Grace.

"No, no, I couldn't," said Orlando.

"Why not?" she demanded with a flash of her acrylic teeth.

He refused to say, but Humphrey and Grace could guess the reason easily enough. They had only to glance into Mooch's bedroom, which Orlando had left untouched, with its black rubber tape on the floor marking out the cardinal directions inside a mystic circle, the grizzly bear poster and sketches of dream animals on the walls, the ceiling speckled with stars, and in the center of it all the spiderweb hammock.

Okeydoke, thought Grace. Dancing around and waving hankies isn't getting us anywhere with this sorrowful bull. Let's grab it by the horns. "You really think she'll come back after they let her loose from that farm, dear heart?"

"Why not?" said Orlando, nettled. "Mooch loved it here."

"But there isn't much *here* left, is there? No mechs. No exhibits. No disney. Nothing but rubble."

"I've still got the shop. We could start over. Make things."

"Who says she'll want to make things? After three years in that pigpen, she might be a pickpocket or a druggie."

"No! It's impossible!"

"Now, Gracie," chided Humphrey.

She persisted. "The Overseers will probably ship her to another city, anyhow."

"She *will* come back!" Orlando insisted hotly. He was quaking, almost dancing with pain. "She *has* to come back! And I'm staying right here, so she can find me!"

Grace relented. The bull was fiercer and crazier than she had imagined.

■

ONCE the fix-it van was ready, each morning Orlando puttered away from the jungle hut when the first arc of sun burned on the roof of the city, before the construction crew showed up to work on the glitzy pleasure palaces. He would park on a street corner, clang the bell, open the rear doors, fold out his workbench, and wait for customers.

In the beginning, people were skeptical. Free repairs? What's the catch? "No catch," Orlando explained. "I'm a public-spirited man." He did not feel compelled to give all the humiliating details of his run-in with the law.

Children and old people—the two groups used to grabbing whatever help they could get—tried him first. Kids would shyly approach with broken toys. Old folks would trundle up cradling defunct appliances in their veiny arms.

Before long, crowds were forming beside the van to watch him work. He might have been an alchemist or a witch-doctor, his movements were so mysterious. Some repairs took only a minute—soldering a connection, tightening a screw, plugging in a chip—but others, the technically sweet ones, took hours. He would become so absorbed that he forgot the onlookers and hummed brokenly to himself. After finishing one of these complicated jobs he would glance up, befuddled, at the ring of watchers. When they saw that the gismo actually worked, they cheered. It seemed like magic to have such skill in one's fingers.

Even if Orlando had never seen a device before and had to ask the owner what it was supposed to do, he could nearly always fix it. He would take it apart and stare at the innards, or run it through a tester, until something looked wrong. He was like a musician hearing a note played out of tune, or like a painter seeing a line out of place. The wrongness was something he *felt* more than understood. And nothing pleased him more than to hunt down the deepest and most subtle flaws and set them right.

Soon his white repair truck became a familiar sight on the nearby avenues. Occasionally an old-timer, fooled by the glossy paint and clanging bell, asked him for a cone or a popsicle. For their sake, and for the toddlers who pressed against his knees to gawk at him, Orlando installed a freezer in the van and stocked it with Neapolitan ice cream, which he began serving to those customers older than seventy and those younger than seven.

"How much?" they asked, their tongues poised for licking.

"Not a penny," Orlando answered. "Free as sunlight."

Wherever he parked, a line quickly formed on the sidewalk—clerks bearing talkwriters and copiers, bureaucrats with office drones, shopkeepers with cash registers, apartment-dwellers with toasters, ovens, phones, videos, cybers, disk-players, robots galore, and countless other gadgets—like so many casualties from a battle in the warehouse of invention. Each customer in turn would place the troublesome item on the fold-out bench, and Orlando would carefully dismantle it. He took extra pleasure in fixing those appliances that bore warning labels: DANGER. DO NOT OPEN. NO REPAIRS. IF BROKEN, DISCARD AND REPLACE.

As his reputation grew, older folks were often elbowed aside by the crowds. So each Thursday Orlando stuck a magnetic sign on his van that declared SENIORS ONLY TODAY. He recognized a few of the SAGites among the oldsters who shuffled up to the van. Some of them brought their gravity-defying contraptions—spring-loaded shoes, helium-filled doughnuts, magnetic belts, traction harnesses, orgone boxes—for him to check over. Usually these gadgets were not broken. They simply failed to work, making no dent in the mountainous burden of gravity. Still, Orlando's authority as a repairman was such that, after he had combed through a contraption—adjusting a knob here, crimping a valve there—the owner would slip it on and feel kilograms lighter.

Saturdays, when school was out, he reserved for children. He recognized few of their playthings, most of which seemed to be designed for blasting their eyes or ears or noses with violent sensations. He was alarmed by the waterguns and zappers and light-sabers, they looked so much like the weapons carried by Overseers. Time and again a little tyke would plop a gruesome object on the bench, and when Orlando asked how it was supposed to work, the child would answer with a screech or a boom.

Orlando never turned anybody away. No machine was too sick. He would try to fix anything. Day after day he tinkered on the avenues of New Boston, his mind contentedly straying among gears and circuits. It was only at night, when he drove back to his shop through the footings and girders of the rising playzone, that he gave in to fret and sadness.

■

GRACE THOUGHT to distract him by giving him a wholesome project to work on in the evenings. "You know what you could do, kiddo?" she proposed one night while Humphrey was in the galley heating up some eggrolls. "You could make me a cat. I am positively dying for a cat."

Orlando shook his head morosely. "Not possible."

"Don't tell me it's too hard for the engineer of beasts!"

"Oh, it'd be a piece of cake. I could do it blindfolded. But the judge told me positively no mechs until my sentence is up. If I monkey with mechs, he said, it's five years in the clink."

"How would they know?"

"They'd know, all right."

Grace aimed a poisonous look at the tracer on Orlando's wrist. The amber light flashed. "They can't hear what you say through that thing, can they?"

"No, no."

"Well, then? How are they going to know?"

"The Overseers snoop around my van and shop whenever they feel like it. If I so much as drew a blueprint for a cat, they'd haul me back to that judge. And I'm not going to give them an excuse to throw me in the clink. Not even for you, Gracie."

Just then Humphrey emerged from the galley with a steaming plate of eggrolls. When Grace and Orlando refused to have any, Humphrey girded himself to eat them all.

"Calories," Grace muttered, clucking her tongue.

"Nourishment," said Humphrey. He lowered himself onto an astro-lounger. "So, Gracie," he mumbled, fullmouthed, "what does our mechanical genius say about wiring the explosives?"

"I decided not to bring it up."

"What explosives?" said Orlando.

"You promised to ask him," Humphrey scolded.

"Well, I didn't."

"Why not?"

"It turns out he's more closely watched than we thought," said Grace. "I think we should leave him out of it entirely."

"What explosives?" said Orlando, more and more bewildered.

"But, Gracie, we need his expertise."

"I say we leave him out of it."

"You know we can't do it on our own."

"If you hadn't put on so much weight we'd do just fine."

Humphrey withdrew half an eggroll from his mouth. "I haven't put on that much!"

"Ten kilos!"

"Seven!"

The old scavengers had a way of quarreling as though nobody else were within shouting distance. Unable to break in, Orlando waited, hoping that when they had simmered down he would find out what was what. But they were still spatting as they piled into their trash-heaped carts and drove away.

Grace prevailed in the argument—as she nearly always did, by sheer horsepower—and after that evening neither one breathed a word about explosives. Orlando tried coaxing answers from them, but they clammed up like a pair of secret agents.

EARLY one Saturday morning, a gaggly line of children stretched away behind the fix-it van. Some kids lugged toys and electronic thingamajigs for repair, others wanted ice cream. All were curious to see the Machine Medic at work. Orlando had just given back a mended telescope to its owner, when the next boy in line towered above the workbench and said, in a wheezy harmonica voice, "Long time no see, Mr. Spinks."

Orlando knew that voice. He looked up expectantly, then had to keep looking higher, up the gangly frame of Garrison Rathbone. The boy had grown even taller and had begun to put on flesh.

"Why, Garrison!" Orlando exclaimed, pumping the boy's hand. "I haven't seen you in donkey's years!"

"I've been after Mrs. Dill to give me a pass, but today's the first time she's let me out since—" The boy glanced over his shoulder at the line of kids, then knelt down in front of the workbench so that his eyes were on a level with Orlando's. He bent close and whispered, "Is your van bugged, Mr. Spinks?"

"Certainly not!" Orlando hissed. "What's on your mind?"

"If Mrs. Dill found out I was here, she'd nail my hide to her wall."

"There's no bugs, I promise you. No cameras. You're safe."

"Well, sir." The boy cast another wary look around and scrunched closer. "I saw Mooch in jail, before they shipped her to the farm. She wanted me to give you a message."

Orlando rose from the stool, his forehead nearly touching the boy's. "What is it? What?"

Garrison drew from his pocket a hand-sized computer interface board and laid it on the workbench. Still whispering, he said, "Pretend you're fixing this. I figured it would look fishy if we just talked."

"So *talk*. What did she say?" Orlando took the interface board and began testing the chips with a probe, but his fingers were shaking so badly that he stopped, afraid of damaging it.

Garrison murmured in a voice almost too quiet to hear, "She wanted you to know she's sorry from the bottom of her heart."

"Why sorry?" Orlando hissed.

"Because she ruined you."

"Ruined me? Do I look ruined?"

"It's what she thinks. And she begs you to forgive her."

"What's to forgive?" Orlando said.

Garrison felt the other kids breathing down his neck. On a neighboring avenue a siren began to howl. Suddenly panicking, he snatched the board from Orlando, thanked him loudly for fixing it, and bolted away.

Like a priest in the confessional, Orlando could only sit there, dazed, and wait for the next person in line to tell him about the woes of machines.

12·

Dr. Bob reserved his expertise for the nuts that were hard to crack. And here, in the person of Emitty Harvard Tufts, was a decidedly hard nut.

The girl attended solo and group healing sessions obediently enough, but therapy bounced right off her. Nothing penetrated her shell. The staff had tried everything short of neuro-juice and chemmies, and those indelicate methods were out of bounds because her escapades in New Boston had not actually killed anyone. Nor could Dr. Bob use an isolation cell or other punishment to soften her up, because she obeyed the matrons, did her schoolwork, played along cunningly with all that was asked of her. She broke neither rules nor heads—as Konga Rue, that lummoxy roommate of hers, was fond of doing. She merely hunkered down inside the shell of her mania and would not come out.

After six months at the Farm, Emitty was more enamored of the wilds than ever before. Having mucked about for most of that time in the stockdomes, doing the filthiest jobs Dr. Bob could conceive, far from despising the brutes she had come to despise their keepers.

"Animals have souls," she told her analyst, one of Dr. Bob's sharpshooters, "and yet they're treated like robots."

To which the analyst replied: "That's very interesting. How long have you been feeling this way?"

In the cafeteria she turned up her nose at meat. Nor would she touch poultry or fish. (To her dining mates she would say, "How can you bear to eat Matilda?" or, "Do you find Larry tender enough?" For she had given names to the indistinguishable cows and chickens and pigs.) She scorned eggs, and even vegetables she ate in moderation. Her idea of a feast was mushroom pizza with kelp salad and a side dish of garbanzo beans. Before eating, she had been overheard to whisper thanks to the green gods.

Far from mellowing on such a diet, she had grown fiercer. Speaking with her was like playing with matches. How she could burn with such an intense fire while nibbling only vegetables was a puzzle to Dr. Bob. Whether he met her alone in the halls or saw her plunged in a crowd, beneath her flame of red hair she seemed to blaze like an inextinguishable torch.

■

"YOU ARE quite sure that animals have souls?" the analyst inquired.

"Absolutely," the girl replied.

"Even pigs?"

"Especially pigs."

"Even fish?"

The girl's alarming green eyes flickered. "Have you ever stuck your face against one of the aquatanks and looked at a catfish?"

"I can't say that I have."

"If you had," the girl insisted, "you'd realize a catfish wants things, just like us. Hungers for things. Runs away from things. Has its own burning center."

"How about crickets?" the analyst inquired, with an ironic hoist of the eyebrows. "Would you say crickets have souls?"

"They sing, don't they?" the girl shot back.

This and other equally neurotic exchanges had been recorded on viddytapes, which Dr. Bob was reviewing in preparation for his initial therapy session with Emitty Harvard Tufts. The time had come for him to wield his expertise. The girl had already worn out the second most powerful shrink on the Farm (Dr. Bob himself, of course, holding first place). This number two analyst, a woman with more tricks than a streetcorner magician, had utterly failed to split Emitty's hard rind of delusions.

The viddytapes documented that failure. Asked to envision a perfect home, the girl described a clearing in a forest. Asked to recount her dreams, she narrated sagas about mysterious beasts, which she illustrated with drawings. In her enthusiasm she acted out these dream-encounters, complete with bestial gestures and blood-curdling sound effects. Confronted with the true story of her laboratory birth, she stubbornly insisted on the "deeper truth" of having been suckled by bears. Shown a book of inkblots, Emitty saw leaves, pawprints, flowers, spiders, and whales. In word-association tests, *dirt* made her think of *roots, liquid* made her think of *rivers, shelter* made her think of *tipis*. Under hypnosis the girl chanted guttural songs and danced in a circle, spreading her palms toward an imaginary campfire. Made to stare at a close-up reflection of her own face in a mirror, and asked what she saw, Emitty described her eyes as ponds, her nose as a mountain, her cheeks as meadows, her mouth as a cave. Altogether she behaved like a monomaniac.

To crack the shell of her mania, it was not brute force one needed, such as that of a sledgehammer, but the precise, concentrated force of needle-nosed pliers. One must know just where to pinch, and then squeeze with all one's might.

Dr. Bob considered himself to be the ideal instrument for the job.

He summoned her file onto his desktop window and browsed again through the pitiable facts. Born in a glass tube, the offspring of germ cells from dead geniuses. U.S. patent number such-and-such. (Figures larger than his salary appeared to Dr. Bob as a blur. He was a man of words, not of numbers.) A failed experiment, the project grant running out seven months after her birth. Given a brief trial and then returned by the pair of psychologists who were to have adopted her. Lodged in The New Boston Home for Little Wanderers. Tumultuous early years. Slow in learning to talk. Persisted in going about on all fours even into her school years. Imagined herself a bear cub. Jittery, secretive, ferocious when cornered. Age nine: diagnosed as having severe eco-psychosis. By turns backward and brilliant in schoolwork. A thief, a sneak, a liar. Hence, given the vulgar nickname of Mooch by her fellow orphans. Age eleven: judged to have insufficient discipline for continued study. Mechanically gifted. Apprenticed five times. Longest hitch the last one, at the disney with the engineer of beasts, which concluded with a massive delusory breakdown, destruction of property, and disruption of public order. Now almost sixteen, and still a wilderness fanatic.

What a hash, thought Dr. Bob. If only he had gotten his hands on the girl in her infancy, at the time she was abandoned by the bio-engineers, he would have known how to mold her into a sweet and reasonable child. Instead she had been dumped in The Home for Little Wanderers, that breeding ground for psychotics and malcontents. With distaste, Dr. Bob recalled having run into—and having nearly been run over by—the Home's director, Bertha Dill. Now *there* was a blunt instrument. The woman had the physique of a sumo wrestler and the voice of a poison-alarm. How could the authorities turn her loose on children, a woman without so much as a single diploma in psycho-management?

Dr. Bob's own several diplomas, glowing in their neon frames, endorsed him silently from the walls.

■

MOOCH APPEARED for her therapy session wearing the Farm's regulation blue overalls, plus knee-high rubber boots that gleamed from a recent washing and a yellow hardhat pulled down to her eyebrows. Fresh from the dung vats, where she had been fixing a composter, she gave off the ripe smell of manure—an aroma she enjoyed, and one that made Dr. Bob take shallow breaths.

He met her in the doorway in his professional outfit of black wig, white coat, and therapeutic smile. Today his slacks were pink and his socks mint green. He reached out a manicured hand. "May I take your helmet, my dear?"

Mooch drew back from him. "I'll keep it on, thanks."

"I can't see your lively eyes beneath the brim!" (He had come dangerously close to saying *lovely eyes*, but had caught himself.)

"It protects my head," she answered.

Dr. Bob tilted his gaze toward the perforated ceiling. "Are you expecting the dome to fall?"

"I can always hope."

He smiled and smiled. "The hat is important to you?"

"My head is important to me."

"Very well, then, whatever makes you feel comfortable," said Dr. Bob, ushering her to a high-backed swivel chair. Her boots left smudgy tracks on the carpet.

Throughout the interview, he paced about the office in his stockinged feet, and she kept him in her sight by swiveling in the chair. Fearing that he meant to grind her up in his psychiatric mill, she kept her muscles taut, ready to fend him off.

By way of overture, Dr. Bob popped the bones of his neck and toes. "So! Emitty! How are you feeling about things?"

"I'll survive."

"Good, good! That's the spirit! And tell me, how are you getting on with your roommates?"

"Better. I made Queen Konga stop messing me over."

Dr. Bob reflected in passing, and not for the first time, that parents named Rue who chose to name their daughter Konga deserved all the misery that amazon had inflicted on them. "How did you manage that, Emitty?"

"I told her if she didn't quit beating on me I'd sneak over to her bed at night and stop her ticker."

Dr. Bob wrinkled his forehead. "Her ticker?"

"She's got a syntho heart, you know."

"Ah, yes. I'd forgotten. Poor child." He shoved his palms together in a prayerful attitude and shone his grin on her. "And is that how we deal with conflicts, Emitty? By threatening other people?"

She glowered at him from beneath the hardhat's yellow brim. "Are you going to call me Mooch, or not?"

"I'd rather not, my dear, because that nickname is attached to your old self, a mischievous and disruptive self, one that we're trying to banish, aren't we?"

"You are. I'm not."

"You don't like your real name?"

"Mooch is my real name."

"Your official name, then. Do you dislike it so much?"

"I hate it. Wouldn't you? Having a bunch of techno-bozos stick labels on you from three universities, as though you were a stupid mascot or something? That name has nothing to do with who I am. Mooch is what my friends call me. Mooch is who I am."

"*Hate* is a strong word, my dear," said Dr. Bob.

"I have strong feelings. I hate and loathe and despise that so-called official name, and I hate anybody who uses it on me." A heavily jowled face, bulging like an over-packed suitcase, filled the screen of her memory, leading Mooch to add tartly, "Like the Pickle, for instance."

"And who might the Pickle be?"

"Mrs. Dill. The boss at the Home."

"Ah, I see! Dill Pickle! Very good!" Dr. Bob loosed a snort of laughter. The last thing he wanted was to be lumped in the girl's mind with Bertha Dill. "All right," he said cheerily, "Mooch it is. And what shall I use for your last name?"

"I won't have any until I earn one."

"And how would you do that?"

Mooch could hear the whirr of the doctor's brainwashing machine. She decided to throw him one of her diamond-hard beliefs, to see what it would do to his gears. "You earn your name by going on a vision quest."

"That's not a procedure I'm familiar with," said Dr. Bob. "Would you mind explaining it to me?"

"When you're a teenager, you go off into the woods by yourself, and fast, and sing, and stay awake, and pray, until a vision comes to you. If you're open to the spirits, and if you're very fortunate, maybe they'll give you a helper, a holy song, and a name."

She crossed arms over her chest defiantly. (Her sleeves were thatched with long brown hairs. Dr. Bob had been told she made a practice of combing the tails of cows.) He knew she was daring him to make fun of her cherished

125 ■

ideas. A less adroit analyst might have done so. But not Dr. Bob. He listened to her nonsense with sympathetic nods, then observed mildly, "An Indian practice, I assume."

"You have a problem with Indians?"

"No, no, certainly not!" Jerking his neck, he popped the uppermost vertebrae. "And where are you going to find a woods for this quest?"

"Outside."

"I see, I see. And how do you propose to get there?"

"When I earn my five-day pass for good time, I can go anywhere, right? So long as I wear the tracer?"

"I suppose. If I give my permission. Should I do that? It's hard for me to imagine you'd rather go outside among the poisons and desolation, instead of visiting your friends in New Boston."

Mooch swiveled away from him, replying in a subdued voice, "I can't go back there."

"Why not?" Meeting with a wounded silence, Dr. Bob pursued her. "Don't you even want to see that queer old fellow, the animal-maker?"

"I *can't*," she breathed, the chair rocking from the vehemence of her denial.

Ah, thought Dr. Bob, here at last was a weakness. He applied more pressure. "You feel guilty toward Mr. Spinks?"

Mooch swiveled back around to glare at him with slick eyes. "I wrecked his life. How do you expect me to feel?"

"Tell me about it," Dr. Bob cooed.

The joys and pains of the last two years roiled in her, and she ached to pour them out. The words rose in her throat like sobs—about finding that sweet old man, almost a father, to love her, and moving in with him at the disney and making her room into a sacred place, about handling the dusty animal skins, about her companion the coyote and the whole menagerie of beasts, and making them wild, and pretending they were alive, and things falling apart, and Orlando's broken leg, and the Overseers coming to destroy the beasts, and her crazy dash for freedom, and leaving everything behind her in ruins.

But she choked down the sobs and flared at this doctor, with his painted-on grin and his pretense of sympathy: "I'm *not* going to tell you about it! Read the file. That's all you're entitled to know. You can't make me confess anything I don't want to. I have a right to my own thoughts. I know the rules."

"I'm asking as a friend, Mooch."

"You're asking as a shrink. I'd rather stay enemies. Your job is to change me, and I don't want to be changed. Not by you, anyway. I want the spirits to change me. All I have to do here is get up in the morning when the alarm goes off, and go to bed when the lights go out, and do my work all day, and study my lessons, and keep out of trouble. If I keep my nose clean, after three years you've got to let me go. I'll stay just who I am, feel what I feel, think what I think, and wait my chance, and go outside and let the spirits change me."

Clearly, this nut was going to be hard for even the gifted Dr. Bob to crack.

13·

Orlando's troubles did not distract Humphrey and Grace from their mission of stuffing Mt. Hexxon with junk. Hunched over the wheels of their zip-carts, they continued to scour the streets of New Boston, gathering whatever had been discarded. They were spurred on by their determination to show that junk and old folks and the muck of feeling cannot so easily be thrown away. Regarding themselves as the wheeled agents of memory, Humphrey and Grace preserved what the forgetful city tried to banish.

At midnight they buzzed up the slopes to dump their loads. They were so zealous in their scavenging that the hollow crown of Mt. Hexxon was quickly filling up.

As the son of a Kentucky coal miner, Humphrey decided that he should be the one to climb down the ventilator shaft and see how much more rubbish the mountain would hold.

"I'd go," Grace insisted, "if I didn't know as sure as shooting that my flexy joints would give out."

"No, no, duckie," he replied in his courtly manner, "you stay up top and keep an eye peeled for the fuzz."

"Don't you and your belly get stuck down there," she warned.

"I am as sleek and svelte as ever," he replied with a sniff, although in truth he had been larding it up a bit lately.

"And don't go snapping any of your brittle old bones."

"And don't you be such a worrywart!"

Fortunately there was a ladder, or Humphrey would never have survived the descent. After a good bit of noisy reconnoitering, he surfaced again to announce between labored puffs, "I figure we've got space for about a month's worth of junk."

"Only a month?" Grace lamented. "Then we'll either have to wire it ourselves or give up the whole cockamamie idea."

"I don't see how we can do it without Orlando," he said.

"I don't see how we can do it *with* Orlando. Those Overseers are stuck to him like glue."

"If only Mooch hadn't gotten herself in trouble. She'd have been the ideal accomplice."

"Well, she's planted on her farm and Orlando's trapped in his fix-it van. They're clean out of the picture."

"Who else can we get to help?" Humphrey unwrapped a chocobar and thrust half of it in his mouth. Chewing, he said, "Everybody in SAG is as decrepit as we are."

Grace resumed her lament. "Only a month, and then no more scavenging!" They had been working toward this moment for years, but now, having nearly reached it, she felt downhearted. Her face, pale and crisscrossed by wrinkles, had the look of a snowy field where animals had cut numberless trails.

Humphrey, who loved every one of those wrinkles, was old enough to remember snowy fields. "Give or take a week."

"When I was a girl, I never dreamed I'd grow up to be a bag lady!" She broke into a fit of corrosive laughter.

"Remember how the scruffy old crones lugged their bags from one trash can to another, picking up bits of sandwich and string—around the Common, you know, and Copley Square, and Boylston Street?"

Flowing easily into his wife's memories, Humphrey said, "And the winos along the waterfront, scratching in the gutters for cigarette butts, their eyes like holes in rusty buckets."

"They were always bent over double, those old scroungers, and one of the bags was filled with newspapers. At night they'd wrap themselves in the funny pages and sleep on subway grates."

"Think of that—people tossing an entire newspaper on the street!"

"Still," Grace conceded, "I'll never cease to wonder at the stuff people will drop, even today. It's a regular cornucopia out there in the avenues." She waved at the sparkling grid of New Boston, which rayed out below them in its geometrical perfection. Then she drew up her sleeve to peruse the dozen watches, talkies, and calculators strapped to her arm. A few of the watches kept time, although no two kept the same time. Out of old habit, she put one of them against her ear. But there was only silence—the vibration of crystals, the lunge of electrons. It was an awfully tidy world, she thought, where watches could get by without ticking.

"What I'll never understand is the lost socks." Hoisting his trousers, Humphrey displayed two plump ankles, each one sausaged into multiple thicknesses of socks. "How do people lose them, just riding around all day or sitting on their tails?"

"You've got me," said Grace. She gave a bewildered shake of her nearly hairless old head, which was enshrouded at the moment in a blond wig. "A body could pick up a whole wardrobe in one day on the streets."

"Shoes I understand," he said. "You can slip out of them without thinking. Your hat could slide off in a crowd. I've seen people lose false teeth and ears. I've seen tires fall off wheelies. No mystery there. But *socks*?"

"Remember when that lady at the lunch counter dropped her nose in the soup?"

"And she fished it out, snapped it on, and kept right on eating!" Humphrey's old brown bag of a face crumpled with disgust. "I don't know what the world's coming to, Gracie. People are getting divorced from their own bodies. First we all move inside these bubble cities to get away from bugs and sunburn and poison rain and radiation. Live without insult from nature! And now everybody's redoing their faces, rewiring their nerves, replumbing their organs, replacing their joints. Where's it going to stop? With brains rolling around in plastic wheelies?"

"Who are we to talk?" said Grace, rubbing her knees. "I'm thankful for my new leg joints. And if you didn't have that ticker," thumping him on the chest, "your blood would turn to sludge and they'd make fertilizer out of you for the farmpods."

"Right you are, my duckie." Humphrey lowered his eyes—his electronic eyes, he could not help remembering—and laced the fingers of his syntho hand into those of his natural one.

They lapsed into silence, feeling the full weight of their ninety-odd years. Gravity, they knew, was gaining on them.

■

ON THE following nights, after dumping their debris, Grace kept watch atop Mt. Hexxon while Humphrey drudged below in the caverns, struggling to lay out the wires and relays and fuses. They had left passages through the rubbish for just this purpose. Over the years, they had pilfered the necessary materials from demolition sites, including the charges of plasty, which would go in last of all.

While the grottoes had slowly filled, a few shorings had collapsed, barricades of cardboard had given way, towers of cans had tumbled down, so that Humphrey now had to proceed cautiously through the labyrinths of junk. As he crawled along, trailing wires behind him, he often found his way blocked by a rubbish-slide and had to backtrack. Twice the walls collapsed on his very heels, and he was forced to grope his way out by side-tunnels.

After the second of these escapes, he slumped beside Grace on the mountain crest, gulping air. "If I don't make it out one of these days," he panted, "I want you to go ahead and throw the switch."

"Are you crazy? With you inside!" Grace's eyes puckered up. "And me out here all by my lonesome to explain things to the Overseers?"

"I was just flapping my tongue," said Humphrey.

Her face darkened ominously under the blond wig. "I don't plan to go on living without you, Hump. So you stick around."

"All right, duckie. Simmer down." He patted Grace's hand.

"I just can't stand the thought of staying on alone. You know that. With you gone, I'd be the only sane person left alive."

"Never you worry, old duck. We've got a lifetime hitch, you and me." He pecked her on the cheek.

Their minds running in parallel grooves, the two ancient scavengers thought of death.

"You know," said Grace after a spell, "when our time comes I still think we ought to hold hands and jump down a recycle chute together."

"Okay by me," said Humphrey. "Mingle our molecules."

She lifted the blond wig to scratch her scalp. "It still seems unnatural to me, dissolving people in a soup of acids, instead of burying them like they used to."

"Even when they planted folks in pine boxes, the worms eventually recycled them. Acids are just quicker."

She patted the wig back in place. "I'd rather feed worms."

"I wonder if there's a single worm inside the Enclosure? Maybe somebody raises them for an experiment somewhere. Or to make protein burgers. We could donate our corpses to a worm farm."

"I don't know about you, kiddo," said Grace, bouncing to her feet, "but I'm not a corpse by a long shot. Let's go scavenge!"

■

IN KEEPING with Humphrey's prediction, one midnight just four weeks later they found that Mt. Hexxon would not quite hold all the rubbish they had collected. Grace mashed as many of the bottles and printouts and broken gadgets as she could into the ventilator shaft, until she heard the junk shifting ominously inside the caverns. Humphrey was down there, crawling through the passages, uncoiling wires. Down he scrabbled, helmet-light wagging, into the deepest recesses of the mountain. He would have been glad right then for a pair of syntho knees. His natural joints were killing him. He wondered how his father had endured the pain and claustrophobia during all those decades in the mines. A pack of hungry kids at home would make a man put up with just about anything, he supposed.

Before even a tenth of the wiring had been laid, Humphrey's rickety old body rang all its alarms. He ground to a halt deep in the labyrinth, gasping. It was all he could do to struggle back up the ladder to Grace.

She took one look at him and said, "No more burrowing for you, Mr. Mole. Let's give it up. I'd rather have a live husband than a dead mountain."

"No," he panted, laying a hand on his chest above the galloping ticker, "I just need a little help, is all."

"You can forget Mooch and Orlando."

"I know, I know. What we need is somebody *like* Mooch. Another spry orphan."

All of a sudden Grace pounded her fist into her palm. "That's it! Remember that giraffe of a kid, the computer freak, who tagged along after Mooch with his tongue hanging out?"

"The one she called Ratbone?"

"He might be just the ticket," said Grace, with a determined snap of her acrylic teeth.

■

"RATBONE'S real name?" said Orlando, answering the question Grace had put to him after supper. (After *their* supper, that is: Humphrey was still eating lasagna.) The three old cronies were sitting around a table in the workshop, beneath the forlorn snouts of Grandfather's stuffed moose and goat and bear. Despite the enveloping chaos of the construction site where the playzone was rising tower by gaudy tower, Orlando had kept his workshop as neat and clean as a hospital. "Ratbone's real name?" said Orlando. "It's Garrison. Garrison Rathbone. Why do you ask?"

Grace had always done well at poker, because her opponents found it hard to believe that anyone who looked so radiant and beatific could be hiding something. She put on her poker face now. "Oh," she replied casually, "Humphrey and I were looking for somebody who could do some crunching on the SAG records for us. We're applying for grants, you know. We have to come up with all these fancy tables and things! And I thought I remembered your saying the boy's a whiz at computers."

"He can make them eat out of his hand," said Orlando.

Thinking this might be an allusion to his own continued assault upon the lasagna, Humphrey looked up from his plate, fork poised. But when the conversation took another turn, he dug in once more. He did have a soft spot for Orlando's cooking.

"How do you think he'd be as an apprentice?" Grace asked.

"I don't actually know Garrison all that well," Orlando admitted, "but I expect he'd be hard working. He's clever, that's for sure. And Mooch told me—with disappointment—that he never makes trouble at the Home."

They had to raise their voices, because the construction crew, pushing to finish the playzone, were still at work under floodlights, and the derricks and welders and riveters made a terrific din. Orlando's small thatch-covered hut, the last remnant of the disney, trembled from the mechanical thunder.

"Can he keep secrets?" Grace asked. Receiving a puzzled look from Orlando, she added hastily, "The SAG records are confidential, you understand."

Orlando thought of how Garrison had stood in line at the fix-it van that Saturday morning to deliver a whispered message from Mooch. "I'd trust him," he declared.

Mindful of the torturous passages in the rubbish through

which the boy would have to crawl, Grace asked, "And would you say he's athletic? Does he have a limber back? Is he spry? Has he got stamina?"

Orlando laughed. "Are you going to ask him to levitate at the SAG meetings, or what?"

Humphrey interrupted his assault upon the lasagna. "We would expect him to work long hours, you see."

"I have no idea about his stamina. All I can say is, he's a teenager, and he's a big galoot."

"Big?" said Grace. "I never noticed that. He must have been sitting down the one time I saw him. Quite big?"

"He makes two of me."

"That could be a problem."

"What does it matter to your computer how big he is?"

"I was thinking of having to feed him," Grace explained. "Feeding Humphrey is hard enough."

At this, Humphrey did push away his plate, eyeing with regret the surviving mound of lasagna. "Well," he said, rubbing his palms together, "Garrison sounds like just the boy for us. Let's go see if we can pry him loose from the claws of that dragon who rules over the Home."

■

THE DRAGON—known to her impertinent orphans as the Pickle—was not eager to let Garrison Rathbone go. She liked the boy for his awkward shyness, his ingenious way with the Home's computers, and above all for his obedience. The only black mark against him, in Bertha Dill's book, was his infatuation with that deservedly banished vixen, the insufferable Miss Tufts.

But this old couple seemed respectable enough. Indeed, the husband bore the impressive title of Exalted Sagamore. They had made a reasonable offer of employment, and Bertha Dill could not reasonably refuse.

The papers were duly signed before Garrison was brought in to meet his new masters. Seeing who had claimed him, he grinned down at them, his big face like a globe high atop an unsteady bundle of sticks.

"You're friends of Mr. Spinks, aren't you?" he said eagerly. "And you know Mooch, don't you?"

Bertha Dill closed her eyes and allowed her lips to pucker from the acrid taste of the name.

Grace and Humphrey were discouraged by the boy's size, which made them feel even more shriveled by age, but they liked the freshness in his voice and the rainwashed look of his eyes. He just might do.

14·

Words are quicker than feet, stronger than muscles, harder than fists. Mooch had learned this from growing up in the Home, where she had usually been one of the smallest kids in any crowd. Time and again she had talked her way out of corners she could never have escaped by running or fighting. Sometimes a joke, sometimes a threat, other times a story would spring her free. Unlike punches, which only bruised the skin, words could bruise or tease or haunt the mind.

Here at the Farm, she relied on her tongue more than ever. There were murderers in this place, brawlers and bruisers who got their kicks from hurting people. Mooch had been cruel plenty of times, mean and stupid, wounding people close to her—she thought of Orlando, and Garrison, and a long list of kids from the Home—but she had known her cruelty for what it was, never enjoyed it, and always felt rotten afterward. In a fight where the object was to inflict pain, she was no match for these tough customers.

During her first weeks at the Farm she had lived in terror, afraid to close her eyes in bed, afraid to undress for the shower, afraid to expose her back in the hallways. Konga Rue was only the first of the burly thugs who tried to pound her into submission. So long as it was a matter of pounding,

Mooch always lost. She was not bulky or vicious enough. Words alone kept her in one piece.

After numerous beatings at the hands of Queen Konga, one night Mooch stole across the darkened room to the other girl's bed, hoping to catch her by surprise. "Don't you lay a hand on me again," she hissed into Konga's ear. Startled, the husky girl flinched and sucked in breath. "You hit me one more time," Mooch whispered, her voice sharpened to a spike by fury and fear, "and when you're asleep I'll sneak over here just like right now and turn off your ticker. You'll never hear me coming. I'll pull your battery, and after you're dead I'll connect it back. Nobody'll know what killed you. Poor Konga, dead in her sleep. Just lie there and think about it."

Konga tossed on her pillow and thought about it, remembering how quiet Mooch could be, how the runt could steal up on you, could practically snatch the shoes off your feet. By morning, she had decided there were punks enough to push around without messing over this lethal geek.

One by one Mooch talked down the bullies on the Farm, not always before losing some blood. Even through split lips, she could mutter something disarming. Between blows, her arm twisted behind, a knee jammed into her back, still she would talk—gasping out her animal dreams, reciting fairy tales, rapping like a clairvoyant, growling like a psychopath. She knew the canary would be protected so long as it sang. She knew the rattlesnake would be left in peace, so long as it made its treacherous noise. She rattled, she sang.

■

HER TEACHERS and therapists, experts at words, did not give in so easily to the charm of her tongue, but eventually she wore them out or won them over, and they quit trying to refashion her in their own image.

Dr. Bob was the last one to surrender. Mooch feared him more than any of the musclebound thugs. He knew his way through the labyrinth of words better than she did, and eventually he would have trapped her, penned her in some deep cavity of language, if only he had concentrated all his wits on pursuing her. But between their solo sessions he was distracted by dozens of other cases, while she thought only about ways of eluding him.

Three times a week they battled grimly in his office, Dr. Bob crackling the bones in his neck and pacing about in his pastel socks, Mooch swiveling in the high-backed chair and fending off his questions. She would have found the battle less grueling had she been able to hate him. True, he was pompous, he looked like an ostrich, the oiled gears of his voice grated on her nerves. She could laugh at him, and fear him—but she couldn't hate him. Unlike the Pickle, who saw the Home as a perpetual riot and herself as chief of riot control, Dr. Bob saw himself as a physician, healing the sick. Mooch granted him that, but she did not believe she was sick, and she fiercely rejected his cure.

"You don't enjoy being an oddball, do you?" he never tired of asking. "Surely you'd rather fit in with the other young people, be one of the gang, and not always be hankering after some preposterous other life? That's no fun, is it? And wouldn't you rather have fun?" At this point he would pump extra oil into his voice and murmur, "I want you to be happy, my dear. I want to help you fit in."

To Mooch this could only mean he wanted to destroy her craving for the wilds. Yet this hunger was all that kept her sane, all that enabled her to feel she belonged on earth and not in some orbiting space station.

Near the end of each therapy session, when Dr. Bob's questions were driving her into parts of the labyrinth she had never seen, he would ease up, his mind drifting toward the next appointment, and Mooch could slither away.

For several months he kept after her, doggedly, shrewdly, and it was all she could do to stay ahead of him. Then, week by week, he seemed to lose interest, he asked gentler questions, a hint of respect—or perhaps it was only the note of dismissal—crept into his voice, and he gave up.

She marked Dr. Bob's surrender from the moment when he told her, cracking his neck for emphasis, "One day a fox crept in through a hole in the dome and began eating chickens. We caught him and put him in a cage, and tried everything we could think of to tame him. But he stayed vicious, biting and scratching whenever anybody tried to handle him. So finally we threw him back outside."

■

No fox had broken into the Farm, of course. The domes were perfectly defended against the wilds. His imagination jogged by the girl's tapering face and ruddy freckles and upslanting eyes, Dr. Bob had merely spun that little fable by way of preparing Mooch for the final stage in her therapy.

Time now for a blunt instrument, he decided. Her shell had proven to be hard indeed. Although Dr. Bob felt as confident as ever that his inspired therapy could have broken the girl, he refused to lavish any more of his strength on this one stubborn nut. A whole pack of delinquents awaited his attention.

Time to invoke what the grandfather of all shrinks, Herr Freud, had called the reality principle, thought Dr. Bob. All that Mooch knew about the wilds she had learned from a handful of mushy books and viddies and feelies, propaganda from bleeding-heart eco-freaks. If she was going to persist in her fantasies about forests and bears, if she was going to cling to her mania even in the face of Dr. Bob's genius—very well, then, let her go outside and wallow in the wilds. Let her go rub that saucy, freckled, dreamy-eyed puss in the muck. She would beg to come in soon enough.

Still, one could not simply open an airlock and shove her out onto the dunes. Dr. Bob was a healer, not an executioner. No, she would need a companion out there to keep her from perishing. And what better companion than Hae Won Gilbert-Chang, the young biologist who ran the environmental monitoring station on the nearby Cape island of Truro? She had called on Dr. Bob for more than one favor in the past—the loan of tools, solar cells, an occasional haunch of beef—and now he could ask a favor in return. Although somewhat of an eco-freak herself, Hae Won knew at first hand about mutations and toxins and other bio-hazards, and therefore entertained a healthy dread of the wilds. She would see that Mooch swallowed enough raw nature to get good and sick, but not enough to die.

"I need a scrambled kid out here like I need a hole in the head," Hae Won told Dr. Bob when he phoned her.

"Would I foist off a problem child on you, my dear?" he replied. "Not at all! I'm sending you a mechanical wizard. Don't your instruments keep breaking down? Aren't you always crying for a repair tech?"

On the phonescreen, Hae Won's face brightened. "She's got the touch with machines?"

"Like a healer. You'll see. Give her a six-week trial. If she doesn't fix everything in sight, ship her back to me."

"But isn't she scared of coming outside?"

"On the contrary. She imagines that's where she belongs! She claims she was raised in a cave by bears! She fancies herself a latter-day Indian who's been uprooted from her native land!"

Dr. Bob laughed at the absurdity of this, but Hae Won stared back at him soberly, hearing through his scorn the echo of a nearly-forgotten cry.

■

TIPSY with excitement over going outside, when she met her new mistress in Dr. Bob's office the next afternoon Mooch still took a hard look at this Hae Won Gilbert-Chang. At first glance the woman seemed too young, too prim and fragile to be managing an eco station. Even in the bulky orange moonsuit she looked no bigger than Mooch herself, with scarcely a bulge at hips and breasts. She could have been mistaken for a schoolie, although she must have been in her late twenties. There were no sun-creases beside her delicate, dark eyes, no gray strands in her lustrous black hair, which she wore in a childish pony-tail. The only visible mark of the outdoors was the burnt almond shade of her forehead and cheeks, set off against the pale triangle of her nose and mouth, which the breather mask shielded from the sun.

In the way the biologist moved, however, there was a coiled alertness, and in her voice there was a ringing hardness of steel.

"Get this straight," said Hae Won. "I don't need a patient. I need a technician. You keep my instruments running, I let you stay. You screw up, even once, and back you come to Dr. Bob. Understand?"

Mooch gave a small nod, fearful that a clumsy gesture might destroy her chance of going outside. She put on the gaudy orange moonsuit Hae Won had brought for her, crimping it snug at wrists and throat, then followed her new boss toward the shuttle-pod.

Dr. Bob strode on ahead with Hae Won, his long ostrich legs scissoring and pink socks flashing, his voice pouring final recommendations into the woman's tiny seashell ear. "I certainly don't want the child injured by the wilds," he was saying, "but I would like her to swallow a healthy dose of terror and disgust."

Hae Won glanced up at him, pressing her thin lips together, lifting her ink-stroke eyebrows. "I hear you," was all she answered.

They arrived at the shuttle-pod. Mooch could not look at the aircraft without remembering how the Overseers had swooped down on her, melters blazing, as she rode ahead of the beasts on the rocking shoulders of the elephant. Those deadly shuttles had gleamed in the arclights of New Boston, polished and flawless; but Hae Won's craft was a dingy old bucket, painted blue at one time but now thoroughly scraped and dented, with aluminum patches riveted here and there like Band-Aids.

"Have you flown before?" Hae Won asked her.

"Sure, plenty of times," said Mooch, although she had never flown anything but playzone copters. Right then she would have claimed to be the reincarnated spirit of a butterfly or bald eagle, would have told any lie to avoid spoiling her escape.

Mooch climbed aboard the shuttle and took her seat beside Hae Won, fastening the belts and fitting the breather to her face as the older woman did.

Dr. Bob waved at them from the launch apron, his therapeutic grin hanging below his beaky nose. Just before the canopy snapped down over the cockpit, he shouted, "Happy hunting!"

Mooch closed her eyes and gripped the armrests. There was a whine of engines from below, and from above the whoosh of air as the doors of the pod retracted. The shuttle quivered, then lurched upward. Mooch felt nauseous and ecstatic at the same time. The ecstasy won out, forcing her eyes open. Overhead, the sky unrolled forever, an impossible blue, and clouds of a stunning whiteness foamed against the actual sun. The sun! So bright, so bright! Below, the domes of the Farm dwindled to the size of soap bubbles, and looked as frail and temporary as bubbles against the tawny flank of the island. The travel tube afloat on its pontoons curved back over the sea toward New Boston. Scattered clumps of trees passed beneath the shuttle, actual trees, dark and mysterious, and the sinuous strands of creeks glinting in the sunlight, and the muscular ripple of dunes stitched through with grasses, then beaches of creamy sand like froth at the island's edge, then the vibrant green of ocean, and beyond she could see the chain of islands curling away like stepping stones toward the mainland.

Mooch felt the tears run down her cheeks and did not wipe them away.

"It's your first time in the air, isn't it?" said Hae Won. Breathing the filtered air of the cockpit, she had removed her mask, but her delicate features were still hard to read.

Mooch tore away her own mask and sobbed. "Yes, yes, the first! First time for everything!"

"Don't be scared."

"I'm not scared," Mooch bawled. "I'm happy! I'm *happy*!"

Hae Won's mouth tightened at the corners. She knew that cry, all right, the cry of the exile returning home.

15·

"Garrison's not exactly a ball of fire," Bertha Dill had warned Humphrey and Grace when they picked up the boy from the orphanage. "He'll seem lazy to you, but it's only because he's putting all his energy into growing."

The growth was easy to believe. He was like a sail filling with wind before their eyes. In the darkened apartment, when the boy finally went to sleep, the old scavengers imagined they could hear the swelling of his muscles, the creaking of his joints. His appetite was in proportion to his furious growth, making even the voracious Humphrey seem, by comparison, like a nibbler.

What they could not believe was Bertha Dill's charge of laziness. During the first weeks of his stay, Garrison nearly drove Humphrey and Grace mad with his industry. Open your eyes in the morning, and there he would be towering over the bed, a breakfast tray in his big spatula hands and the newsfax clamped under his arm. Close your eyes at night, and there he would still be, knocking about in the closet, putting away a load of laundry. Between what passed for sunrise and sunset in this electric city, whenever he was not in the den untangling computer records for Seniors Against Gravity—a daylong job in itself—he was cleaning the apartment, filing bills, shampooing rugs, labeling photos, greasing the zip-carts, mending clothes, all without being asked. No drone ever worked harder.

The only times they actually saw him grind to a halt were during meals, when, between prodigious forkfuls, he would mention Mooch. He was ingenious at dragging her in, no matter what the topic of conversation, and once her name floated above the table he would pause in his chewing, grow very still, and gaze into the distance like a shipwrecked sailor longing for land.

After snapping out of this amorous daze, Garrison would hurry through his meal and rush back to work.

To escape his constant bustle, Humphrey and Grace went tooling around the streets of New Boston in their carts. But it made their scroungy old hearts ache to pass by perfectly good trash without picking it up, and they could not pick it up, had no place to dump it, since Mt. Hexxon was full. Why else had they saddled themselves with this eager boy? Yet they dared not rush him straight to the mountain and let him in on their little plan, not until they were confident he would keep his trap shut. Garrison did not seem the blabbing type. On the other hand, he did seem compulsive about rules and regulations. Who knew how he might react when they handed him the wiring plans? He might run squealing to the Overseers.

Even Grace, dynamo that she was, found the boy wearying. One of the reasons she had always preferred cats to dogs was because cats, after beguiling what they wanted from you, would go on their snooty way and leave you alone, while dogs clung to you, their long syrupy tongues hanging out, their dark eyes fawning. Garrison, in his eagerness to please, was like a gigantic, bumbling mutt.

"He's done everything but offer to scrub my back in the shower," Grace complained to Humphrey in bed one night.

"That's because you're a female of the species and he's a modest boy," said Humphrey.

"Don't tell me he offered to scrub yours?"

"Three times, before I persuaded him I could still manage very well on my own."

From the living room came the whine of the vacuum cleaner.

Grace flopped over on her pillow to face Humphrey, the cellophane tape on her forehead (stuck there nightly to discourage wrinkles while she slept) catching the green light from the alarm clock. "As I remember from our teen years, boys were all posturing, muscle-flexing, lust-filled egomaniacs. Why is he so sweet?"

"Do you include me in that description?"

"No, no, kiddo. You were sugar itself. You still are." She patted his cheek. The sag he made in the mattress, familiar to her from seventy years of sharing a bed with him, had grown noticeably deeper of late. Now was not the time, however, to bring up his diet. "But it isn't natural for a boy to grow up in an institution and turn out so . . . so . . . *kind*."

"Maybe he's a genetic freak. Another experiment, like Mooch. Only she turned out wild and he turned out tame."

Grace flopped onto her back and did some belly tucks, reminded by the sag in the mattress of gravity's onslaught. Between abdominal contractions, she said, "I think he craves affection, that's what."

"From two old geezers like us?"

"From anybody."

Beyond the door the vacuum kept whining.

Grace began thrusting out her chin to firm up the turkey wattles beneath her jaw. "I think that Dill woman has convinced him nobody will ever love him."

Humphrey recognized his wife's neck-stretching exercise from the way it distorted her voice, and this, coupled with the mention of love, made him think tenderly of her old body, that ever-mysterious landscape.

■

WHAT HUMPHREY and Grace did not realize was that Garrison had needed only five hours on his first day to thoroughly cook the SAG records, and since then, whenever he shut himself in the den with the computer, he had been taking naps. Superstitious about computers, they never broke in on him while the door was closed. Within minutes after waking from a nap Garrison could churn out a graph or holo that would astonish the elderly couple, persuading them he must have been slaving away over the keyboard the whole time.

Refreshed by his naps, he would then truly slave away, at whatever jobs he could find to do around the apartment. His aim was to become indispensable. Love was too much to expect, but if he could steal into the outer hallways of their hearts, if he could make it difficult for them to imagine getting through a day without him, that would be enough.

The trouble was, by the end of his first month as their helper, Garrison had all but run out of jobs. Every appliance was purring. The walls and rugs could not stand any more scrubbing. The cooker and refrigerator gleamed. The junk that used to fill the apartment in knee-high drifts had been sorted into boxes, the spoons with spoons, watches with watches, socks with socks, each item with its own kind. Nor could he squeeze many more days out of the computer job—an elementary piece of network breeding— without making the old couple suspicious.

Before long they would realize they had no need of him, and back he would go to the Home.

Desperate for something to do, Garrison was cleaning the plastic bonsai trees one day, going over each leaf with a toothbrush, when Humphrey and Grace suggested they all go picnic in Natureland Park.

"Have you ever seen the view at night from the peak of Mt. Hexxon, when everything's newly washed and shining?" Grace asked.

"No, ma'am, I haven't," said Garrison. "But I sure would love to."

At midnight they puttered up the mountain slope, Garrison riding with Humphrey and the hamper of food riding with Grace. They spread a tablecloth between two inflated boulders, and as they sat down Humphrey complained of the arthritis in his knees.

"Which reminds me—" he began.

Grace cut him off. "Not quite yet, dearie. Grub first."

They ate, and while eating they talked about music, books, vitamins, gravity, Mooch, and life in the immaculate city. New Boston's million lights glittered below them in honeycomb towers and crystalline streets. Where the disney used to be, the playzone now sprawled amid a garish pool of neon. Orlando's hut was lost in that welter of noise and explosion of lights.

"The poor dear must grind his teeth," said Grace.

"But think of all the boffo games he can play right outside his door," said Garrison.

Humphrey gave a rumble of distaste. "It's hideous!"

"What, sir?"

"The city! The whole electrical plastical shebang! After all these years inside the bubble, it still gives me the creeps, everything's so regulated and squeaky-clean!"

This baffled Garrison, who dreamed of building habitats

far cleaner, tidier, more rational than the Enclosure, this web of cities clinging to a wet ball of rock. He dreamed of utterly pure colonies in space, uncontaminated by earth, small worlds entirely sprung from the human mind.

There was an awkward silence. Humphrey kept rubbing his knees. At length Grace told him, "Now's a good time, dearie."

After calming himself with a forkful of macaroni salad, Humphrey said, "Garrison, my boy, I was wondering if you could do me a favor."

"Sure thing, Mr. Tree. You name it."

"Well, you see, I was poking around one of these puffed-up boulders the other day—that one right there, in fact—when it rolled aside to disclose this deep shaft going down into the mountain, and as I peeked over the edge, my sunglasses—family heirlooms, handed down from my grandmother, who lived back when there was a sun to look at—these glasses fell out of my shirt pocket. And I was wondering, young and limber as you are, if you'd mind climbing down in there to have a look—"

Before Humphrey could finish, Garrison bounded to his feet and shoved the boulder aside. "Glad to. You bet."

"Hold your horses! Let me get you a light!" said Humphrey.

He fetched the antique miner's lamp from his cart. Garrison strapped it on, then lowered his lanky frame into the ventilator shaft.

Half an hour later he surfaced with oil smears on his cheek, a rip in the sleeve of his T-shirt, the sunglasses in hand, and a look of amazement on his face. "Holy smokes," he breathed, "that mountain's full of garbage!"

"We know," said Humphrey.

"We put it there," said Grace.

"And it isn't garbage, my boy," Humphrey corrected. "It's what the city thinks it has thrown away."

■

AFTER SHOWING Garrison the blueprint and revealing their cache of demolition materials, which they had stored in a grotto among the disused rubbery stalactites and albino crayfish, the scavengers observed him shrewdly, to see how he would react.

At first he was puzzled, and then, grasping their plan, he shook his head vigorously. "I couldn't do this. It's against the law. I'd get my skin nailed to the wall."

Humphrey sighed, and flung up his hands.

"Right you are, sweetie," said Grace, her wrinkles deepening with disappointment. "It was only a thought. We'll just forget all about it and trundle on back home." She reached for the wiring blueprint.

But Garrison held on to the slick, incriminating paper. A chill spread through his bones. He was about to leap from a window into the treacherous air. "I'll do it," he announced impulsively, his voice breaking like an untuned harmonica.

"We wouldn't think of forcing you," said Grace.

"I want to. Mooch would have done it, and gotten away with it, too."

"You're sure?"

"I *want* to do it. I *have* to do it."

"Wonderful!" said Humphrey. He gave a hop of satisfaction, which the pain in his knees immediately caused him to regret. Wincing, he added, "Just be careful you don't jostle things too much down there, my boy. Those tunnels are very ticklish. And leave this final connection for me." With a blunt finger he indicated a junction of lines on the blueprint. "It's the only dangerous one, and I should be able to handle that much."

Exchanging conspiratorial smiles, like prisoners trading hacksaws, the old scavengers kept watch atop the mountain while Garrison swung down the ladder carrying load after load, coils of wire over his shoulder, relays and switches in his pockets. Last of all he carried down the plasty, in its two dozen innocent-looking pouches.

The phony sun was rising on the dome and early hikers were climbing Mt. Hexxon when Garrison dragged himself out of the shaft. Sweaty, bloody, filthy, and bruised, he looked as though he had been mugged in a junkyard. "Done!" he gasped. "All but that last junction box."

"You are an absolute sweetheart," said Grace. "If you weren't such a big galoot, I'd kiss you."

Garrison took the sopping wet hem of his T-shirt and scrubbed a spot clean on his cheek. "I'm not all that big," he said shyly.

It was a clumsy kiss, Grace on tiptoe, Garrison stooping. "Bless you," she said.

∎

THAT EVENING they left Garrison in the apartment, his cuts painted with germicide, his alarm set for midnight.

"You can watch from the window," said Humphrey in parting. "Just don't stir from here. We'll take our chances with the Overseers, but we don't want you getting mixed up in this."

After supper Grace led the way in her cart up Mt. Hexxon. The summit was empty of visitors, so Grace took her usual place on a cushiony boulder, and down the shaft climbed Humphrey, his skeleton complaining at each rung of the ladder.

The delicate job of hooking up the detonator took him

the better part of an hour. Finished, he sucked in his belly and started the long trudge back toward the surface. Whenever he bumped the sides of the tunnel, the mass of junk shuddered above him. He made his way gingerly, thinking of his father crushed in that Kentucky mine. From the walls on either side of him protruded the necks of bottles, rims of cans, strings, sleeves, artificial limbs, the edges of books, the corners of pictures, all compressed into strata like the mud of an ancient sea, but Humphrey scarcely looked at them, he was so intent on escaping. Then he noticed the bowl of a soup spoon jutting out. How could he have missed it? Gracie must have dumped it when he wasn't looking. Without thinking, he yanked the spoon from the drift of junk. A small quake buckled the props in front of him, lowering the ceiling.

That was royally dumb, thought Humphrey. He sank to his knees and crawled forward.

Another tunnel collapsed nearby, then a third, a fourth.

A few meters above him, Grace was perched on her boulder, listening to the mountain as if it were a colicky baby. Each time it grumbled and heaved, she groaned. The rubbish-quakes sent tremors up through the aluminum slope, through the elastic boulder on which she sat, through her bones.

"You all right, kiddo?" she whispered into the talkie strapped to her wrist.

A moment later his voice blurted from the radio plug in her ear. "Little queasy down here, duckie. But I'll make it."

"Mind you don't go collecting spoons or anything."

"Don't be ridiculous!" he panted. "Now hush."

She drew the talkie away from her lips. The Overseers could hear you blink your eye, if they happened to be listening in your direction. They could monitor your heart, and tell if one of your valves was sticking.

Grace kept an eye on the park gates, where tonight's visitors were streaming out and tomorrow's visitors would begin arriving soon after midnight. Most young people would ride the conveyor up the side. But the old people would climb on foot, mouths groping for air like stranded fish. She understood well enough why they labored up these metal slopes, their hearts thumping, spots dancing before their foggy eyes. She was one of them, a young spirit in a battered carcass, a caricature of her true self, patched together with electronics and plastic. The new portions of her were numb, as if the surgeons had implanted a gob of emptiness in place of her knees, her liver, her right foot and left shoulder, all the failed organs and bones. Her own surviving flesh ached about these empty spaces, and her soul moaned through them like a ghost flitting through the chambers of an abandoned house. There was nothing like a jaunt up the mountainside to rouse the ghosts.

She checked her watch. Half past twenty-one. "Hurry it up, kiddo," she whispered into her talkie.

For a moment only gasps leaked through the earplug. Then Humphrey muttered, "Going as fast as I can. Got to rest a bit."

"You're not prospecting? Hunting for socks or cutting pictures from magazines?"

"Heavens, no!"

"Nothing the matter with your ticker?"

By way of answer, the thump of his heartbeat came slushing into her ear.

"Sounds too fast!" she said. "How far do you have to go?"

A rasping noise smothered his reply as a quake shook the mountain.

"Humphrey?" she hissed.

"It's all right. A little slide. I'm digging through."

"Where are you?"

"The golf-and-garter tunnel. Midway somewhere."

"Here I come."

"Stay put."

"Not on your life!"

She grabbed a flashlight from her cart, flung the boulder aside, and hobbled down the ladder. If someone discovered their secret, so be it. Plan or no plan, she was not about to lose Humphrey. At the base of the ladder, where the rubbish tunnels began, she switched on the flashlight and shuffled away into the gloom. From Humphrey's description, she recognized the mouth of his tunnel by the golf club elbowing out from the wall and the garter belt dangling from the roof. She slithered in, careful not to touch anything but the well-packed floor. Another slide, she thought, and we'll both be sardines.

Within a few paces she came up against a blockade where the ceiling had collapsed. Through the avalanche she could hear the sound of Humphrey's quiet scratching, like a mouse trapped in a heap of cans. She began working from her side, removing a pot, a crushed hat, a picture frame.

His ragged voice curled in her ear. "Gracie?"

"You were expecting a troll?" She pried loose a clump of streetmasks, a bag of hair clippings. "I hope your daddy was better than you at shoring up mineshafts."

"His mountains were made of rock," Humphrey wheezed, "not skittery junk."

The sound of his scratching drew closer. Grace got down on her knees and clawed her way forward. A chunk of roof fell on her. Shrugging the debris from her back, she kept going. Presently she cleared away the crumpled chassis of a wheelie, and there was Humphrey's light, dancing in hectic circles. In a moment his hands appeared through the opening, the fleshy one bleeding and the synthetic one leaking oil. Then his lovely crumpled bag of a face appeared. She squirmed forward and hugged him fervently, even though his breast pocket was full of spoons.

■

IT WAS nearing twenty-two hours when they rode their junk wagons down Mt. Hexxon for the last time. They parked beside the light-fountain in Cascade Plaza, too excited to fret over their abundant aches. They sat on the fountain's edge, with colored lights swarming at their backs and the four mountains rising in the park before them. The mountains were deserted, for the gates had closed. Soapy water began pouring from each peak, streamed down the slopes, and vanished through drains. The mountains gleamed. The entire city looked as though it had been hatched that very minute, the pure architecture of thought.

They waited for midnight, to make sure Garrison would have a chance to watch. When the hour arrived, Humphrey drew the switchbox from his pocket and said, "You want to do it?"

"Let's both," said Grace, placing her hand on his.

Together they pressed the button.

The sides of Mt. Hexxon bulged, cracked, the top burst open, smoke and ash and clots of junk spewed into the enclosed sky of New Boston.

Traffic stopped. Riders leapt from pedbelts and stood gawking as the air filled with shoes, wigs, forks, spinning bottles and glinting cans, film snarled like spaghetti, posters, printed circuits, all the leavings of their lives. Melted globs of plastic settled on the walkways. Grease filmed the windows. Twisted scraps of metal clattered on the gleaming tiles. The citizens were struck motionless, gaping at the burst mountain, their avenues grown suddenly hazardous, while ash and cinders rained down on their wigs and white gowns, on their measured noses, on their painted masks. A blizzard of forgotten things descended upon the city.

Holding one another's hand, Grace and Humphrey huddled together solemnly beside the fountain, two old-timers with long memories.

The city ground to a halt. Gears and switches and relays seized up, the pedbelts froze, lights flickered whimsically off and on, fountains shot their spray at crazy angles, smoke alarms wailed, fire extinguishers doused stores and offices with foam, overturned wheelies blocked the avenues and no one dared even to walk through the clutter. The Overseers' shuttles could barely navigate through the soupy air. Their cones of light shone down on chaos. Cleaning drones made little headway against the mess, their wheels skidding on oil smears, their brushes gumming up, their pincers snagging. In the end, soldiers were called out to deal with the emergency using those primitive tools, shovels and brooms.

Over a week passed before New Boston purred smoothly again, and even then a new anxiety nagged at the citizens. If an innocent mountain could be turned into a volcano, what other catastrophes might erupt without warning? Were they going to suffer once more the hazards of weather? Earthquake? Germs? During those troubled days the newsfax and viddy spoke of little aside from the blizzard of junk. How could all the safeguards have failed? Might there be a flaw somewhere in the machinery of the

Enclosure? The culprit was identified soon enough, yet doubts still lingered in the city's dreams.

After their initial glee, Humphrey and Grace observed this turmoil and soul-searching with heavy hearts, for on returning to their apartment the morning after the explosion, they had found a note from Garrison: BY THE TIME YOU READ THIS I'LL BE IN JAIL. BUT DON'T WORRY ABOUT ME. I KNOW WHAT I'M DOING. What the crazy boy had done was to enter the nearest Overseer station while debris from the eruption was still floating down, and with the wiring diagram in his fist as proof of guilt, he had confessed to blowing up the mountain.

16·

Mooch dreamed that she had found, in the bottom of Orlando's trunk, a musty bearskin. Somehow the scuffed black metal trunk had made its way into her old room at the Home. She could tell it was her room from the revolting color of the walls, a sugary pink, but there was no bed or dresser or chair, no window, there was only a closed door and, in the middle of a bare vinyl floor, the open trunk.

Hauling out the bearskin, she held it against her body to check the fit. Then she noticed that she was wearing a frilly white dress with puffy sleeves and lacy hem, one of Bertha Dill's ridiculous gowns. It was far too large for her and slipped off easily, and so did the frothy underthings. The coarse black fur burned against her nakedness.

She thrust her feet into the hindlegs of the bearskin, her arms into the forelegs, her face into the bear's empty head. It reeked of dry blood, mildew, the musk of old shoes, but it was a comforting smell, the right smell. For a moment the tanned skin felt loose and dry against her, and then with dreamy quickness she grew to fill it, hands thickening into huge paws, shoulders bunching, chest and stomach swelling, until the black fur was her only skin, snug and true.

She looked out through the bear's eyes, and the world

grew dim. The pink walls of her room changed into sun-fired banks of falling snow. She lifted her muzzle and snuffed at the breeze, which brought news of danger. The hair stiffened on the back of her neck. Through the blizzard she could see an upright figure approaching. It was Orlando, more bowlegged than ever, waddling along in his safari suit, his bare knees and scalp dusted with snow, and he carried his grandfather's double-barreled shotgun aslant over his shoulder.

Mooch reared back on her haunches and raised a paw in greeting. "Orlando!" she tried to say, but it came out as a growl.

He stopped, braced the gun against his shoulder, and lifted the barrel. "I warned you to leave me alone," he said with eerie calm. It was Dr. Bob's clinical voice. "I don't want anything more to do with you."

"I'm not a bear! It's me, Mooch!" More fierce growls.

"You just couldn't leave me alone, could you?" Orlando squinted along the barrel.

It grieved Mooch to hear Dr. Bob's voice come oozing from Orlando's kind old leprechaun face. Giving up on speech, she fell onto all fours and turned away, to show how peaceable she was, but he waddled after her, waving the shotgun.

"I didn't build you, that's the trouble," he said icily. "If I'd built you, rigged your wires and programs, you wouldn't have run wild like this, you wouldn't keep threatening me."

A surge of her great swollen bear's heart made her stop, swing about, and fix the puny man with her black stare. She bared her fangs, grimacing with sadness, and a deep belly-rumble broke from her.

"I'm going to kill you and eat you," Orlando murmured

coldly. His white beard was powdery with snow. "You're the last beast. I'm going to kill and eat the last beast."

Mooch took a lunging, mournful step toward him. The gun boomed. A sudden fire lit in her chest. Then she gathered her enormous legs and sprang at him, the other barrel booming, a flame scorching her throat, and she came thundering down on him. His bones snapped under her weight like a cage of twigs.

Mooch awoke screaming, clawing at her pajamas to pluck them off. "I'm not a beast! Not a beast!"

Her screams rang through the station, rousing the five crew members. Four of them grumbled and dove back into sleep, but Hae Won leapt from bed, threw on a robe, and ran toward the screams. She hugged Mooch, cooing to her, stroking her wild red hair, until the shudders ebbed away.

■

HAE WON could remember having felt every needle of the girl's fear. She had come outside for the first time herself only seven years earlier, at the age of twenty-two, while a graduate student in ecoscience. Nothing she had studied at M.I.T. had prepared her for the vast buzzing confusion of the wilds, the endless sky, the swift clouds, the seething metallic grate of the surf, the sinuous dunes and murky woods, and above all the black, unfathomable nights.

During her own first weeks outside, Hae Won had felt the nights would never end. The sound of wind hissing over the roof of the station, blown sand scritching at the windows, gave her nightmares. If she had wakened screaming, maybe somebody would have comforted her. But her mother's training reached even into sleep and made her swallow the terror, hide her feeling behind the stiff mask of her face. Even now, after seven years outside, some nights Hae Won would jerk upright in bed, chest heaving, lower lip bleeding where she had bitten herself to keep from crying out.

Growing up in New Boston, she had never experienced true darkness, not even while shut up inside her mother's closet with the silken kimonos that smelled of sandalwood. Those kimonos, along with her mother's poetry, gave Hae Won the nudge that eventually shoved her out here onto the windy exposed islands of Cape Cod.

She explained this one day to Mooch, when the two of them were lying side by side on their bellies, chins propped on their palms, staring into the shallows of a freshwater pond. It was a scorching July afternoon, relieved by a salty wind off the ocean. Only regulations kept them from taking off their orange moonsuits and wading into the pond. Lily pads crowded the surface. Frogs hunched on the slick green saucers, croaking. Russet-bellied swallows crisscrossed low over the water, snaring greenhead flies.

"Why did I become a biologist?" Hae Won's reflection shone up from the water, a smile visible in her eyes above the white triangle of the breather mask. "Because of my mother, I suppose. When I was a girl, once in a great while she would take me to her room, lock the door, put on one of her lovely kimonos, and recite haiku to me."

"Haiku?"

"Tiny poems. Like this:

> *In its eye*
> *are mirrored far-off mountains—*
> *dragonfly!*

Or this:

Song of the cuckoo—
in the grove of great bamboos,
moonlight seeping through.

"The sounds were beautiful," said Hae Won, gazing between lily pads at the rippled sandy bottom of the pond, "and my mother's face reciting them was beautiful. But I couldn't understand the words. What was a dragonfly? A cuckoo? Bamboo? How did moonlight look? I'd never even seen pictures of these things, because my father was an indoors man, a New Newyorker, who loved the Enclosure and hated the wilds. He didn't believe in stuffing my head with what he called the moldering rubbish of nature. That was why Mother never let him see her wearing those kimonos. They were made of gorgeous, shimmery silks, embroidered with pictures of mountains and twisty, ancient trees, butterflies, waterfalls, flowers bursting into bloom, cranes wading in streams, flocks of birds wheeling in the sky. I wanted more than anything in the world to see those wild things whose names Mother sang in her poems, whose pictures she wore on her secret dresses."

"Say another haiku," Mooch begged.

Smiling, Hae Won chanted the poem in her mother's gay, wondering voice:

"A sudden shower falls—
and naked I am riding
on a naked horse!"

"I can *feel* that," said Mooch. The amber light of the tracer flashed on her wrist, but she looked hastily away, fixing on the yellow-hearted starburst of a water lily. Since coming outside she had felt rain on her skin, and she could almost imagine the horse carrying her away, utterly free, the huge muscles flexing and surging beneath her. To have a mother at all, let alone one who would sing such pictures into your mind! "Have you seen all the wild things from her poems?" Mooch asked.

Hae Won gave a sad laugh. "A lot of them! But a lot more died out before I had a chance to see them. Whales. Most of the cranes. Most of the butterflies. Tigers. Pandas. Crows. Mother taught me a haiku about the look of crows against a field of snow. That's something I'll never see. Nobody will ever see. The crows are gone."

"Because of poisons?"

"Poisons, habitat destruction, shifts in climate, plant die-offs. Hundreds of reasons. That's why we're out here—to see how many strands in the web of life are still holding."

There was a flutter in Mooch's chest as she asked, "How about bears? Aren't there still bears?"

"Yes, a few. In fact the healthiest population in the world is in the White Mountains of New Hampshire and Maine. Black bears. *Ursus americanus*. The IR satellites pick them up, their big hot bodies glowing like boilers against the cool woods."

"Have you ever flown in there to look for them?"

"Three or four times. It's not my territory. I've got my hands full with surveying these islands."

"But could we go? Would you take me?"

Their gaze met on the pond's surface. Hae Won frowned, her inkstroke eyebrows drawing together. "I understand you were raised in a cave by bears. Is that so?"

Mooch was trembling. "Don't make fun of me."

"I'm not making fun."

"Dr. Bob thinks I'm crazy." Curling her left hand into the shape of a water strider, Mooch lightly stroked the skin of the pond with her fingertips. "But I'm telling you I *wasn't* born in a test tube. I wasn't bred and raised in a lab."

"I don't think you're crazy," Hae Won answered gently.

"When I look inside myself, I don't find any lab and test tube. They're not part of me. But I've met bears in dreams. I've smelled them. I've felt their fur against my face and drunk their hot milk. They're *real* to me. They're as real to me as words in poems, as real as pictures on dresses."

"I believe you."

Mooch lifted her fingers from the water. "I have to go to those mountains and find a bear. I'm going if I have to walk."

As the pond smoothed out, the reflection of Hae Won's face gathered into a sober dish. "You won't have to walk. I'll take you. Not now—I can't get away in the growing season—but in the fall, when the trees begin to turn and the air cools off."

Mooch looked searchingly at the watery image. "I can stay that long?"

"The way you've got my instruments humming, you'd better not even think of leaving."

During the silence that followed, Mooch noticed the silver blades of minnows veering in the shallows. She could not stop trembling. The minnows turned and darted, their sides glinting. Back at the Home, and back among the sullen, clumsy beasts on the Farm, she would never have dreamed that anything so tiny could possess such wisdom of motion.

■

THROUGH the rest of July and all of August, Mooch stayed inside much of the time, overhauling equipment. Like an invalid regaining the use of her legs, she also took walks outside, brief and shaky ones to begin with, then gradually longer and bolder ones. At first she always kept within sight of the station, that gleaming shelter, with its white, petal-shaped ring of workrooms and sleep-chambers encircling a greenhouse of smoky glass. She would go out for an hour to pick blueberries, and the taste of them on her lips and the stain of them on her fingers would make her cry. She would zigzag after butterflies in the meadow. She would lie on her back and watch clouds. On clear mornings she would climb a nearby hill to look out over the rumpled dunes, beyond the salt marsh, to the gray hem of the ocean.

Eventually, she grew bold enough to walk by herself to the nearest beach, two kilometers from the station. Ankle-deep in the surf with her back to the island—Turtle Island, the crew members called it, in honor of its shape—watching the waves surge in, Mooch could imagine herself riding on the back of a great sea turtle, trusting the generous beast to keep her afloat.

By September, after two months at the eco-station, Mooch still woke up some nights from terrifying dreams, but less and less often. Now she could spend entire days outside, tagging along after one or another of the researchers. She took notes, carried gear, fixed probes and monitors.

With Steen—a husky and tight-lipped Australian who wore a blue bandanna for a headband—she would go out at sunrise to study the tracks of birds and crabs on tide-smoothed beaches. Instead of humming, as Orlando used to do, Steen made soft muttering bird cries deep in his throat, or burbled the watery songs of fish. With Cynthia and Hojo, a blond and conspicuously married pair of graduate students from the University of New Chicago, she ran soil tests, charting populations of mites, beetles, fungi, bacteria and nematodes. With jumpy, fast-talking Lucas, who came from New Oregon, Mooch spent her days cataloging plants, everything from algae to oak trees. Best of all she loved the secretive bog plants that Lucas would point out to her with a quivering gesture of his velvety, chocolate hands—wild sarsaparilla, mayflower, sphagnum moss, cranberry, sweet pepperbush—the names were as lovely as Hae Won's poems.

Cynthia and Hojo scarcely spoke with anybody else, they were so wrapped up in one another. But it seemed obvious that Steen and Lucas—the hulking, quiet bird-caller and the wiry, chattery plant-seeker—would have loved Hae Won, if only she had let them.

"Don't be ridiculous," Hae Won replied, when Mooch passed along her insight.

"But you can see it in their eyes!" Mooch protested.

"Nonsense. We're friends and colleagues, working on a project together. That's all." There was no room in Hae Won's life for romance. She managed the whole survey, but specialized in mammals, which was why she could justify going to the White Mountains to look for bears.

Early mornings, while dew still clung to the grass, Mooch walked out from the station to a nearby woods, to see if any leaves had begun to change color. She knew the pines and cedars would keep their needles through the winter. But oaks, cherries, shadbush, the few beeches, and above all the sumacs, these she inspected anxiously, hoping for the promised yellows and reds. But well into September the woods remained stubbornly green.

Then one morning there was a tinge of red in the sumacs, a lick of yellow on the beeches. Mooch was practically dancing when she told the news to Hae Won.

■

HAE WON herself had news that day. Dr. Bob had called from the Farm with a plea for help. The pumps had gone haywire, and catfish were dying in droves. And since Mooch had fixed them before, would she please come see what she could do?

"What if it's some kind of trick to lock me up again?" said Mooch.

"He could order you back any time he wants," said Hae Won, "because you're only on loan to me. But he's asking."

Mooch considered. "All right, tell him I'll come, if he'll promise to give me back my medicine bundle."

It was a brief trip in the shuttle, the small craft skimming on its air-jets low over the water like a stiff-winged swallow.

Dr. Bob met them at the shuttle pod, his black wig fluffed up into a thunder cloud, his toothy smile flaring like lightning. He scrutinized Mooch, to see if a spell in the wilds had shaken a bit of sense into her. But the only changes he could see were a thickening of her freckles and a narrowing of her green, unreadable eyes.

"How good it is to see you, my dear! And looking so healthy!" He popped the vertebrae of his neck. He cracked his lavender-stockinged toes. "We've certainly missed you and your ingenious hands around here. Machines are breaking down left and right!"

Mooch was polite, even though his oily voice brought back the chill of her nightmare. She felt the bearskin tightening around her, saw the dream-Orlando raising the shotgun, heard the boom, felt the flame in her chest.

Dr. Bob took Hae Won aside for what he called a chummy little chat, while Mooch went to the fish dome.

She felt odd, tramping through the tunnels in her bright orange suit, among the blue uniforms of the imprisoned kids. She knew about half of the faces she met, including two of her old roommates, who ran up squealing and gave her bouncy hugs. Mooch was glad to see them, but anxious to break away, afraid of becoming entangled in this place again. She had felt the same about her friends at the Home, even about Orlando and the disney. Every place she had lived before going to the station, every one she had known, had been a net, binding her.

The pump was easily fixed, so easily that she felt certain one of the Farm's own technicians could have handled it. Dr. Bob had some other reason for bringing her back.

On her guard, eager to escape, Mooch was hurrying to the shuttle pod when she saw, approaching down the tunnel, a familiar gangly figure.

Her first impulse was to spin around and flee, her second was to fling herself at him. Confused, she merely stopped.

In that moment Garrison spied her. He came loping, even bigger than she remembered, less clumsy, his great pie of a face bursting with delight. The other kids in the tunnel jostled aside to give him room.

"Mooch!" he bellowed. He flung his arms wide, but dropped them self-consciously as he drew close to her.

Mooch did not know what to do with her own arms, her face, her voice. She almost yelled *Ratbone*! but caught herself, that nickname no longer fitting, and instead cried, "Garrison! How did you land in here?"

He reddened. "I blew up a mountain."

"You *what*?"

Breathless, too busy looking at her to keep his sentences from snarling, he told about Grace and Humphrey's patient scavenging, the laying of wires in the caverns, the explosion of Mt. Hexxon, the blizzard of trash falling on New Boston, the stunned faces in the street.

The image delighted Mooch. "You big galoot! And here I always thought you were the one Little Wanderer who was sure to go straight!"

"Now just look at me. A hardened criminal."

"Look at you!" Mooch grabbed his hands, surprised at the weight of them, his fingers the size of knife-handles. Why hadn't she ever seen before that his eyes were ocean-gray? She hardly noticed his big tremulous ears, or the yellow sprawl of his hair. "How much time did they give you?"

"Only a year. My first offense."

"Why didn't Grace and Humphrey get caught?"

"After I was locked up, they tried confessing, but the Overseers thought they were a couple of publicity-seeking old crackpots and sent them home."

"How'd you get arrested?"

"Just dumb, I guess."

"Come on, tell me. Did they track you down?"

"Not really."

"Give, give. I want all the gory details."

He looked away, answering quietly, "Well, I turned myself in. They believed me, because I had the wiring map."

"Turned yourself *in*? That's the craziest thing I ever heard! Why'd you do a stupid thing like that?"

Only when he swung his gaze back to her did Mooch feel again the weight of his hands in hers.

"I hoped they'd send me in here with you," he said.

"You're kidding."

"I'm serious."

"You're lying. Nobody'd get locked up for me." She dropped his hands. "This is a trick. You're trying to *catch* me."

"No. Listen. I had to see you."

"Nobody's going to catch me again."

"Hey, look, you're the one who's running around out-side, and I'm the one in the cage," said Garrison, thumping a fist on the base drum of his chest.

"That was your idea. Don't blame it on me."

The two of them formed an angry knot in the tunnel, the blue waves of Farm kids flowing past, as Dr. Bob and Hae Won came up.

"Ah, I see you've found one another!" said Dr. Bob.

Hearing that greased purr, seeing that calculated smile, Mooch knew for certain that Garrison was another net, flung out to snare her. She backed away from him, flustered, panicky.

"You can stay here with your friend if you'd like," said Hae Won, who had been primed for this by Dr. Bob. She was holding Mooch's medicine bundle, the red fox fur still zipped in plastic.

"I'm ready to go," Mooch declared vehemently.

Garrison stood there without speaking. His big body slumped as though his flesh had grown too heavy for his bones.

17·

Peeping out from the door of his workshop into the frenzied crowds and flaring lights of the playzone, Orlando felt as he imagined a space traveler might feel who had lost his way among the stars and crash-landed on a hostile planet.

Like New Boston itself, the playzone never closed, so the noise kept up around the clock. Dodgem cars banged together. Shrieks and moans gushed from the eros parlors. Giddy laughter poured from the feelie booths. The motors of amusement rides revved at a hysterical pitch. Chemmie vendors cried out the virtues of their wares. Sirens, loud-speakers, amplified music, human voices keening in transports of pleasure and pain—it was all so loud it made the stuffed heads quiver on the workshop walls.

Orlando's own bald head ached from the perpetual racket. He lined his bedroom with baffles and wore spongy protectors over his ears, yet still he could not sleep. Day and night, revelers pounded on the doors and windows, thinking the round thatched hut was another pleasure palace, or maybe a disguised toilet.

Locked inside, Orlando felt like the last member of a tribe, besieged by a relentless enemy. Warily opening the garage in the mornings, he would often find chemmie-freaks slumped across the driveway, their faces goofy with stale joy. Before rolling the van out for his daily fix-it tour, he would have to drag aside the limp bodies.

It was a relief to putter off in the glossy white van each morning, wearing crisp overalls and a gambler's eyeshade. He parked in the quietest neighborhood he could find, clanged the bell on the roof, and gratefully watched people line up on the sidewalk, their arms cradling broken gadgets. All day he lost himself in the work, fixing whatever the customers plopped down onto his bench. Hunched over ailing machines, he listened to the telltale grate of gears and clack of switches, fingered the cracks in worn-out tubes, smelled the burnt insulation of fried circuits. Thinking of the machines as patients, he opened their metal skins and stared into their bowels and replaced their botched parts and put them back together again, all the while handling his tools with the deftness of a surgeon. He interrupted his work only to chat with onlookers or to dish out ice cream and popsicles to oldsters and kiddies. Tinkering soothed his frazzled nerves.

But when he returned home at night he would find lunatic messages spray-painted on the walls of the hut, garbage trampled into the plastic lawn, smashed windows, jimmied locks, the whole place like a battered fortress.

The noisier the nights, the more dangerous his days. Idling at stoplights, he dozed at the steering wheel and woke to the blast of horns. He began nodding off while seated at his workbench behind the van, in the middle of repairing some gismo or other. He ruined more than one appliance this way, by shorting wires and burning out the delicate chips and cryodes. Once he nearly lost an eye, his sleepy head tumbling forward onto the point of a screwdriver.

Instead of returning home at night, he tried parking in

alleys and stretching out on the seat for a nap, the green eyeshade pulled over his face. But passersby, reading his red-lettered sign—

ORLANDO SPINKS
THE MACHINE MEDIC
EVERYTHING FIXED FREE

—plucked temperamental watches and talkies from their wrists, cranky cybers from their pockets, staticky music hats from their heads, and thumped on the windshield, demanding repairs. If he ignored them, within minutes an Overseer would turn up, gold helmet reflecting a dwarfed world, pockets bulging ominously. Terrified, Orlando would scramble up to unlock the van.

The dial on his tracer reminded him there were still six months to run on his sentence, half a year more of obedience if he wanted to become a free man.

■

DROPPING BY the workshop one evening while the playzone was in full uproar, Grace and Humphrey invited Orlando to sleep at their apartment, a quiet little box on the forty-second floor in a noise-control district.

"I'd take you up on that in a minute," Orlando told them, nearly shouting to make himself heard, "but the judge ordered me to spend my days on the streets and my nights in the hut."

"Let the judge eat fudge!" yelled Grace, who had not lost her spunk.

But Humphrey said nothing. He slumped on a stool against a wall, as torpid as the stuffed moose above his head. Since Garrison's arrest, the zip had gone out of him.

"I don't like the way he's been looking," Grace confided

to Orlando. "You can just see him wilting, like soggy lettuce."

Indeed, Humphrey was no longer the jovial butterball Orlando had known since childhood. Almost overnight, it seemed, he had become a precariously old man. His face had aged so as to resemble a brown sack that was not merely crumpled, but squashed and tattered and worn nearly through at the creases. He wheezed. He stooped. His white caterpillar eyebrows drooped. He shuffled around in slippers and forgot to brush his teeth and let the stiff rootlets of his whiskers straggle out from his chin.

Most troubling symptom of all, Humphrey had gone off his feed. At meals he pushed the food around his plate with a listless fork. Between meals he scarcely thought of eating. It was plain to see that he was melting away.

Grace, to compensate, munched continuously. As Humphrey dwindled, she grew.

"How could we have known the boy would turn himself in?" she grouched to Orlando that evening in the workshop, for the umpteenth time. She raised her voice above the din of the playzone, carrying on as though Humphrey were not propped there on a stool within arm's reach. "Could we help it if the boy wanted to go to jail? You can't separate a fool from his folly!"

"Who can understand teenagers?" said Orlando, thinking of Mooch even more than of Garrison.

"We never meant to land the poor, sweet giraffe in trouble. And after he was arrested, didn't we go straight to the Overseers and confess? Was it our fault they took us for a pair of cranks and laughed us out the door?"

Orlando could see how the eccentric old couple might be mistaken for a pair of cranks, but this did not keep him from sympathizing with them. "Don't blame yourself, Gracie," he said.

"I'm not blaming myself! You think I'm blaming myself? Not on your life! All I want to know is why Humphrey's taking it so hard."

They both looked at the rumpled old man, whose glum expression seemed to echo that of the moose on the wall above.

What Humphrey needed, in Grace's opinion, was a good rousing dose of Seniors Against Gravity.

"That would stir up his juices," she predicted. "Dress him in his robes, plop that balloon hat on his head, stand him in front of an audience, and before you know it he'll be his old peppy self again, feeding his face and kicking up his heels."

Motionless on the stool, Humphrey seemed to be lost in revery. His electronic eyes drifted aimlessly in their sockets.

"SAG could meet here in the shop," Orlando suggested. "It'd be crowded, but I could shove the benches aside and leave the van on the street."

"We could all fit in and still have room for dancing," Grace replied, "as few of us as there are left."

The secret lodge had fallen into disarray since the closing of the disney. A few members had lost the battle with gravity. Others had been locked away in nursing towers. Still others had grown so reckless at the wheel they were no longer permitted to drive, and thus were forced to limp around on their tottery legs or else ride on the crowded tubes and suffer the rude elbows of youngsters.

"Pick a date," said Orlando.

Grace sidled up to her husband and put her lips near his

withered old ear. "What do you say, duckie? You ready to play the Exalted Sagamore?"

Fingering a crooked whisker, Humphrey did not answer.

■

ON THE NIGHT of the lodge meeting, the SAGites picked their way cautiously through the playzone, their floppy orange hats and long black capes giving them the look of Halloween gremlins. Meeting one another, they exchanged indecipherable winks and split-fingered handshakes. They craned their wrinkled necks to gaze through the neon-lit doorways of pleasure booths. The squeals and bursts of laughter made them jump. Scooting in wheelies or hobbling on canes, they entered the jungle hut. Soon their ancient voices filled the workshop with a gay croaking that pushed back against the roar of the playzone.

Still not an initiate, Orlando watched the proceedings from a monitor in the control room, perched on his astro-lounger. Humphrey had indeed regained some of his old vim. He stood in front of the orange and black crowd of old-timers and led the chants, the windmill arm gestures, the curses against gravity. From the first row, Grace's leathery voice rose encouragingly, cheering him on. As Humphrey grew more and more animated, his face turning the rosy color she loved, Grace felt the moths of happiness fluttering in her throat. At the conclusion of these rituals, the SAGites all fingered the buttons of aerosol dispensers and their balloon hats quickly inflated, carpeting the room with a bobbing mass of clenched fists.

Embarrassed to be spying on this occult ceremony, Orlando turned away from the monitors. When he turned back, the air had gone out of the hats, Humphrey had taken a seat next to Grace, and two SAGites were demonstrating their new levitation belts. The demonstrators rose jerkily into the air, spun about, bumped heads, and crashed back to the floor.

During their moment of flight, Humphrey reached over and fumbled for Grace's hand, squeezed out her name in a final astonished breath, and died.

FOR THREE DAYS Grace remained speechless with grief. She felt as though a cleaver had sliced her down the middle, and one of the halves had been thrown away. This time surgeons could offer no replacement for the part she had lost.

After the funeral she recovered her tongue. "That rascal promised to wait for me," she complained to Orlando. "He promised never to leave me alone."

Orlando had put away his threadbare sentences of comfort. *He lived a good life. He died without pain. You were there beside him. Think of all your happy years.* Such worn sayings, mumbled so easily, could not stifle the heart's howling. Not believing his own consolations, Orlando said nothing, merely squeezed Grace's hand, as Humphrey had done at the end.

"If either one of us felt it coming," she continued, "we were going to jump down a recycle together. Mingle our molecules."

Orlando thought of Humphrey's molecules, reduced by now to their elements, stewing in vats beneath the city. It made him feel peculiar to think of the old gentleman's carbon, say, turning up in a tire, his phosphorous in a vitamin pill.

Grace muttered, "I told him I wouldn't keep on going without him, so he'd better not quit on me. And look what he did!"

She railed and Orlando squeezed her fidgety hand all the

way back to the workshop, where she had moved the night after Humphrey's death. SAGites and other old friends offered to keep her company in her own apartment, but Orlando was the one she needed most, and he was still bound to the shop for the remaining few weeks of his sentence. He made up the hammock for her in Mooch's room. Grace promised to leave untouched the animal pictures on the walls, the taped symbols on the floor, and the girl's other mystic paraphernalia.

Mornings, not wanting to be left alone, she rode out with Orlando on his fix-it tours. She would sit beside him at the fold-down bench, occasionally fetching him tools and parts from inside the van, dishing out ice cream and popsicles, chatting with customers, watching the city go about its day. The electric sun arched along its customary path over the roof of New Boston, bathing the streets in perpetual high summer, and lavender clouds squirted from the peak of Mt. Pepsicoke, and the breeze changed direction once an hour, and fountains danced to music in all the plazas, everything on schedule, as though nothing had changed.

At night, to buffer the noise from the playzone and to distract her thoughts from Humphrey, Grace listened to the girl's tapes of whalesong, waterfalls, Indian drums. After some weeks of this, there came a night when she slept right through until dawn, and she awoke to the smell of breakfast and climbed out of the hammock and took several gimpy steps before she remembered that she had been cut in half. Remembering, she felt the cleaver slash through her once more.

■

ONE EVENING Orlando and Grace returned to the workshop to find that revelers from the playzone had broken in, toppled the cabinets, ripped down Grandfather's stuffed heads, and strewn clothing and papers and tools everywhere. To Orlando, who could not stand the sight of a mussed bed, the shop was a nightmare.

It hurt him even more to see Mooch's room. The hammock had been cut to shreds. Her dream animals, painted in all their mystery on ceiling and walls, had been scrawled over with obscenities. The tape on the floor—marking the wind's four quarters inside a holy circle—had been peeled up and mashed into a ball. Orlando forced himself to enter. He found stuck in the torn webbing of the hammock one of the gray turkey feathers that Mooch used to wear behind her ear when she danced. Closing his eyes, he saw her spinning, her moccasins flashing, her fringed skirt and red braids whirling, and he heard the strong rain of her singing. Then he opened his eyes on the havoc, and his ears filled with the din of the playzone. She would never set her dancing feet here again. The bedroom, the workshop, the disney were all dead to him now. Putting the feather in his breast pocket, he took a final survey, remembering how Mooch in her doeskin dress had made the painted chamber seem like a sacred cave. Then he turned his back on the desolation and walked away and shut the door behind him.

"Those filthy oinkers," said Grace, who was straightening up the workshop. "No," she corrected herself. "That's an insult to pigs. We're the only animals who would do this." She lifted the head of a mountain goat by one horn, and the spiraling horn came away in her hand. "How much of this stuff do you want to keep?"

Orlando sat on the floor amid a scree of microchips and threw back his head and wept.

Swiftly Grace went to him and put her flabby arms about his thin shoulders. While he sobbed, he was a child again and she was a young woman, not quite a mother, but as close as she would ever come.

■

Over the next month, working late into the evenings, using scrap metals, recycled wheels, and portions of the jungle hut, Orlando built a house-trailer. It had a tiny bathroom, a bedroom for Grace and a fold-out couch for himself, a galley kitchen, and a parlor that doubled as a miniature shop. The parlor was jammed with all the animal skins and electronic parts he had salvaged from the ruins of his old workshop. On the outside of the trailer, which was electrified to discourage vandals, he painted red letters a meter high, announcing THE ORLANDO SPINKS ANIMAL CIRCUS.

"That's the cat's meow," observed Grace, standing back to admire the little rolling house.

"It gives us something to look forward to, anyhow," said Orlando.

For now, he and Grace could take refuge at night inside the trailer, inside the devastated jungle hut. When his sentence was up, he would build a new menagerie of mechs. Then he would load his beasts in the trailer, shake the dust of the disney from his feet, and take his show on the road.

18·

The airjets hissed like welding torches. The cockpit smelled of hot oil. Mooch pressed her cheek against the shuttle window and gazed down at the smoldering mountains. On this cloudless, sunstruck October morning, the golden beeches and scarlet maples seemed to blaze up from the cool green of hemlocks and pines. She could almost hear the crackle of flames. The world might end this way, in a ball of fire.

"It would be terrifying if it weren't so beautiful," she told Hae Won.

The biologist lifted her eyes from the flight controls and studied Mooch, alert for signs of wilderfear. "Are you sure you're ready for this?"

"I've been getting ready my whole life," said Mooch.

"So you think. I'll admit you've done well on the island. But that's just a cozy garden compared to the White Mountains. The land stretches away farther than you can imagine, and all of it—except the travel tubes and cities and poisoned zones—has gone back to wilderness. No amount of equipment or maps will ever make you feel at home there. I've been outside for years now, and I still get jittery when I come to the mountains."

Watching the fiery autumn slopes roll past below, Mooch felt a cramping in her stomach. A few minutes from now, after landing, she would be a speck down there, a flickering candle in the vast conflagration of the wilderness. Nervously she fingered the birdbone whistle, which she had retrieved from the medicine bundle and wore again about her neck. The bundle itself she carried in the zippered pouch of her jumpsuit. On her left wrist the tracer gave its telltale amber flash, and she jerked the sleeve down irritably to cover it. "Tell me a haiku," she said.

"What kind?"

"One that makes you calm."

Hae Won thought a minute, calling up lines that brought back the fragrance of sandalwood and the silken feel of her mother's kimonos. At length she said, "Here's one I've always found soothing:

> *Though it be broken—*
> *broken again—still it's there:*
> *the moon on the water.*"

Mooch savored the image. The water she pictured was the shimmery pond on Turtle Island, and instead of the moon she pictured Hae Won's round face. A pebble thrown in the pool or a breath of wind or a leaping fish rippled the surface, shattering the reflection; but as the water smoothed out, the jostling scraps of light gathered again to form the lovely moon of Hae Won's face. Holding to that image, Mooch, like the pond, grew calm.

They flew on, the airjets whispering, and soon came within sight of the New England eco station, which looked exactly like their own base on Turtle Island, a daisyish cluster of white domes surrounding a greenhouse. Instead of perching on a hill overlooking marshes and dunes and sea, however, the domes had been wedged into a river valley between two mountains. Caught there in the land's grip, flanked by shaggy dark slopes tinged with the flames of maples, even now at midday the station foundered in shadow.

As the shuttle banked toward the landing pad, Hae Won said, "Remember, there's no guarantee we'll find a bear."

"We'll find one," Mooch said passionately. "We have to."

Reminded again of herself as a teenager and her own fierce desire to know the wilds, Hae Won smiled. If desire were fuel, Mooch could have spread her arms and flown across the continent.

The shuttle touched down. The man and woman who sauntered from the station to greet them wore the familiar bright orange moonsuits and gauzy breather masks, but on their hips they carried stunners.

Mooch whispered, "Why the guns? For animals?"

"Two-legged ones," Hae Won replied, flipping switches for shut-down. "The mountains are full of tribals. Renegades from the Enclosure. Usually they mind their own business. But if they run low on food or medicine or solar cells, they sneak in here to grab what they need. Like foxes attacking a chicken coop. Winter's their desperate time."

Hae Won opened the hatch, letting in a slap of cool air. Not winter yet, Mooch told herself. Cold enough for bears to be digging their dens, though. She climbed down from the shuttle, torn between anxiety and hope, and for the first time stood, not merely on the shifting sand of an island, but on the broad stony back of North America.

■

THEY WOULD have no more than five days here, all that Hae Won could spare from her work on Cape Cod. The remainder of the first day was taken up with briefings, Hae

Won and the director of the White Mountain station exchanging reports about their surveys. This director—a thickset, gruff man named Ike Ortiz, with a scorched outdoor face and shoulder-length gray hair and a rich Hispanic way of rolling his r's—was the mammal expert, so there would be no hunting for bears until he was free to go.

Restless, Mooch tagged along that afternoon with a pair of scientists who were cataloging plants. She found that all the research teams worked in pairs, one person always keeping watch.

"Just a precaution," explained one of the botanists, a stolid woman in her thirties with raven hair chopped close to the skull. "You never know what might come out of the trees."

"Like mountain lions?" Mooch suggested hopefully. "Or wolves, maybe?"

The woman shook her close-cropped head. "No more lions. And we're not going out far enough to see any sign of wolves."

Mooch was left to imagine what else might lurk under the trees. Following the botanists into the shadowy woods, along a trail that was dimpled with the split-hoofed prints of deer, she kept glancing nervously back, not wanting to lose sight of the station. When the reassuring domes finally vanished behind the flank of a hill, she almost cried out in panic. Steady, she thought. You know this place. You carry the mountains in your blood. You belong here. Swallowing the cry, she moved on.

The chipmunks darting stiff-tailed across the path and the fluted mushrooms pushing up through the leaf duff gave her courage. The merest beetle or curling grass blade put to shame the most intricate device she and Orlando had ever made. By fixing her attention on ferns, counting the white stripes on hemlock needles, staring at mosses through a hand lens, she was able to gather herself, like Hae Won's moon making itself whole again on the rocking water.

That evening, alone with Mooch in the sleep-chamber they were sharing, Hae Won noticed her tight lips, the bloodless patches on her cheeks, the smoke of uncertainty in her eyes. "How was it?" she asked.

"Harder than on the island," Mooch conceded.

"To reach bear country, we'll have to hike out for a day, maybe even two. We'll have to sleep overnight in the woods. Are you going to be able to stand that?"

"I'll stand it."

"Wilderfear is nothing to be ashamed of. You don't have anything to prove."

"Nothing to prove, maybe. But something to find."

At meals, Hae Won had noticed that Mooch only pushed the food around on her plate and drank nothing but water. "Why are you fasting?" she asked.

Mooch glanced at her sharply, then looked away, exasperated. "You don't miss a thing."

"You're bone and muscle to begin with. You haven't got a gram to spare. How do you expect to hike on an empty stomach?"

"The Indians did. When they went looking for visions."

Hae Won's inkstroke eyebrows tilted. "What do you really hope to find out there?"

"A bear."

"I mean besides the bear. Behind the bear. What?"

A name, thought Mooch. A helper. An outward and breathing visitor from my dreams. A picture of how things are. But she could not bring herself to say these wishes aloud, not even to this deep and accepting woman.

■

WARY of humans, and for good reason, the black bears in their slouching travels through the mountains gave the station a wide berth. Ike Ortiz could map where dozens of them rambled, for he had traced them to their dens in winter and shot them with tranquilizing needles and buckled radio collars around their fat necks. These tagged bears would not do, however, for his two visitors. For the severe Dr. Gilbert-Chang and her quicksilver, nervy apprentice, Ortiz wanted to find an uncompromised bear, a wily old sow, maybe, or a surly boar, one never drugged and labeled. He knew to look during these crisp October days on north-facing slopes where nuts and rotted logs were abundant, and where granite outcrops or dense brush or the splayed roots of fallen trees offered prime sites for denning.

Nor would it do to spot these elusive bears from the sky. Ortiz had seen too many beasts cringe and jerk their heads and blink fearfully up at him in the shuttle. In that moment of bewilderment they lost their dignity. Confronted by the hissing machine, which was unimaginably larger and more lethal-seeming than any hawk or eagle, an apparition from outside the boundaries of their ancient knowledge, the beasts were robbed of grace. If the girl wished to meet a bear on its own ground, she would have to walk.

On foot, the party might also run into the occasional tribal, out grubbing roots or trapping squirrels. Like bears, these skittery renegades would only attack if you cornered them. They nicknamed Ortiz the Orange Engine, because of his bright coveralls and squat shape and the chugging way he moved over the land. He left them alone, and, except for the occasional winter raid or stand-off in the woods, they did not bother him or his crew. Given a choice between crossing a city at night and crossing the mountains, Ortiz would always choose the mountains.

■

EARLY on their second morning at the station, Hae Won and Mooch awoke to boisterous singing.

"Going on a bearhunt!" Ortiz sang with full lungs. "Going to catch a big one! I'm not afraid!"

They shouldered their packs and set out well before sunrise, Ortiz charging ahead, his gray scarf of hair streaming, Hae Won and Mooch hastening to keep up. Fog thickened the beams from their belt lamps. As they followed the river north toward unsullied country, the hooting of owls laced the chill air. Then with first light came the ragged songs of day birds, songs grown tattered from neglect since the avid chorusing of spring. The midmorning sun burned away the fog and stilled the birds, revealing the purr of the rain-swollen river, the clatter of wind-shaken leaves.

Mooch kept her eyes on the ground, to avoid the dizziness of staring into the dark throat of the woods or seeing the muscled mountains range away endlessly from green to misty gray. She was lightheaded to begin with from not having eaten for two days. Even with eyes on the trail, she kept stumbling. Roots flung like knotted ropes across the path snagged her toes. Twice that morning a root flinched under her boot and turned into a snake and wriggled away. The rustle of squirrels in the leaves or the sudden hammering of a woodpecker or the explosive blue flight of a jay made her stagger.

As the day wore on, the weight of the pack gouged into

her shoulders. Her legs complained, then after a few hours they went silent, moving only from stubborn habit. The breather mask grew clammy from her panting.

Every little while Hae Won glanced back to check on her, but she could read nothing except determination in the green eyes.

For long stretches, lulled by his own burly motion, Ortiz forgot his two companions. He stopped only to inspect animal signs. A bruised clump of moss or a nibbled mushroom or a five-toed pawprint spoke to him of raccoons, mice, wolves.

Late that afternoon they climbed up from the river, along a trail that was scarcely more than a faint groove in the brown carpet of hemlock needles. Partway up, Hae Won stopped, arm pointing, and then Ortiz, and then Mooch. From the shadows a deer stared back at them, a plume of grass caught sideways in its narrow muzzle. Mooch let out a gasp. The deer, her first one, more astonishing than a unicorn, flicked its ears and swung away and bounded off, white tail flung up in alarm. For a long time afterward Mooch glided over the ground with the ease of dream.

On top of the ridge they crossed the twin beds of an old superhighway. Waist-thick trees grew up through the buckled concrete. Alongside the road a pylon that must once have carried high-tension wires, overlooked by salvage crews, lifted its rusting, cross-hatched girders above the spires of the tallest pines. The far side of the ridge had been scoured bare, either by erosion or by earth-moving machines from the highway era. Ortiz picked a cautious route down over the scrabbly exposed granite. The valley below was a spoil zone, blackened stumps jutting like rotten teeth from poisoned gray soil.

Without needing to exchange a word, the walkers hastened away from these reminders of that desolate time, climbing the next ridge and the next.

The sun inflamed the maples with a final guttering intensity before it disappeared. Darkness oozed from the woods.

The charm of meeting the deer had long since worn off, and Mooch was tottering under the weight of the rucksack, holding back tears, when Ortiz finally stopped for the night.

"Look," he said, shining his lamp on the trunk of a white pine.

Just above eye-level the bark had been slashed. Sap rose in golden beads from the deep claw marks. Lower down, the trunk was matted with coarse, black hair. Plucking one of the tufts, Mooch held it to her nose, and the rank, wild smell tore through her like a gust of wind.

■

THEY SLEPT in the open that night with an alarm wire strung around the camp but without burning a flare, Ortiz and Hae Won agreeing that it was preferable to break regulations rather than to spook the beasts. There was no moon, and the stars were hidden by clouds, leaving the night as black as an underground river.

Seconds after saying goodnight, Ortiz began snoring.

In her sleepsack, the hood drawn up, Mooch squeezed her eyes tight and felt the darkness lapping over her. She fought for breath. Her legs twitched, as though treading water.

Hearing Mooch pant, Hae Won rolled toward her and whispered, "It's all right. I know what you're feeling. But nothing's going to hurt you."

Mooch could not unclench her teeth enough to speak. Her breath made an owlish whistling.

"Here, give me your hand," Hae Won murmured.

Pulling her left arm from the sleepsack, Mooch groped toward the other woman. Her fingers brushed over twigs and leaves and finally met a warm hand. She clung to it. Safely tethered, she let herself go into the annihilating waters.

19·

Dream carried her into a moonlit night. Wrapped in the musty old bearskin from Orlando's trunk, lumbering through woods on her four thick legs, Mooch came to a pond. A black muzzle gazed up from the water with her own grassy eyes. The pockmarked golden coin of a full moon rippled on the surface nearby, within reach of her paw. It was an innocent moon. As she bent down to lap at the pond with her long, red tongue, the moon became Hae Won's face. Not weather-darkened and tough, but the fragile porcelain face a Japanese artist might paint on a fan.

Mooch paused in her drinking. Breath chafed in her throat.

After a moment Hae Won's midnight hair turned white, the scalp showed through, the delicate lines of her cheeks and lips turned coarse, and now Orlando's rumpled old mug quivered in the moon's place. He looked hurt. His lips parted and his beard trembled, but he did not speak. Mooch was unable to call, knowing her voice would emerge as a growl. She reached out a paw to comfort him. Instead of skin she touched water. Orlando's face broke into a hundred scraps of light, each one carrying a blood-shot eye that stared back at her.

Breath roared in her throat. Hunched there beside the

pond in the hulking bear flesh, Mooch waited for the water to grow calm, waited for Orlando's face to mend itself.

She was waiting still when a bellystab of hunger jolted her from sleep. She awoke to daylight, bird song, the yeasty smell of multigrain cooking.

Dressed, her glossy black hair drawn back in a ponytail, Hae Won was kneeling over the stove and stirring a pot. "Are you going to eat today?"

Mooch rocked her head against the sleepsack. The hand with which she had clung to Hae Won through the darkness now lay across her chest. She absently rubbed that wrist, then sat up with a jerk, startled. The arm was bare. She tugged up the sleeve and still felt nothing but her own skin.

Hae Won tasted from the spoon, then lowered it, watching her. "You lose something?"

"My tracer! Where's my tracer?"

Hae Won beamed. From her pocket she drew the woven steel bracelet, its amber crystal gone dark. "I took it off."

"How? Why? Now I'm in big trouble."

"No you aren't. The Overseers phoned me the combination right after you moved out from the Farm. They told me I could take it off whenever I thought I could trust you."

Mooch nervously rubbed at the bare wrist. "But what about the rest of my sentence?"

"Excused for good time."

"You mean I'm free to go where I want?"

"I hope you'll want to stick with me."

"Why take it off here? Why now?"

"I couldn't stand seeing you wear it in the woods, like a tagged animal. It's an ugly thing, a shackle."

Just then Ortiz came back to the campsite, his gray hair bristling damply in a halo about his ruddy face. "The pond's all yours," he said to Mooch. "It's clean enough to drink."

"Seriously?" Hae Won asked.

"Seriously. I checked."

Neither was wearing a mask. The deep woods made them both impatient with regulations.

Following where he pointed, beyond a screen of golden aspens, Mooch found the tiny pool. Sight of it brought back her dream, and she thought of Orlando, his face broken into a hundred bloodshot eyes. Instead of a bear's muzzle, the reflection gazing up from the surface was her own insufferably familiar one. With a glance over her shoulder to make certain she could not be seen from camp, she peeled off the bodysuit and thrust a toe in the water. It was shockingly cold. She plunged in anyway, squealing with pained delight. Two strokes carried her to the middle. The encircling trees, like lashes around the clear eye of the pond, opened onto a blue dish of sky. She dipped her chin, hesitated, worrying about poisons, then drank. There was a taste of iron and sunlight. Buoyed by the water, free of rucksack and clothes, free of the tracer, free at last of the Enclosure's entanglements, Mooch felt a ballooning lightness.

■

THAT MORNING they ranged out in a spiral from the scratching tree, and then at night, having seen plenty of smashed logs and fresh prints but no actual bears, they spiraled back in to camp again at the base of the gouged and fur-matted pine.

Ortiz was apologetic. "I thought sure we'd run into an old grayback out here. We're in a sow's territory. But that's eighty square kilometers, and she could be anywhere inside it."

"We'll give it one more day," Hae Won said.

"What if we still don't have any luck?" Mooch asked in a panic.

"Maybe we can come back and try again in the spring."

Giddy from lack of food, clinging once more to Hae Won's hand, Mooch slept as though in a fever. Three times she woke in the darkness and looked up between the black feathery branches to see the constellation of the Great Bear wheeling about the North Star.

Next morning again she was the last to bathe. The smell of breakfast cooking and the chill of the water made her cry aloud. When she came out of the pond and saw the limp bodysuit and luminous orange coveralls lying on the bank, she could not put them on. They were gaudy, alien skins. No bear would let itself be found by anyone dressed in such clothes. She was cold, cold. She wrapped herself in a towel, but she could not stop shivering. From the waistpouch of the coveralls she retrieved her medicine bundle, and clutched the fox fur against her belly. Needles of hunger pierced her stomach and skull. She could not think. The encircling trees danced and glowed. The sky was a whirling blue plate. Birds shot by overhead like meteors. The roaring in her ears was the call of a bear.

The call yanked her into motion as though by a rope. Naked under the towel, her bare feet wincing on twigs and stones, she staggered up from the pond, away from the camp, into the seething shadows of the forest.

Later, going to see what was keeping Mooch so long at the pond, Hae Won found only the clothes on the bank, like a castoff chrysalis.

■

DEER SAW the pale two-legger stumbling through the woods. Fox and raccoon sniffed at her. Jay and hawk spied her from overhead. Frog watched her splash through a creek. Moth and mantis and bee, sluggish with cold, snared a hundred images of her in the facets of their eyes. An old woman dressed in wolfskins and moccasins, one of the mountain fugitives, away from her village digging sassafras roots, also watched the girl stagger by. All the creatures drew back and let her pass, all except the old woman, who left off digging and trailed along behind.

With each dizzy step, the birdbone whistle pecked at Mooch's throat. Her braids came unraveled. Twigs and leaves caught in the loose hair, which spilled over her back. She fell, picked herself up, fell again and again, always rising and blundering onward. A brier snagged the towel from her shoulders, and she let it go. She was cold, cold. Hugging herself, pressing the fox fur against her breast, she went on. Went where? She had no idea. Part of the way she flew, or seemed to fly, her feet losing all sense of the ground. The trees turned cartwheels before her. The wind sawed at her ribs. The mountains clapped.

Bear bear bear, Mooch thought. Aloud, she did not say the word, but only chanted, "Mother! Grandmother!"

She would make a welcome new bride for the village, thought the woman who was trailing her. With her flame of hair, the girl must have come from a distant tribe. No people in the nearby mountains had such hair. She would bring in a trickle of fresh blood. A bit crazy from wilderfear, but that would pass. In need of some fattening. Otherwise, she looked healthy. The hunters would be pleased. The old woman hurried to keep up with the girl's frenzied pace.

Mooch felt a burning in her legs and looked down to see a dozen bleeding scratches, as though she had been clawed by the forest. Her feet also were bleeding. She stopped. The trees kept spinning around her. Burning, freezing, she opened her eyes wide, trying to steady the world.

Bear, she thought. *Come to me. Save me.*

Where did the girl live? wondered the old woman, panting from the chase. Maybe she escaped from the orange-suits. If so, they would come searching for her in their great metal birds. Thought of those machines terrified her.

A mouth opened before Mooch. It was the hollow beneath a granite outcrop in the side of a hill, calling to her. Beyond fear, she pitched forward, slithering down into the hole and landing on a softness of leaves and pine needles. The rank wild smell stole her breath. She gasped and gasped, heart a frantic bird in her chest.

Appalled, the old woman saw the girl disappear into the bear's den. The she-bear must have been away, speaking with the animals, fattening on acorns and hickory nuts, or by now the girl would have been screaming. A shout of warning would frighten the girl, make her run again. And the old woman could not hold a girl possessed by wilderfear. It would take a hunter to catch and subdue her. Let my four grandsons race here to see who should own her. Stay there, you fiery-haired bride, thought the old woman, as she began trotting back to fetch her grandsons from the village.

Mooch burrowed into the leaves, making herself a nest. She curled into a ball, her fingers surprised by the feel of her own skin. The raw stench of bear no longer gagged her. At every breath the leaves rustled. Gradually her shivers died away. Her teeth stopped clicking. She thought of the pond, the waters calming, the shattered moon gathering itself. Her stomach was numb from hunger, her throat was parched. Dimly it came to her that she might die.

Hearing the news from the old woman, the four grandsons took their bows and knives and set off at a run toward the she-bear's den. Every hunter in the village knew the bear who wintered there, a huge black sow with ginger paws and a face like a dish of flint. They left her in peace, for she was Keeper of the beasts. Without her permission, the deer would not come to the bow, the rabbits and quail would not come to the trap, and the village would starve. So it was with fearful hearts that the grandsons ran toward the she-bear's den, racing one another to claim this naked girl whose hair blazed like a torch.

Mooch ached, without remembering clearly what it was she ached for. She only knew she must wait. She must not close her eyes. She must not sleep. From between her thighs she drew the medicine bundle, untied the shoelace, and opened the fox fur. In the gloom, by touch more than sight, she identified the owl's skull, the smooth round compass, the squirrel's paw, the pouch of tobacco and corncob pipe, the prickly starfish, the hard crystal of quartz, the turtle shell with its clatter of bones inside. The compass and pipe offended her, and she hurled them away into the woods. She tore open the foil pouch and sprinkled tobacco around her as an offering. The owl skull spoke to her then with Orlando's voice, saying, "Good, good. Sing to the earth. Sing, darling, sing." With split lips and scorched throat, Mooch sang. Curled in her nest of leaves, rattling the turtle shell, she sobbed the chants of praise.

The bear answered her call. Nearing the den, the hunters saw the great humped back, the lifted face like a dish of flint, and they stopped, trembling with awe. The she-bear sniffed at the den and tilted her massive head as though listening to the girl's thin song.

To Mooch, looking out with feverish eyes from her nest

of leaves, the day seemed to have been swallowed by night. The blue-black shape covering the mouth of the den was a doorway opening onto the nothingness of space. The song dried in her throat. "Mother?" she whispered. "Grandmother?"

"Daughter!" rumbled the she-bear.

"I am thirsty," Mooch cried.

"I bring you drink."

"I am hungry."

"I bring you food."

"I am lost, Grandmother."

"I have found you, Daughter. You are here with me."

The grandsons heard the she-bear snapping her jaws, clacking her teeth, chuffing and grunting, all signs of her fury. They watched her pace on stiff legs before the den, her upper lip peeled back. If the girl did not heed these warnings and come out of the den and run away, the bear would charge in and smash her with a forepaw and crush her neck with a single bite. They had seen the Great One kill fawns and dogs and even wolves just that way. The girl did not come out. Thinking of the pale-skinned bride with the flaming hair, the hunters were tempted to chase the bear away. But they knew better than to anger the Keeper of the beasts, and so they looked on.

"I accept you, my daughter," Mooch heard the bear say.

"Thank you, Grandmother."

"You are a blade of green-eyed grass rooted in the earth. You burn with the sun's fire. We two are at peace. You must go make peace with those who love you."

"Orlando," said Mooch helplessly. "Garrison. Hae Won."

"You must answer their aching."

Mooch wept, unable to speak.

"Now come to me and eat," rumbled the bear.

Closing her eyes, Mooch rubbed her lips over the silky fur until her mouth found the fat nipple. She sucked the hot milk. It streamed through her like a river. Tears warmed her face.

Seeing the bear surge forward into her den, the hunters knew the girl was doomed. They listened for her sharp cry.

When Mooch had drunk all the milk she could hold, the bear licked her face and hair and throat with a raspy tongue.

"Daughter," said the bear, "I give you the rain and snow to be your helpers. You must live where snow and rain fall free."

"I will, Grandmother."

"The song I give you is the sound of wind through trees. You must sing it always."

"I will, I will."

"Daughter," said the bear, "I give you a name. You shall be called Moon Waters."

From that instant, Mooch thought of herself as Moon. Broken and mended. No longer a sneak, a skulker. No longer an orphan. Now she was daughter to the Earth.

■

EVEN TRACKING the girl's barefooted trail from the air by infrared, Hae Won and Ortiz and the two men who had quickly flown out from the station in the shuttle still did not find her until late afternoon. She had zigzagged crazily through the woods, covering more than fifteen kilometers. Hae Won could not imagine where she had found the strength for such a journey after half a week of fasting. Perhaps the force of desire truly had enabled her to fly.

As the shuttle hovered above the granite cliff where the girl's trail had ended, a bear came waddling backward from a hole in the rock face.

"That's the old grayback I was looking for," said Ortiz. "She's making her den in a new place this fall. The poor girl must have stumbled into it."

The bear gave one irritable skyward glance and took off at a run, the front legs and the rear ones gallumphing along parallel paths.

"Tribals!" Hae Won called sharply. She pointed down through the windshield at four thick-bearded men who were dashing away into a grove of flame-colored maples. They wore skins and carried bows in their fists. Knives glinted from their belts.

"She's dead," Hae Won cried. "I know she's dead."

Ortiz brought the shuttle down onto the cliff. Hae Won leapt from the cockpit and was clambering over the rock even before the airjets stopped hissing. She slipped and slid, tearing holes in her suit, ripping her fingernails on the granite. The last two meters she let herself fall, dropping with bent knees onto the lip of the den. She could see claw marks where the bear had been scraping leaves and grasses for bedding. She imagined the same slashes on the girl's mangled body.

"Mooch!" she wailed. "Mooch?"

From the black throat of the den came a whimper. Hae Won shone her lamp into the hole. Two green slits caught the light. "Mooch?"

A voice like the rustle of dry leaves whispered, "My name is Moon."

Hae Won scrambled in on hands and knees. Murmuring, she gently brushed the leaves and grass and weeds aside and touched the curled-up body. Tenderly she felt the girl's neck, and found no mark of teeth. She groped along her bent legs, her spine, her arms and ribs, and found no bones jutting through the sleek skin.

"She's alive," Hae Won called out to Ortiz and the other crewmen, who had reached the den. "Weak and delirious, but alive."

Before moving her, Hae Won gave her a shot of nutri and trickled water into her mouth. She wrapped her in a blanket and lifted her gently onto a stretcher. Only then did she let two men carry her from the den and up to the shuttle. Ortiz punched in coordinates for a flight to New Boston, the nearest place that could provide intensive care.

Above the ocean, the last rays of sunlight bloodying the water, Hae Won peeled away the blanket for a moment to reassure herself that the girl really was intact. The green eyes were closed in sleep. A red spray of hair veiled both cheeks. The ribs flexed with each breath. Lying on her side, knees drawn up to her chest, the girl was a milky ball, captivating, lunar.

PART THREE•

20·

Within minutes after the Overseers removed his tracer and put an end to his term as roving fix-it man, Orlando was hard at work building a new menagerie of beasts. Instead of having to gad about the city at the beck and call of strangers, repairing whatever lame contraptions they chose to plop in front of him, now he could stay home and tinker with his own mechanimals. The house-trailer, still parked inside what was left of the jungle hut, resounded with his cheerful humming. He scarcely heard the hullabaloo of the playzone, except when zonked-out revelers came pounding on his door, and even the pounding ceased when he trickled a charge of electricity into the trailer's walls.

He was alone once more, for Grace had moved back to her cluttered apartment in the Golden Years Tower.

"You're more than welcome to stay here with me," Orlando had told her before she left. "As soon as the beasts are finished, we'll take our show on the road. Think of it—spotlights, roaring crowds, the smell of grease! A new street every night!"

"Thanks bundles, duckie," Grace replied, "but if God had meant me to roll all over creation, I'd have been born with wheels. My gypsy days are over. Besides, I've got a slew of friends in the Golden Years. Most of them are in worse shape than I am. It gives me a kick to shoot by their rooms and light a fire under them."

Orlando carried her suitcases into the apartment, which looked like a salvage yard that had been convulsed by earthquake. Grace kicked aside a pile of socks and a carton of spoons to make way for the opening of the door.

"Would you believe that sweet boy Garrison had this place as neat as a pin?" she said.

Surveying the bundles and stacks and boxes, the drifts of paper, the tangles of clothing, Orlando found it hard to believe that even a regiment of robomaids could have brought order to this chaos. "What happened?" he asked.

"Humphrey is what happened. After we blew up the mountain and the boy got jailed, Humphrey came unzipped. I hate to say it, but the dear man went haywire. Loony tuny. He emptied the closets, pulled everything out of the cupboards and down off the shelves. He dumped boxes. He kept digging through all this stuff and throwing it every which way."

Following Grace over the top of the skittery junk—there being no other path to the bedroom—Orlando asked, "Was he looking for something?"

"His heart!" she declared. "He had an artificial ticker, you know. Had it fifteen years. Never a minute's trouble. Then after the boy was locked away, Hump started getting these pains in his chest. Doctors couldn't find a thing wrong. But Humphrey swore he was going to die unless he got back his real heart. I told him they'd turned that soggy old pump into fish food years ago. But would he listen? Not on your life. He swore it was hidden somewhere in the apartment. And he turned this place upside down looking for it."

Orlando flopped the suitcases onto the bed, between a

mound of wigs and a leaning tower of books. The jouncing from the suitcases toppled the books onto the floor.

"What a klutz," Orlando muttered.

Before he could kneel to pick them up, Grace seized him by the arm. "Leave them, leave them. What's a few more flakes in a blizzard?"

The clutter made him break out in a sweat and take shallow breaths, yet he offered to stay and help straighten up.

"Oh, no you don't," she sang out. "I need something to keep me busy. You go on home. Build your animals."

"Isn't there *something* I could do?"

She pressed an upright forefinger across her withered lips. After a moment's reflection, she announced, with a flash of her gay old eyes: "There *is* something. You can make me a cat. A saucy, purring, fluffy-tailed, persnickety puss."

"What color?"

"Surprise me."

Orlando promised her a cat.

At the door on his way out, he paused. "I'll come say hello whenever I bring my circus through the neighborhood."

"You do that, duckie."

"Sure you'll be all right?"

"You mean, have I gotten over losing Humphrey?" She gave a laugh that sounded like breaking glass. "Heavens, no! Nothing's ever going to fill the hole that man left in me. But I've still got my breath, don't I? I've still got a few beans in the pot!" She rapped knuckles on her forehead. "When you were a kid in Boston, did you ever walk through the Public Gardens and see one of those old beech trees that had been struck by lightning, and the top was broken off and the trunk was hollowed out and all it had left were a few limbs, and still, when spring came round, it squeezed out fresh green leaves? Well, that's how I feel."

◾

ALL BY himself, therefore, using parts scavenged from the disney and pelts inherited from Grandfather Spinks, Orlando tinkered away at his beasts. First he made a fluffy black and white calico cat for Grace, who clapped for joy when he delivered it. Next he built a lion, in memory of Mooch. (He would never forget the sight of her scrawny legs sprouting from that previous lion's jaw.) Then he built a monkey, programming it with all the smarts he could muster, so he would have somebody to talk with. He went on to make a rhinoceros, a gorilla, two pandas, a Komodo dragon, an abominable snowman, a unicorn, a porcupine, a griffin—twenty-four beasts in all. He took liberties with scale, so that the gorilla and snowman, for example, were no taller than he was; the dragon and elephant came up only to his shoulder.

To identify specimens from the taxidermy collection, Orlando relied upon the labels that Grandfather Spinks had sewn onto the pelts. Even to Orlando's untutored eyes, however, some of the items appeared rather improbable, as if they had been pieced together out of scraps from various antique animals. There was a suspicious-looking seam, for example, where the griffin's wings joined to its muscular torso. The horn was secured to the skull of the unicorn with a bolt, not at all a common feature in biology. The pale fur of the abominable snowman bore a striking resemblance to a bleached raccoon coat. It would be ungrateful as well as inconvenient, Orlando concluded, to peer too closely at Grandfather's legacy.

He left the monkey running all the time, for the sake of its chatter.

"Hey, Boss," the monkey asked in one typical exchange, "why did the baby cross the road?"

"I don't know. Why?"

"Because he was stapled to the chicken."

Orlando remarked dubiously, "Is that right?"

"Mighty righty. And, hey-the-day, Boss?"

"I'm all ears, Monkey."

"How many robocops does it take to eat a plate of spaghetti?"

"How many?"

"Three. One to read up on how you squishies do it, one to grease the slitheries, and one to arrest the meat balls."

Later on, Orlando would regret having endowed the monkey with a joke generator and slang receptor. The russet-furred, curly-tailed rapscallion picked up the most obscure sayings from kids in the street, so that listening to him was like overhearing bits of a slapstick opera sung in Chinese by a chemmie-freak. For the present, however, Orlando was glad of the company.

He could never fire up more than two or three of the other mechanimals at once, because there was so little space for them to do their tricks inside the trailer. "Not room enough to swing a cat in," his father would have said. Certainly not room enough for a gorilla to beat on its chest without hammering dents in the walls. To accommodate his expanding menagerie, he used the few remaining panels and beams from the jungle hut to build another pair of trailers. These were little more than rolling boxes, with compartments inside for stowing away the beasts. He painted the new trailers a dazzling peacock blue to match the old one, and stenciled the flanks of the fix-it van to match the trailers, so that now the entire caravan proclaimed, in ruby letters a meter high: SPINKS' ANIMAL CIRCUS. As a final touch, he furnished the trailers with grass-colored rugs and plastic trees and inflated stones, to give the effect of wildness.

When the last of the mechs were tuned up, Orlando hitched the trailers on behind the van, opened the workshop doors for the last time, shook the dust of the disney from his feet, and set out to astonish the population.

■

THE POPULATION—chiefly in the persons of gawking youngsters and hawking oldsters—felt something several degrees milder than astonishment. When the caravan glided to a stop in a neighborhood, loudspeakers blaring with calliope tunes, a crowd of mildly curious onlookers gathered round. The spindly, white-bearded, bald-topped man who climbed down from the van and announced himself in an age-cracked voice to be Orlando Spinks, Ringmaster, did not promise to be much of a showman. But once he got cranked up, hooting and hollering about the wonders of his mechanical beasts, he wasn't half bad. He wore shiny black boots, white tuxedo and top hat, lavender shirt and a glowing neon bow tie the color of stoplights. One by one his beasts lumbered down the ramps from the trailers, ambled onto the sidewalk, and did their turns. A wolf sat up and begged, a lion roared, an elephant balanced on its trunk, a dragon blew smoke rings, a moose did back flips, a monkey shot off wisecracks.

"All authentic!" the ringmaster yelled while skipping among them, prodding the beasts with his whip, now and again thwapping an unruly pet over the skull.

But no sooner had this sidewalk show begun than the

tuxedoed ringmaster was herding the beasts back into the trailers and crying, "See the whole show inside, folks! Admission only one hundred smackeroos!" When no customers stepped forth, he lowered the price to ninety—then eighty—fifty—all the while bellowing, "Mechanical marvels simulate the jungle! Wildness on stage! Secrets of the woods revealed!" Only when the price dropped to fifteen, and the ringmaster in despair began climbing into his van, did a few people grudgingly purchase tickets.

These rare paying customers decided there wasn't much more to see inside the rented hall than they had already seen for free on the sidewalk. By far the liveliest part of the show was the bow-legged ringmaster himself, this Orlando Spinks, who waltzed and cavorted among his sluggish beasts. He balanced on the spine of a zebra, wrapped himself in a boa constrictor, made a tiger jump through a hoop. The audience yawned. The wider the yawns, the more frantic the ringmaster became, revving his beasts to higher and higher speeds so that they twitched through their routines in a blur of hairy limbs. When a rhino thrust its horn through a tire and stopped dead, as if shot in its tracks, and a wolf began gnawing on its own hind leg, shorting wires and producing a billow of smoke, the audience stood up to leave.

"Wait!" the ringmaster yelled, "it's not half over yet!"

Ignoring him, the customers shuffled outside to find some juicier entertainment.

Orlando loaded up his scorned menagerie and drove the caravan to a new neighborhood. There he met with pretty much the same reception. "My kid's got dolls that can do more tricks!" somebody might yell during the tease performance on the sidewalk. "When's the show gonna start?" somebody else was bound to holler midway through the gala performance inside the hall. It was discouraging. People had no eye for art, and even less of an eye for nature. On his first swing through the precincts of New Boston, Orlando earned just enough to pay for recharging the battery on his van and restocking his larder.

Early in his second tour, a heckler cried, "That all they can do, is jump around and growl?" Remembering how Mooch had scolded him for corrupting the beasts in the disney, Orlando shouted back, "Did you maybe expect them to play the organ? Glow in the dark and sputter like fireworks? Drive motorcycles?"

After weeks of such heckling and after wrestling with his conscience, Orlando reprogrammed his beasts to perform such foolishness, and worse. The pandas now played calliope duets. The tiger's stripes blinked on and off like signs in a sleazy diner. The gorilla sped about doing stunts on a zoomcycle. The porcupine launched its quills at targets. The dragon swooped through the air, sprinkling audiences with confetti. Waving its long snout like a baton, the anteater tossed rings at the unicorn, which caught them upon its threaded horn. And so, one way and another, all two dozen beasts were turned into buffoons.

Even though the audiences grew larger and more attentive for a while, attracted by these unbeastly antics, Orlando took little joy in his success. Mooch would despise him for what he had done to the animals. His ears burned with shame to think what the girl might say, were she to witness these shenanigans.

■

No LONGER calling herself Mooch and no longer considering herself a girl since her encounter with the bear, Moon Waters did indeed witness these shenanigans one evening from the back row of a sparse crowd. Her telltale flaming hair was tucked beneath a yellow hard hat and her green eyes were hidden by mirrorshades. The hat was part of the uniform she wore at City Recycle, where she had found a temporary job after leaving the hospital.

Hae Won had stayed beside her bed in the hospital for three days, only returning to the eco station when it was clear that Moon was out of danger. When Moon had recovered enough strength for talking, she called Hae Won and described as well as she could the powerful vision she had experienced in the murk of the she-bear's den. "It must sound crazy," she conceded.

"Not crazy," said Hae Won. "Only mysterious."

"Most of it I still don't understand."

"Understanding it all may take your whole life."

"One thing I know right now, the bear gave me some business to do here in New Boston. Could I stay for a while, after I get out of the hospital?"

Tactful as always, Hae Won did not ask what the business might be. She merely inquired, "How long?"

"A month. Two months at the outside."

"What'll you do for money?"

"With hands like mine, I can find work in half an hour."

"And when you're done, you'll come out to the eco station?"

"I promise," said Moon. "That's my future."

The phone was silent a moment, before Hae Won said, "I suppose, if the bear told you to do it, you'd better do it."

The doctors had pronounced Moon fully recovered, although even now, a week out of the hospital, she had still not gained back all the weight lost during her ordeal in the mountains. Her cheeks were saucers of shadow. At her job down in the bowels of New Boston, lifting parts from conveyor belts and sorting them into piles for salvage or melt-down, her slender arms quickly grew tired. When she curled up to sleep in the cubbyhole provided by City Recycle, below the streets in a workers' dormitory, far from the wind and rain the bear had promised, her bones felt like taffy. Only by reminding herself that these arrangements were temporary was Moon able to face the shrill conveyors each morning or the stifling cubbyhole each night.

Make peace with those who love you, the bear had said. Orlando and Garrison loved me once, Moon felt certain. But do they still?

She had chosen to start by making peace with Orlando. On several evenings since her release from the hospital she had trailed his caravan through the streets. Disguised in the mirrorshades and hard hat, she had watched the sad little sidewalk performance. Twice, drawing near to Orlando as he trudged back to the van, she had tapped him on the padded shoulder of his tux, but each time before he could turn around she had run away. She was terrified that, on recognizing her, his face would brim with hatred.

Tonight she had finally worked up the nerve to buy a ticket from the smart aleck monkey outside the hall where the Spinks' Animal Circus was playing. It seemed to her the monkey took longer than necessary over the transaction, and its black button eyes seemed to examine her with a knowing look. Moon shrugged off the impression and hurried into the auditorium, past garish posters showing Orlando with his boot planted on the head of a lion.

And now she perched in the back row, frowning as beasts in gaudy costumes went through their dipsy-doodle routines. Orlando must have stuffed Grandfather's moth-eaten skins with old memory chips, for the acts were all familiar.

She remembered this boxing kangaroo and yodeling moose from her first days at the disney, remembered these panda twins playing duets, the stunt-riding gorilla, flying dragon, tap-dancing elephant, operatic penguin, and philosophical tortoise. Such had been Orlando's vision of beasts all along, not the wild, mysterious creatures she had dreamed of. Relieved of her, the harmless old man had simply returned to his own way of seeing, as though she had never charged recklessly through his life. What would be the point, now, of barging in on him again? What could she bring him except confusion and pain? Nothing, nothing whatsoever.

Moon was gathering herself to slip away, before he could penetrate her disguise, when soaring music announced the finale. She hesitated. A lion came bounding into the spotlight. In his blinding white tuxedo and tophat, Orlando circled about the tawny beast, snapping a bullwhip. After a flurry of jokes, he cracked the whip and shouted, "Down!" Obediently the lion pressed its chin to the floor and suffered the ringmaster's shiny black boot to rest on its skull. In that moment of servility the lion's fierce yellow gaze searched through the audience and came to rest, with a cool glare of recognition, on Moon.

21·

The lion was the first of the animals to desert Orlando.

A hint that something was amiss had come to him the previous night, following the show. Orlando had parked the caravan behind a drive-through church, the quietest place he could find. The keening of hymns and murmur of prayer tapes muffled the city's racket. As usual, he stowed the mechs away in their compartments and shut off their juice. He was in the house-trailer, hanging up his tuxedo jacket, noticing with dismay the ripped seams and the sweat stains under the sleeves, when the monkey came frisking in.

"There's grumbling back in the wagons, Boss," the monkey piped with a flurry of its cinnamon arms.

"What grumbling? How can there be grumbling? They're turned off."

"I hear what I hear," said the monkey sagely.

Since he had stripped down to his gray flannel longjohns, another item inherited from Grandfather Spinks, Orlando threw on a robe before venturing outside to investigate. He limped past a queue of wheelies loaded with yawning worshipers. To block out the drone of a broadcast sermon, he squeezed a hand over his left ear, then pressed his right ear against each wagon of the caravan in turn. Sure enough,

■ 218

through the aluminum walls there came a sinister muttering, like the quaking of an upset stomach.

"What are they saying?" he whispered to the monkey.

"You got me by the big toe, Boss."

"Who turned them on?"

The monkey flipped its long fuzzy tail into the shape of a question mark, its pantomime of ignorance.

When Orlando flung open the door of the first wagon, a hush fell over the beasts. "All right, you guys," he demanded, "what's all this chattering?" No answer, only a heavy shifting of limbs. Their glass eyes glinted. Angry and more than a little frightened, he rushed down the aisle throwing switch after switch until every last mech was stilled.

"You keep a sharp eye," he told the monkey, "and if anybody comes messing around with them, give a howl."

"Affy daffy, Boss."

Orlando took this to signify agreement. The rascal's thickening slang made every statement a puzzle.

Later that night the lion slipped away.

Swearing up and down that it never saw the great cat slink off, the monkey advised, "You want things peepered, you ought to build a bow-wow." The small frizzy head tilted back and let out a bark.

"If you don't keep a sharper eye on things," Orlando threatened, "I might just do that. Build me a watch dog out of leftover monkey parts."

He made discreet inquiries in the neighborhood, referring to the escaped lion only in the vaguest of terms, so as not to spread alarm. But nobody had seen any manner of creature stalking about on all fours. Orlando was baffled. A lion, even a mechanical one, could not just go rambling unnoticed through the streets of New Boston.

Next day the mystery deepened, for the rhino and griffin vanished during Orlando's afternoon nap.

"Could be they eloped, hey Boss?" suggested the monkey, trying to cheer him up.

Orlando was not cheered. He was downcast. He was mystified. It could only be a judgment on him for having made fools out of his animals, and now they were abandoning him like sailors jumping ship to escape a mad captain.

He doubled the locks, shortened his naps, and dozed at night sitting up on his astro-lounger. But still the beasts crept away. While he was counting the skimpy gate receipts after an evening performance, the gorilla and the big-footed shambling snowman disappeared. The dragon flew off while he was in the shower. During a stop for groceries, the tortoise and the porcupine scuttled away. When or how the elephant lumbered off without giving itself away was more than Orlando could fathom.

The departures soon reduced the menagerie to an even dozen, and reduced Orlando himself to bewildered repentance. It was indeed a sign. Mooch had warned him against violating nature, and here he had gone and done it, just to put on a flimflam show.

Remorseful, he began reprogramming his animals, erasing their silly tricks.

The audiences dwindled. Who wanted to lay out good money to watch a herd of grungy animals sit around and scratch imaginary fleas? After a while, only hecklers showed up. They ignored the lazy beasts and focused their mockery on the little ringmaster who fidgeted about in his threadbare tuxedo. He strayed among the animals like a laboratory rat nosing through a maze. The onlookers flung taunts at him, and he flung them right back. He was plucky, you had to give him credit for that. While the circus animals lounged and gaped and snored about him, the ringmaster danced. He juggled rubber coconuts. He twirled his baton. He performed feats of derring-do with butcher knives and static electricity. At the conclusion of his act he removed the top hat to make a sweeping bow, and the house lights struck reflections off his bald scalp, sweat flew from his white beard, his legs trembled with fatigue. Occasionally some few onlookers would clap halfheartedly. The rare laugh of a child at one of his tricks set up currents in Orlando's heart like the motions of fish. But more often he would hear only the scuffle of departing feet.

■

MOON tried reasoning with the lion, the first of the animals to show up at City Recycle.

The huge slouching beast made quite a sensation as it emerged from a tunnel into the sorting room at the start of morning shift. The blond mane stood out in a ruff surrounding its massive head, its heavy flanks rubbed against the conveyors, its yellow eyes slashed the air. Except for Moon, every worker in the place fled to the Safe Room, as though a toxin alert had sounded. They looked on through shatterproof glass as the lion nosed up to Moon and licked her outstretched hand with a pink tongue the size of a scarf. Only when she had lured the beast away into a storage vault, locking the door behind her, did the workers cautiously return to their posts.

Inside the echoing steel-ribbed vault, which held stacks of rubber tires awaiting a batch melt-down, Moon tried reasoning with the lion, but to no effect. It refused even to consider going back to Orlando.

"He needs you," Moon said. "He built you. He owns you."

"I have found the Liberator," the lion kept repeating in a worshipful tone.

"What's with this 'Liberator' jazz?"

"You led our ancestors to freedom."

"You mean the stampede?" Moon thought with shame of that bungled exodus, Orlando shouting from his wheelchair at the gate, the sway of the elephant beneath her, the pedestrians scrambling out of the way, Coyote loping beside the elephant's feet, the Overseers swooping down in their shuttles with melters blazing. "I led your ancestors to the scrap yard!" she exclaimed. "I led them to annihilation! How do you know about that, anyway?"

"It is in our memories," the lion answered gravely. "Your face, your voice, your deeds, everything is in our memories."

All it would have taken to keep her alive in their brains was a single chip salvaged from those doomed beasts. Further questioning of the lion convinced Moon that word of her had spread like tribal legends among the new generation of mechs. She was a goddess in their eyes. They believed her fingers had thrown the switch that started the world. They believed the electricity in their circuits had sparked from the flame in her hair. She had brought them visions of shadowy forests and open plains and tossing seas, a real and substantial world beyond this illusory city. She had taught them to hunger for wildness. They knew she would come again to lead them to freedom.

"And you have come," the lion rumbled.

Spotting her when she bought a ticket, the monkey had whispered the news to the lion, which had picked her out from the crowd, its haughty stare penetrating through the mirrorshades to recognize her legendary face.

"Does Orlando know?" Moon asked.

The blond mane swept the floor as the lion shook its head.

"Good," said Moon. "Then maybe I can get you back to him before any of your buddies decides to follow."

"I will stay with the Liberator," the lion insisted.

True to its word, the beast would not let her out of its sight. It blocked the door of the vault to keep her from leaving. When she darted behind a stack of tires, hoping to slip away, the lion shook the chamber with its roar and came charging after her, nostrils flaring. She could not very well take it back to stand beside her at the conveyor while she sorted through junk. There was nothing else to do but shut it down.

"You're a beautiful beast, you are," she murmured, patting the giant head. The lion sat back on its haunches and blinked rapturously. Feeling once more like a betrayer, Moon wrapped her arms about the thick neck, stroked the broad rumbling chest, then flung open the control panel and jabbed the emergency shut-off. The rumble ceased. The yellow eyes clicked shut. The massive frame stiffened.

It wasn't murder, Moon kept reminding herself as she returned to work. You can't murder a machine. It can always be started again.

Her neighbor at the conveyor, a bleached, fiftyish woman who looked as though she had sprouted here in the depths of the city, like a pale, forked root, asked, "What the devil was *that*?"

"Just some scrap," Moon said.

"Scrap's supposed to ride in here on the belt, not walk in on its own legs."

"Big city like this, you never know what's going to turn up."

What turned up next, near the end of that same shift,

were the rhino and griffin. Their appearance cleared the room again. Again the workers looked on through the shatterproof glass while the menacing creatures sidled up to Moon and rubbed horns and wings and clawed feet against her slender frame. Again she led the brutes away into the vault, and emerged alone after a few minutes, her face grimly set.

This time Moon's work partner only said, "Must be a lot of that scrap walking around."

Moon bent over the conveyor, sorting feverishly, and did not reply. It was clear she had set in motion another stampede. How on earth could she halt it?

During the next week, so many queer things crawled or leapt or slithered from the tunnel that the workers lost count. A gorilla waddled in, scraping its knuckles across the floor. Along came a dragon, its toothy jaws wreathed in smoke. A creeping tortoise bestowed philosophical glances on all sides. A porcupine scurried in with a rattle of quills. An elephant, squeezing its bulk through the aisles, carried a fat snake wound like an anklet around one foreleg.

Realizing that these were only machines dressed up to look like animals, the workers eventually quit fleeing and stayed at their posts, nervously watching as Moon led each furred or feathered or scaly hulk into the storage vault.

By the end of that bewildering week, the vault was crammed full of worn-out tires and disabled beasts. Not even a rabbit could have been squeezed in. When the wolf showed up, stripped of its hide, Moon had to lead it back to her cubbyhole apartment, where she turned it off and propped it in a corner. The naked glittering chassis disturbed her. What had become of its skin? The chips and switches and wires, the springs and gears, the nylon joints were harsh reminders of how deluded she had been. This ingenious device had never been anything remotely like a wolf. The whole menagerie of mechs had been nothing more than clumsy imitations of nature, mere playthings, toys. She draped a blanket over the contraption.

Next morning on her way to the recycle works, she was still trying to figure out how to stop this new exodus, how to restore the dumb, devoted machines to Orlando. But the first thing she heard in the locker room, while donning her coveralls and goggles, was that the night shift had melted down the tires, and, finding the queer, fur-covered robots, had dismantled them as well. Moon slumped on a bench and stared at her hands through a glaze of tears. For a second time she had ruined the innocent old man.

■

AFTER an especially dismal show, during which a heckler had pelted him with ice cubes, Orlando was stitching a tear in the wolf's mangy hide when the monkey sidled in to announce that the wolf itself had vamoosed.

"Without its skin?" said Orlando, raising the shabby pelt from his lap.

"You got the number on that ticket, Boss," said the monkey, whose jargon was becoming ever murkier.

Orlando shut his eyes and thought about the unclad wolf slinking through the spick-and-span avenues of New Boston, its aluminum chassis gleaming in the fluorescent light, the wires in its belly snarled like noodles, computer chips encrusting its forehead like jewels. Blinking his sad eyes open, he said, "Did you see it go?"

The monkey turned its palms toward the ceiling and hoisted its shoulders. There was a faint whining of motors, a gritting of metal on metal, and the monkey was paralyzed midway in its shrug.

"We're getting old together," Orlando said with a sigh. He was feeling as though he himself could use an overhaul. This news about the wolf only made him ache the worse. Opening a door in the monkey's belly, he fiddled with the controls. When this did no good, he slapped it between the puny shoulder blades.

Immediately the monkey finished its shrug, inquiring with amnesiac vagueness, "What's happening, Boss?"

"You were telling me the wolf had run away."

The monkey thrust a finger to its chest. "Ego mego? Do say wolfie toodle-oodled?"

"Yes, you did," said Orlando wearily. He could almost see the circuits unraveling in the monkey's brain. "Now please go back to the wagons and keep watch on the others."

There were not many others to watch—the kangaroo, the anteater, the twin pandas, the penguin, the unicorn, and the moose. These seven, plus the monkey, were all that remained of the Spinks Animal Circus. One by one they were deserting him. Where could they possibly go? He imagined the hairy snowman shoving its way onto the pedbelts among the commuters with their briefcases, the boa constrictor coiling its great length into elevators, the elephant blocking the doorways of trains at rush-hour, the gorilla swinging from balcony to balcony on apartment towers. None of them had ever been caught and returned to him, even though his name was clearly stamped on the control panels. He was afraid to ask the Overseers for help, having run afoul of them already once too often.

He sold the wilderness furnishings and the extra wagons to pay his bills. He moved his clothes and tools and astro-lounger into the van and put the few remaining beasts in the house-trailer, which he did not even bother to lock. If they were so eager to go, let them go. Some nights he tried to conjure up new tricks. Other nights he let himself peek into the future, where he saw only a great dark hole: his entire menagerie run off, the empty rented halls echoing to his solitary voice.

■

IN DESPAIR, Orlando turned for comfort where he had always turned. One day, on the pretext of dropping by to check on the calico cat, he left the monkey in charge of the menagerie and, lugging his tool kit, rode up to the forty-second floor of the Golden Years Tower for a visit with Grace. She welcomed him with her customary bounce, cleared a spot for him on the couch by heaving aside three lumpy garbage sacks, and then listened indulgently to his woes.

"Poor boy, poor boy!" she murmured, patting his hand.

The couch was surrounded by Himalayas of trash. From where he sat, Orlando could not see the opposite wall, his view obscured by mounds of paper, crumpled aluminum foil, shredded plastic, and snarled cloth. The whole land-scape was covered by a woolly stratum of dust through which the calico cat, in perfect running order, pranced and gamboled. Orlando was too distracted by the mess to carry on for long about his own miseries.

"Gracie, you can't enjoy living like this," he said at last.

"No, as a matter of fact, I don't," she admitted, her wrinkled lips turning down. "But the recycle's broken and the disposal's jammed. My knees don't scoot me around like they used to. I run out of gas before I get started. And everything I touch reminds me of Humphrey."

This time Orlando pitched in without asking if she

wanted help. The recycle was easily fixed and the disposal unclogged. She protested when he began flinging armfuls of junk down the chute, but then she resigned herself.

"Everything can go except the spoons," she agreed.

Orlando, working himself to the quivery brink of exhaustion, cleaned the apartment from end to end, stowing things in closets, vacuuming, scrubbing, throwing away all the prize rubbish that Grace and Humphrey had saved from their scavenging.

"Any time you can't think what to do with yourself," Grace told him at the door as she planted a kiss on his bald dome, "you come right back here."

In truth, scorned by audiences and deserted by his beasts, Orlando had less and less of a notion what to do with himself.

22·

Within a few days following the wolf's departure, all the remaining beasts except the twin pandas and the monkey stole away. Orlando sold the house-trailer and moved the remnants of his circus into the van. He slept up front in the cab, when he managed to sleep at all.

With two sluggish pandas and one sassy monkey he could not do anything very flashy, but he tried nonetheless to put on a show. Four bums made up the entire audience, and they only sat through the performance because Orlando had given them boxes of popcorn along with free tickets. Having gobbled the popcorn, the bums fell asleep. Orlando shut off the lights and left them to snore. The pandas and the monkey shuffled out behind him, nylon elbows and aluminum ribs showing through rents in their hides.

Later, parked for the night in an alley, he was soaking his feet in a tub of hot water and staring down at his bunioned toes as if reading tea leaves in the bottom of a cup, when the monkey scampered in on a mission of consolation.

"You were dynamite tonight, Boss."

"Is that what put them to sleep?" said Orlando, refusing to be consoled.

"You had them fagged out from pounding their palms,

Boss. You razzled them and dazzled them. You wore down their buzz buttons. You tuned their eyebulbs for them."

"Buzz buttons? Eyebulbs? Have you lost your dictionary altogether?"

"What I'm saying, Boss, is when you slung those lariats and noosed the pandas, why, the crowd was wowed. You made a quartet of beeries cheery. You fed them lizard gizzards. You ironed out the wrinkles in their tickertapes."

Orlando frowned skeptically. "It's kind of you to say so."

"Nilly dilly," proclaimed the monkey, which exited by swinging from the fluorescent lamps.

Perhaps it was only a sign of age, but Orlando scarcely understood a thing the monkey said. Mooch would have been able to translate for him. She had always possessed an uncanny rapport with the beasts. Thinking about her, he felt a cold wind howling through the corridors of his heart. She had kept him young, right up to the moment of the stampede. By now she must have served out her time at the Farm. He wouldn't have been surprised to learn that she had liberated the cows and pigs, leading them away into the woods. He liked to imagine her living outside, red hair in defiant pigtails, hunting in the forest with bow and arrow, breathing air that was no longer poisoned, sipping from creeks that were no longer foul, her bare feet dancing over soil that was no longer radioactive. Did she ever think about him? He supposed not. She would be seventeen by now, primed for life, sniffing the breezes of the future. Why would she bother to think about a run-down old coot? For all she knew, he was dead and gone.

Orlando peered down at his pink toes. Water dripped from his whiskers into the tub.

He was still sitting in this mournful posture when the

twin pandas sauntered up and squatted before him. Unequipped for speech, they gazed at him in silence, four dark melancholy eyes. Feeling a bit foolish, Orlando pulled his feet from the water and lowered them with a squish onto the vinyl floor.

"What are you two after?" he scolded, to break the silence. "You can't be wanting juice, you beggars. I just charged you up yesterday."

The pandas gathered into their faces all the primordial sadness of their kind.

Orlando was on the point of calling the monkey, which could often interpret these enigmatic silences, when the pandas quit gazing at him and set off waddling down the aisle. Instead of returning to their compartments, however, they nosed out through the van's rear door and flumped down into the alley.

"Hey, you two!" cried Orlando. He rushed to the door, leaving wet footprints on the vinyl, and peered out.

The monkey was in the alley beside an open manhole, a wrench in its fist, impatiently waving at the pandas. As they waddled up to him, the monkey opened their control panels and punched buttons. Brilliant saffron lights came on in the pandas' eyes. Orlando's own eyes opened wider with a sense of outrage. The monkey whispered in their ears, and then down the pandas went, through the hatchway, into the basement of the city.

Before the monkey could tug the cover back into place, Orlando sprang from the van, shouting, "You pile of scrap metal! You scummy sack of gears! You traitorous babble-box!"

The monkey hoisted the wrench above its head to ward off blows. "Whatever you're thinking, Boss, you got it all wrong!"

"Wrong!" Orlando danced in a furious circle, looking for an opening where he could land a punch. "Didn't I just see you help the pandas run off? You think I'm blind? Thief! Rustler! Is that where they've all gone, sneaking away under the city?"

"Hey, Boss, lay off! Listen one little ticktock!"

"Lay off? I'll lay you out! I'll douse your lights!" But the monkey was quick with the wrench, and Orlando could land only glancing blows.

Attracted by the commotion, an Overseer came trooping into the alley, stunner drawn, helmet lamp swiveling to fix Orlando and the monkey in its glare. A thought of how he must look—bare feet, shabby tuxedo trousers rolled up to the knees, suspenders dangling from his waist, white hair spun out in a ragged aureole about his gleaming pate—quickly sobered Orlando.

"What's the problem?" growled the Overseer.

"Not a thing, sir," Orlando babbled, smacking the monkey's shoulder. "I'm just exercising my pet here."

"Loud exercise, Gramps. And late. It's zero two hundred hours."

"My goodness!" said Orlando. "Far past our bedtimes!" He grabbed the monkey by a thin wrist and yanked it after him toward the van.

"My boss is going to skivvy me down into screws and gears and CPUs," the monkey whined.

Orlando gave a dismissive laugh. "One of our little jokes!"

"Joke indoors," the Overseer grumbled. He kept the stunner and the harsh light focused on them as Orlando lugged the monkey into the van and slammed the door.

While Orlando peeked out from behind the curtain to

make sure the cop had left, the monkey wriggled free and clambered up among the light fixtures.

"I can explain everything, Boss! Just promise you won't undo me!"

Orlando turned from the window. The anger was gone out of him. He felt old, lost inside his skin. So what if they were deserting him? He would hold nothing against its will, not even a lying, traitorous machine. "Come on down," he said wearily.

"You won't fry my circuits? Divvy my switches?"

"I won't. I promise."

Orlando sagged onto his bunk, slumped against the pillows, drew a comforter over his bare legs. The monkey swung down from the ceiling and hunkered beside him. Its liver-colored face loomed a handbreadth from his own.

"Hey, Boss, don't open the valves."

"I'm far too old to cry," said Orlando stiffly.

"They made me spring them loose, Boss. They threatened me."

"You were intimidated by the pandas?"

"Not just the pandas. The lion, the griffin, the porcupine, the moose—the whole pack of them. They said if I blabbed to you, they'd come back and dice me up and feed me to the vapor hole." Panic had stripped away the monkey's inscrutable slang. It crawled onto Orlando's stomach and clung to the rumpled front of his shirt. "You won't let them do me that way, will you, Boss? I never told on them, did I? You spied out the truth for yourself."

Running a hand over the monkey's frizzy skull, Orlando said, "Nothing's going to hurt you." Still, the paws did not let go their hold on his shirtfront. With a tone of resignation, he asked, "Did they all steal away under the city? Even the elephant?"

"We had to take apart the elephant and dragon, and the gorilla carried them down in hunks. Even then it was a tight fit."

"And what do they plan to do down there? Start a junkyard? Who's going to juice them up? Who's going to keep them running when their gears seize up and their circuits short out?"

"Oh, *she* will, Boss."

"She who?"

"The girl, you know. The Savior. She's almost as handy with tools as you are." As soon as the words had escaped, the monkey slapped both forepaws over its mouth.

Orlando jerked his head from the pillows. "What girl?" The monkey's eyes grew larger and larger. Orlando peeled the fingers away from its lips. "I said, *who's this girl?*"

"They'll rip me apart if I tell," the monkey whimpered.

"I'll rip you apart if you *don't!*" Sitting up with a lurch, Orlando seized the monkey by its scrawny shoulders and twisted, as if he meant to execute the sentence right then and there.

"The Liberator!" the monkey gasped. "The one who led our ancestors out of the disney!"

"Mooch?" said Orlando, incredulous.

The monkey trembled, yanking its head up and down. "She's what they all ran off to."

Orlando flung the monkey aside and heaved up from the bed and hustled from one end of the van to the other, looking for his socks and shoes, lifting the suspenders into place with his thumbs, roaring, "Where is she? No—don't tell me—show me!"

From where it had flounced onto the pillows, the monkey

regarded him with an expression compounded of terror and hope. "You mean we're going to Mooch? Right now?"

"Right this minute."

"It's a long way, Boss, and hard."

Orlando wriggled his arms into the sleeves of his tuxedo jacket, clipped in place the neon bow tie. "If those fat pandas can make it, I can make it."

"You're going to get your duds all filthy."

"Who cares? They're rotten anyway."

"We'll need a light, and some food, and maybe you'd better juice me up," said the monkey, but Orlando was already in motion, seizing an electric torch, stuffing grub into a satchel, hooking the charger to the monkey's electrodes.

Within minutes they were climbing down through the manhole, Orlando groping for the rungs with his feet, the monkey swinging down effortlessly by its tail. They paused long enough to drag the cover back in place above their heads. As they made their way down the echoing passage, the monkey skipping ahead with its eyes ablaze, Orlando thought fleetingly of the white van parked above, SPINKS' ANIMAL CIRCUS painted on the side in ruby letters, its doors unlocked. He hoped somebody would steal it. He could let it go, and gladly, for now he was on his way, the last animal to desert his own circus, headed for Mooch.

■

EVERY now and again during that long trudge through the tunnels of New Boston, Orlando's body recollected its age and the time of night and sat him unceremoniously down. While on the floor, he noticed a foul breeze flowing in the direction of their travels. It smelled of exhaust fumes and clothes dryers and moldy refrigerators. After sniffing it, he decided these clammy pipes must be drains for sucking away the city's used-up air. Fortunately, there was a current of fresh air near the ceiling, so that by walking tall he could avoid gagging.

The monkey had no use for air, foul or pure, and little patience. Whenever Orlando sat down for a rest, it fidgeted constantly, running up the sides of the tunnel, darting glances forward, its illuminated eyes casting spears of light into the gloom. All it cared about was getting to Mooch.

"How did you ever find her?" Orlando panted during one of these giddy halts.

"She found us, Boss. She came to the show one night, decked out in a hard hat and shades, doing the old incognito. But I ogled right through that get-up. Her face did a kaboom in my brain. The Liberator! Just like in your photo albums. A little older, maybe, but it was the number one gal, all right."

How could she have sat in the audience and made no signal to him? How? Easily, Orlando admitted. He saw himself through her eyes, a pitiful old clown in a shabby tuxedo making fools of animals. "Then what?"

"Lion trailed her to the rag-and-bone shop where she works, and then came back and lipped the directions in my ear, and I've been piping them to everybody else from that time on."

"What's the rag-and-bone shop?"

"You know, the electro dump, where they give burned-out juice-jewels and frazzled magic boxes the old divvy-do."

As the monkey's fear ebbed away, its language drifted back toward street lingo. Orlando did not have the energy to frighten the scamp into lucidity. "So you all conspired to desert me?"

"That night when she peepered the show, after you sacked out I fired up the gang back in the wagons and we chewed the grease. We buzzed on about Mooch and how she'd goose our gears for us and unkink our circuits and set us all purring and lead us outside to the green grassy-o."

"Of course, of course," said Orlando absently. His mistake had been to reuse old memory chips in building the new mechs, and then to regale this jabberbox monkey with endless affectionate stories about Mooch. "You knew all about her."

"She ran in us like electrons, Boss. Compared to the stunts she pulled with our ancestors, your circus was Podunk City. Rinky-dinky-doo-doo."

"I see," said Orlando. The air down near the floor where he sat was growing thicker and more sour. Soon he would have to take out his pocket knife and slice cubes of it to swallow. He dragged himself to his feet and staggered for balance.

"You got a hitch in the get-along, Boss?"

"No, I'm just fine. Go on ahead. I'll follow." He panted in the stale air. He could have done with a few spare parts for his own chassis—some knee joints, say, and a right foot, and a pair of air-bags for his wheezing chest. But he reckoned the original equipment would last him as far as the recycle dump. He had been there once on a field trip during college, and he remembered the conveyors heaped with broken appliances and ruined gismos, the workers sorting through the junk and testing each scrap, the bins crammed with salvaged parts. It pained him to think of Mooch down in that clanking inferno.

Would she want to see him? Not likely, if she had visited

the circus without even saying boo. What was he to her, anyway? Just a chump who had let her run amuck in his disney for a spell when she was a kid.

Orlando's steps began to drag. His chest burned. Feeling more and more a fool, wishing he had never seen the pandas escaping down the manhole, he said to the monkey, "Why did you stick around after the others took off?"

The monkey flashed its brilliant eyes around at him, then looked away down the tunnel. "Oh, I thought about high-tailing it, but I knew you'd croak if we left you alone."

"You were going to stick with me no matter what," Orlando suggested hopefully, "even if that meant being cut off from Mooch forever?"

"Not forever, no. Just until you cashed in your chips."

Orlando's feet were turning to lead. He could barely clump along. "And Mooch never sent back any word?"

"Well, there was one thing," the monkey admitted.

Orlando used all his scant breath to set the tunnel booming: "What? A message?" He grabbed the monkey and shook it like a rag doll. "She sent me a *message* and you didn't *tell* me?"

Through clacking teeth the monkey answered: "She said . . . don't any beast . . . dare blab . . . because she was . . . afraid . . . to see you."

"Afraid? Of me?" Orlando dropped the monkey and stood gasping, as if he had pushed a boulder as far as he was ever going to push it.

"She said she'd been cruel to you," the monkey chattered, frisking and gesturing madly. "The gang told her you'd never breathed a mean word about her in all our days. Oh, she said, you weren't the sort to talk mean. But underneath, in your heart, you just had to hate her."

"Me hate Mooch? All this time she's been thinking *that*?"

Orlando sagged against the wall of the tunnel and slithered down to sit on the floor. The air seemed thick enough to chew. It smelled of parking lots, overheated circuits, mildewed closets, the ravaged trays of cafeterias. He imagined that millions of people had already breathed this air and left in it whatever they had no more use for—the wool of worn-out thoughts, the poisons of the soul.

The monkey jumped around him, tugging at his elbows, jabbering in that incomprehensible lingo. When the monkey's eye lamps played over his outstretched legs, Orlando noticed the stains, the ragged patches, the holes where his blue knees showed through. It used to be quite a fine tuxedo. He could not remember now just why he had bought it. A funeral? No, no, one did not wear white to funerals. Black for funerals. Must have been a wedding. Whose? His? But there was no bride. Never a bride. Never a wedding. A daughter once, but she was long gone.

Sitting down felt so good that he decided to lie flat, and he did so in one dizzy glide, rapping his head on the floor.

The monkey's jabbering played around him like a bunch of kids yelling, and then it was gone.

Sprawled on his back in the pipe, his face churning with pain, Orlando breathed in gulps. He imagined the used-up air inflating him with its secrets, its kisses, its curses, its lies and murmurs. He imagined himself swelling with vapors, floating up through tunnels, seeping from the manhole, rising into the sky of the city and hovering there beneath the dome, an unforgettable sight, a man the size of a thundercloud, black with a rain of loss.

23·

When light divided momentarily from darkness in Orlando's groggy head, the first object to appear was a girl's face, screwed up with worry, green, foxy eyes uptilted. He blinked. "Mooch?"

The face disappeared, as if jerked away by a rope.

"Mooch?" He ordered his muscles to prop him up, ordered his arms to reach out for her, but his body was on strike and did not move. He lay flat as a sidewalk and felt about as trampled over. There was a choking sound, a word caught rattling in his throat. Then fingers brushed his chest, on the very spot where the burning from the poisoned air had been so fierce.

Was it Mooch, or a dream of Mooch? The bullying darkness smothered him again before he could decide.

It was Moon, all right. The monkey had fetched her, after Orlando passed out from exhaustion and toxic fumes within a hundred meters of her dormitory. In her pajamas, pigtails flying, she had come rushing down the tunnel with a cylinder of oxygen and a wheelchair hastily retrieved from the first-aid closet. She had been amazed, lifting Orlando into the wheelie, at how little of him there was. She remembered him as being, not large, but weighty, substantial, and she found it hard to believe that this dwindled, wispy doll of a man was the mighty engineer she had loved and betrayed.

Small though he was, still it had been a trick to squeeze him into her cubbyhole of a room, which already housed the moose and unicorn, the anteater and penguin and kangaroo, the skinless wolf, and the twin pandas. As these newcomers had arrived over the past few days, Moon had not dared leave them at the recycle works, for fear that they, too, would be dismantled. Instead, she had brought them back to the dorm. Frozen in whatever postures they had assumed at the moment she turned them off, the mechs encircled Orlando's bed like a deputation of well-wishers.

"Are you boiling mad at me, Your Holiness?" the monkey jabbered, clinging to her knee.

"I told you to quit calling me that," Moon whispered.

"The boss made me show him the way, Your Holiness!"

"Hush. Let him sleep."

She gave Orlando a few more whiffs of oxygen, to clean the muck from his lungs. She pulled the blanket up to his whiskery chin. His old face, as cracked and stained as an antique leather purse, was beautiful to her. The rim of white hair fringed his bald scalp like frost-covered bushes around a winter pond.

The monkey held on to her knee, chattering in a high-pitched whine. "The show kept getting worse, Your Holiness. It was Pity City. An old bozo and his rinky-tinky stooges."

I reduced him to that, thought Moon. To the monkey she only whispered, "You hush now."

"But everything's hunky-dory now, isn't it, Your Holiness? You'll save us, right? You'll lead us outside, won't you? Park us beside the stilly dilly waters, lay us down on the green grassy-o, restore our circuits?"

Moon hissed, "You want me to hammer you flat into a cookie sheet?"

"Your Holiness—"

"Shut up!"

"But Your Holi—"

Moon seized the monkey, slapped a hand over its wagging jaw, and turned it off. Then, without ceremony, she hooked the stiff body over the moose's antlers.

For what little remained of the night, she hovered beside Orlando, smoothing the wrinkles on his forehead as if the skin were a letter that had been folded too many times. His eyes twitched beneath the lids but did not open. She felt deeply ashamed, thinking of the pain she had caused him. Each time one of his mechs had stolen up to her, shabby and confused, telling stories about the sad circus, calling her Savior and Liberator, a new layer had been added to her guilt, like a winter's snow on a glacier. She could hardly move under the weight of it.

Since leaving the hospital, Moon had been telling herself that she would face Orlando as soon as she had recovered her strength. Weak or strong, now she would have to face him. Bent over the bed, she waited nervously for him to awake.

■

ORLANDO, meanwhile, was dreaming of his beasts. One by one they were returning, crowding about him, their pelts glistening as though newborn, their eyes lit up with a secret they could hardly wait to tell.

This time when the light of consciousness dawned in his brain, he forced himself up onto his elbows and looked around. There were his beasts, all right; a few of them, at least. The moose, the monkey, and half a dozen more. But their pelts were as shabby as ever, and their eyes held no secrets. Their glass eyes, in fact, were dead.

Perhaps I'm dead as well, thought Orlando. He sat up and asked the silent room, "What now?"

From behind came a deliciously familiar voice. "You okay?"

Swelling with a bubble of joy, Orlando twisted around on the bed. There she was. Older, nearly a woman now, still marked by a girl's freckles and pigtails, still slender, but with a woman's curves showing through her rose-print pajamas and the weight of knowledge showing in her face. Maybe I have died and gone to heaven, he thought. He reached out a trembling hand. "Mooch? Is it really you?"

Moon grabbed the hand, then his arm, his neck, and seized him in a hug, rocking and sobbing and laughing. Orlando fumbled at her cheek with dry lips and hummed one of his old nonsensical melodies.

They were a long time in finding words.

When at length words did come, they both spoke at once, Moon asking, "You don't hate me?" and Orlando asking, "You didn't forget me?"

"How could I forget you?" she said.

"How could I hate you?" he chided.

Moon gripped him by the shoulders and pushed him away to arm's length. "You should hate me because I wrecked the disney. I destroyed your work. I ruined you."

Hearing those words, Orlando recalled when Garrison had stood in line behind the fix-it van and delivered this very message. Now Orlando repeated what he had told the boy. "Poppycock! Do I look ruined?" He flung out his arms in their tattered sleeves and nearly fell off the bed.

Moon caught him. "Easy now. Save the heroics. You had a bellyful of bad air."

Orlando straightened his tuxedo jacket, recovering his balance if not quite his dignity. "I did suffer a temporary setback, I'll admit. The disney's gone. Turned into a playzone! Here's all I managed to rescue from your old room, I'm afraid." From an inside breast pocket he produced the gray turkey feather.

"You're a sweetheart," said Moon. Taking the feather, she thrust it in her hair at a jaunty angle.

Orlando rubbed his palms together with a sandpapery sound. "But now we're back in business again. Who needs a disney? I've still got my tools, and a few beasts, and a van. At least I had a van last night, unlocked in some alley. I've been keeping the ship afloat, you see, until you came back. And now you're here! We can get things rolling again. Set up a repair shop, maybe. Start a museum. Give classes to school kids. Build a new menagerie and go on the televiddy. What do you say?"

In a quiet voice, Moon answered, "I'm not staying."

Orlando grew so agitated that he fairly bounced on the edge of the bed. His arms in their ragged sleeves sawed the air. "What do you mean, not staying? How about this room here? And your job at City Recycle?"

"I've just been hiding out here for a while, working up my nerve to see you."

"You had to work up your nerve to see me? Am I such an ogre? Am I?" He grinned desperately and shook a finger at her. "Ah, ah! You fox! None of your teasing! You really are staying, right? You just wanted to surprise me!"

"Oh, God," she moaned, turning away.

"Hey," said Orlando, hearing the tears in her voice, "hey now. Come here." He opened his arms, careful not to tip over. She turned back to him and knelt beside the bed and pressed her cheek against his rumpled shirt. He clasped her tenderly, stroking her luminous hair. For a long while he merely hummed one of those broken, wordless melodies. At length he murmured, "You're going back outside?" and when she nodded wetly against his throat, he said aloud what he had known but never admitted all these mournful months: "It's where you belong, isn't it? I've kept imagining you out there, dancing in the woods, the wind on your face." Beneath his fingers, her wild hair was a feathery blaze. "Do you have a place to go?"

Still pressed against him, so that her voice echoed back from inside the frail cavity of his chest, Moon told him about the Farm and Hae Won and the eco station and her dreams of becoming a biologist. "If I study hard and keep my eyes open," she said, "maybe I'll learn to see. It's what I want more than anything. To glimpse the power that drives the universe. To understand some bit of creation— even a mouse, even a mustard seed."

"You will, you will," whispered Orlando.

Then she told him about the shimmer of moonlight on ponds, the cry of gulls, the croak of frogs; she described how grass stitched the dunes together with vivid green threads, how the tide left a sinuous chalky line of crab shells on the beach, how the maples caught an icy fire in October, how the mountains arched their bristling backs against the sky, the actual sky. Finally, she told him in a rapt voice about her meeting with the bear, who fed her on hot milk, who licked the film of blindness from her eyes, who gave her the wind and snow and rain, who called her by a new name.

"What did the bear call you?" Orlando asked softly.

"Moon Waters."

He whispered the name back to her, saying, "It fits you."

■

MOON CARRIED in a backpack the few things she had acquired in New Boston. Orlando carried the monkey, the only one of his mechs he chose to keep. The others—the forlorn moose, the punchdrunk kangaroo, the morose pandas—he left behind for dismantling at City Recycle, when Moon stopped by there to quit her job.

"I want a fresh start," he explained. "I'll just hang onto this fuzzball for company," he added, tapping the monkey's knobby skull. Still switched off, the tiny figure drooped over his shoulder like a frizzy towel.

In the artificial daylight they returned to the alley where Orlando had parked the van, but the van was gone, and with it had disappeared every last thing he owned, all his tools, his tapes and holos and books, his extra teeth, his grandfather's trunk, everything except the tattered monkey he carried on his shoulder and the shabby tuxedo he wore on his back.

"Maybe it was towed away," Moon suggested.

"Good riddance," said Orlando. Much to his surprise, he was feeling buoyant, as though gravity had relaxed its grip.

"What are you saying? It's awful. You've got to report this to the Overseers."

He shook his head. "I'm not going anywhere near the Overseers. I don't want to remind them I'm even alive."

"You sure you won't come outside with me?" Moon begged.

She had already asked him this question every way she knew how, and Orlando had kept giving her the same reply: "No, no, sweetheart. I belong in the city, just like you belong in the wilds. I'd be miserable out there. I'd go crazy. No use kidding myself about that."

"Then what are you going to do? Live in one of those

elderhomes? Wander the streets? Sleep on benches? Dig food out of dumpsters?"

A smile bloomed on Orlando's face, realigning the wrinkles. "I know somebody who needs me. You remember Grace Palomino and Humphrey Tree? They used to scavenge as a hobby, and puttered by the disney in zip-carts loaded with junk."

"Of course I remember. Two wacky fireballs."

"Well, dear old Humphrey cashed in his chips, as the monkey here would say. But Grace is perking right along."

■

DRESSED in rainbow tights, her white hair whirling like a cyclone, Grace was exercising in time with a muscular gal on the viddy when Orlando and Moon arrived at her apartment. Scarcely puffing, she yelled for them to come on in, then she bustled around making tea and biscuits, collecting armfuls of debris that had freshly accumulated on every flat surface ("I don't know where all this stuff *comes* from!"), and pausing now and again in front of the viddy to jounce through a few more exercises. She still had breath enough to rave over what a full-blown *person* Moon had become.

"You'll have to swat the boys away with a tennis racket!" Grace clapped her hands. "My! What would that poor lovesick Garrison make of you now? One look at you and he'd forget his name! Oh, my!"

When Orlando managed to slip in a few words about his situation, Grace boomed, "Stay with me? Of course you'll stay!" and immediately set about making up the spare room. She dragged Humphrey's clothes from dresser and closet, holding immense garments against Orlando's meager frame to check for size. "A little tuck here and there," she remarked, "and you'll have a new wardrobe.

Humphrey always was a spiffy dresser, when he wasn't grubby. Look at this blazer! And these polka-dot trousers! And just look here, Humphrey's Exalted Sagamore outfit!" She flung the black robe around Orlando's shoulders, engulfing him, and she flattened the rubbery orange hat onto his head. "What do you think of that?" she demanded, turning to Moon. "Isn't that the cat's meow?"

Moon's eyes shone like damp grass. She could say nothing.

"Speaking of which," said Grace, craning around, "where is that persnickety cat? Tempest!" she yelled. "Tempest! Come here and say hello to your maker."

The black and white cat stole into the room on soundless feet, took one look at the monkey, which Orlando had deposited on the couch, and began spitting.

Grace declared, "She thunders, too, when she gets mad, which is why I call her Tempest. Turn on your chimp and you'll see."

Always curious, Orlando thumbed the monkey's on button. The furry lump took on life, sat up, spun its head, blinked, and said, "Whatty-boo's the news, Boss?"

The cat hunched its back and roared. The monkey leaped in one bound onto Orlando's head, where it clawed for purchase on the slippery hat. Grace snatched the wriggling cat by the scruff of the neck.

"Have you got a screwdriver?" Orlando asked her, shouting to make himself heard above the monkey's frantic chatter. "Our noisy friends could use a few adjustments."

"Humphrey left a whole toolbox here someplace. Lord only knows where it is in all this mess! But it'll turn up."

The promise of a toolbox brought a host of schemes thronging into Orlando's mind. He could become a fix-it man for the SAGites. He could rig up his own anti-gravity contraption and float around the city. He could fashion birds and launch them from Grace's balcony. He could tinker with a new generation of beasts. Or why not insects this time, a whole zoo in a shoebox? Or why not try his hand at the vegetable kingdom and whip together some flowers and trees? No telling what he might do with a few tools.

That was how Moon decided she could bear to leave them: Grace the uproarious matriarch in her rainbow tights dangling the cat, Orlando the wizard in a voluminous black robe balancing a hysterical monkey on his head, the two of them burning with a fire as old as the universe.

"I'm going," Moon said gently.

"Not without a hug," Orlando protested.

Biting her knuckle, Moon went to him. She felt his quick, sure hands on her back.

"And not without promising to come visit us," said Grace.

"I'll come when I can," said Moon.

The monkey jabbered. The cat hissed. Grace was laughing too hard to scold them.

Moon stirred in Orlando's arms. She had feared he would scorn her, despise her. And then, discovering that he loved her, she feared he would try to keep her. But he let her go. Loving her, he spread his arms and set her free.

24·

Without handcuffs or tracer this time, without a grunting Overseer to drag her about like a mutt on a leash, Moon rode the tube train away from New Boston, over a stretch of sea, toward the outermost island of Cape Cod. She had on a fern-colored parka and jeans that were the lionish color of sand dunes, and in her unbound hair she wore the turkey feather. Every other thing she owned was in the backpack on the seat beside her. She felt by turns light as a windblown seed and heavy as a stone. Her mood kept shifting between sadness and euphoria, as her thoughts darted back and forth between the life she had left behind and the life to which she was going. When other passengers gawked at her, even the men and boys making their blunt appraisals, Moon stared right back, a free person.

She got off the train at Refarmatory Station, along with a crush of workers and a few visitors bearing gifts and several gold-suited cops who were towing sullen kids. Approaching the security gate, she felt a moment of anxiety. What if some authority still claimed her—the scientists who cooked her up from a frozen egg, say, or Bertha Dill at the Home, or the Overseers, or Dr. Bob here at the Farm? Her palm quivered as she spread it on the detector at the gate; but no alarm sounded and she passed on through.

The matron at the reception desk eyed her with efficient coldness and treated her like any other visitor. Moon had to leave the pack behind and undergo a scan for weapons before she was allowed to proceed to a cubicle. There she waited, chewing her lip and gazing around. White walls, camera on the ceiling, twin chairs bolted to the floor: a duplicate of the tiny chamber where Garrison had visited her in jail, except that here the two chairs were not separated by a wireglass partition. Nothing to divide the free soul from the prisoner.

The door opened and Garrison stepped in, ducking his head to fit through the frame. He wore knee-high rubber boots and the lilac Farm overalls, which were splotched with brown stains, and he brought in with him a whiff of cow manure. When he stood up, there seemed to be too much of him for the cubicle to hold. Surprise flickered in his face, then he glared at her without speaking.

Moon rose nervously from her seat. She had prepared a little speech to deliver, a comic apology for all the times she had been cruel to him, but now she managed only a faint, "Hi, there, stranger."

"What do you want?"

She was taken aback. "I want to see you."

"So here I am. As ridiculous as ever." He spread his arms, the way she had seen a cormorant drying its wings in the sun, and his fists brushed the opposite walls of the cubicle. "Have you got your laughs ready?"

"I didn't come here to laugh."

"Then why did you come?"

She swallowed. "To make peace. To say I'm sorry."

Lowering his arms, he tightened his jaw, which glistened with the fleecy beginnings of a beard. His face had filled out, along with the rest of him. Not a handsome face,

Moon supposed, but warm and rugged as a sandstone cliff, one she could imagine looking at again and again without growing tired. His big head, the splayed ears hidden by waves of straw-yellow hair, loomed above her. He said nothing.

Under the weight of his presence, Moon sank onto a chair. She patted the other seat. "Please sit."

Garrison lowered himself warily to the edge of the chair. His knees pointed at her like cannons. Still he did not speak.

Trying to relieve the tension, she gave a counterfeit smile, which promptly slid from her lips. She meshed her fingers and twisted them until they hurt. "So. Friends meet after long separation and grind their teeth. Anyway, you're looking good. If I didn't know better, I'd say life on the Farm agrees with you."

"I'll survive."

"Do you see Dr. Bob for therapy?"

"I'm not screwed up enough for him to bother with."

Since Moon had been Dr. Bob's patient for several months, she took this as another challenge. "When do you get out?"

"Thirty-seven more days."

She looked at him searchingly. "You blame me for landing you here, don't you?"

"I blame myself, for being stupid enough to care about you when you didn't give a damn about me."

"If I didn't give a damn, would I be here now?"

"How do I know why you're here? To toy with me some more? To jerk me around by my strings? To wipe your conscience clean?" His voice was growing too large for the tiny room. "Whatever the reason, forget it. You don't owe me a thing. Not an apology. Nothing. You never asked me to chase after you. You never asked me to stand under your window at the Home and watch your shadow on the curtain, to hang around the disney on the chance of saying hello, to spin after you like a yo-yo, to blow up a mountain and wind up scrubbing cows for a year. I was the lovesick dope who did all those things. I was the fool."

Without flinching, Moon shot back: "If you don't blame me, why are you yelling?"

"Who's yelling?" he roared.

"*You're* yelling!"

"I'm talking! I talk and you get hysterical."

"I'm *not* hysterical!" Her voice broke, which made her even more furious.

"You *are!*"

"*You* are!"

The cubicle reverberated with their shouting. Suddenly they both fell silent, their trembling faces so close they could feel one another's breath. The silence took on weight. Garrison was the first to give way, leaning back in his chair. In a hushed voice, he said, "Ah, what's the use? I can't cut the strings. You pull, and I jerk." He lifted his arms, puppet-fashion, and let them fall, his elbows landing on his thighs, the hands dangling slack between his knees.

Moon reached over and clasped one of those big hands in her two small ones. "Do you remember," she asked, in a voice as muted as his, "when you came to see me in jail, and we couldn't touch because of that glass partition?"

"I remember." His fingers lay inert in hers, as though rolled from clay. "I remember every single time you so much as glanced my way. I tried to forget. I worked at it— while I was scrubbing cows or eating hash in the cafeteria or tossing in my bunk—worked hard at forgetting you. Fat lot of good it did me. All you had to do was show up here, say a few words, and now you've got me spinning round and round again. Is that what you came to prove? Are you satisfied?"

"I missed you," Moon said, only discovering the full truth of it in the saying.

He asked banteringly, "Missed poor Ratbone?"

"I haven't called you that ugly name in years. Not since I realized how much you loathed it. I truly missed you, Garrison. The whole time I was outside, whenever I saw something beautiful or amazing, I wanted to show it to you. I wanted to have you there beside me where I could grab your arm and say, 'Look! Look! My God, what a world we live in!' "

Still cupped between her palms, his fingers twitched. He studied her, his gray eyes like windows opening onto fog. "Don't play with me, Mooch."

"I'm not playing, and I'm not Mooch."

"Then who are you?"

"A bear gave me the name of Moon Waters."

Now it was his chance to mock. Instead, he asked her solemnly where she had run into a bear. She told him about her fast, her trek through the mountains, her vision, her recuperation in the city, and her parting from Orlando, all the while holding his weighty hand.

He listened with tender patience. When she finished, he said, "So now, remembering that, you have something real to measure everything else by."

"I do."

"You've touched the source, found out where you come from."

"I have," said Moon, startled by his insight.

"Nothing even close to that has ever happened to me. I don't suppose you can *make* it happen. You've just got to be ready, keep yourself open, and wait. You can chase the bear all you want, but you'll never catch it. In the end, you can only sit still, and hope the bear will come to you."

Moon leaned forward and kissed him on the mouth, clinging to him in astonishment, and then she drew back.

His free hand closed over hers, and their four hands knotted as though to mark a promise. The strength of his grip brought back her dread of traps, making her stiffen, her muscles coiled for flight. Garrison held on. After a moment she relaxed.

This time the silence was not heavy, but light, the airy silence of falling snow. They breathed it with open mouths. At length, aware that her time with him would soon be up, Moon asked urgently, "What are you going to do when you get out?"

"Go back to the Home, I guess. I won't be allowed to walk around loose until next year, when I turn eighteen."

"How about another apprenticeship?"

He laughed, his cheeks flushed behind the downy beard. "Doing what? Blowing up mountains?"

"I was thinking of something more like data-crunching at an eco station. I'd love to have you out there on Turtle Island with me." Once more she only recognized what she had been feeling as she uttered the words. "My boss keeps begging for a cyber jockey. You'd like her. She's got a head full of poems."

"She wouldn't touch a juvie, a jailbird."

"She took me."

"But she doesn't know me from Adam."

"She knows all about you," said Moon.

"How?"

"I told her. More than once. More than a few times! What do you say? Will you give it a try?"

He filled his chest with a swift intake of breath, held it

for several beats, gazing at her, and then, letting it slowly out, he whispered, "Yes."

With an uncertain hand, Moon brushed the hair from his cheek and ran a finger along the whorls of his ear. "I'm so glad."

Suddenly frowning, he said, "But I'm a city boy. I've never seen a blade of grass. Never heard a cricket. Never felt the wind on my face. What if all that wild and woolly stuff out there drives me nuts?"

"The station's got walls, you know. A roof. Windows. You can sit snug indoors as long as you need to."

"But I can't stay cooped up forever. What happens when I finally go outside?"

"I'll feed you the universe in tiny bites." Moon's finger drifted from his ear, along his cheekbone and jaw, to his lips.

Garrison closed his eyes, accepting her touch. "Can you remember any of your boss's poems?"

"A few." She thought a moment, searching for the right one, then chanted:

> *"They have the guise*
> *of being married just today—*
> *those two butterflies.*

Can you see that? The two of them spinning circles in the air?"

A look of bewildered pleasure broke over his face. "Not quite. I won't really be able to picture it until I've seen a butterfly. When I get outside, will you show me one?"

"In the spring," she promised.

"What is it out there now?"

Reckoning up the weeks gone by since her vision of the bear, Moon said, "It's winter."

"And spring comes next?"

"It always has."

A buzzer sounded. The clumping footsteps of a matron approached their cubicle.

"Time's up," said Garrison.

"Time's just beginning," said Moon. Again she kissed him, quickly, their lips meeting and then parting with the sound of rain dappling a pond.

■

MOON scarcely spoke during the flight back to the station, for she was feeling a turmoil of hope and regret and elation that would not clarify into words. Hae Won, sensing her need for quiet, did not push for an accounting of her time in New Boston or at the Farm. From the landing pad at the station, the rest of the crew hurled shouts of welcome, making a warm, affectionate fuss over Moon's return, before they, too, recognized in her stillness a brimming-over of emotion. Then, like Hae Won, they held their tongues and cradled her in a zone of quietness where she could wheel about for a spell on her own axis.

Moon felt deeply grateful to Hae Won and the others for accepting her into their circle of work and thought, here in this outpost of the Enclosure. Or perhaps the station did not belong to the Enclosure at all, but was a feeler pushed out from nature itself, a wild, reasoning eye turned back on the wilderness.

She reclaimed her old room, put away her few things, then stretched out on the bed. Charged with expectation, she was a long time in falling asleep. With eyes closed she listened to voices, footsteps, the low babble of electronics, the sizzle of windblown sand against the dome. She tingled in sympathy, as though a single wind blew over the station and over her skin and over the delicate membranes of her cells. It came to her that cells and body, along with domes and towers and the proudest cities, were no more than bubbles adrift on a stream of mystery. Who knew, who could ever know, what power buoyed us up or pulled us down? At last she had come to her true beginning, here in this place of questions. Ancient though it was, the world beckoned to her with fresh energy. She was eager to learn all that a single mind could know about the universe, and to leave behind some record of her knowing.

The winter's first snow fell during the night. By morning the sky had cleared, and Turtle Island was a brilliant white hump rising from the gray metal of the sea. At sunrise, Moon bundled up against the cold and went outdoors, shuffling through ankle-deep snow, making her way over the hidden, rolling dunes to the beach. Salt spray stung her nose and cheeks. Her eyes watered. Scanning the eastward horizon, not far from where the sun was burning up from the ocean she spied the snow-brightened shape of Garrison's island. In her thoughts it would continue to be Garrison's island until he left that place to join her here. New Boston, where by now Orlando would be stirring, lay farther east, hidden from her beyond the earth's curve. She flung ropes of longing to both her men, the old one and the young.

Then she turned back toward the station and the day's work. Last year's grass and reeds and the bare frames of trees stood out against the snow like secret calligraphy. The land was a blank page, written over delicately, waiting to be read, waiting for rebirth. Hurrying up the slope, the snow yielding sensuously to her feet, Moon gave a shout and broke into a bearish dance.